RELICS

JOHN J. DESJARLAIS

THOMAS NELSON PUBLISHERS
Nashville

Published in Nashville, Tennessee, by Thomas Nelson, Inc., Publishers.

ISBN 978-0-8407-6735-6

Printed in the United States of America

1 2 3 4 5 6 7 — 99 98 97 96 95 94 93

For Matthew

A wise son brings joy to his father.
Proverbs 10:1

Introit

We do not worship the relics of the martyrs, but honor them in our worship of Him whose martyrs they are. We honor the servants in order that the respect paid to them may be reflected back to the Lord.

Jerome
Reply to Vigilantius

In pilgrimage, one's journey takes him not to a far place but toward his deep self, where God waits to accept him.

Paulinus of Constantinople
Memoirs of a Sinner

Anno Domini 1251

1

The cathedral bells tolled for midnight *Matins,* the prayer ending the eve of the Feast of Saint John the Baptizer. The music rippled through the still summer night of the village of Auxonne like the lazy lapping of the nearby River Loire, awakening Jean-Michel d'Anjou.

He scratched the stubble on his cheek, then in the dark reached from beneath the woolens to grasp the handle of Purity, his sword. He pulled the hollowed hilt to his lips and, with a sleepy kiss, invoked the aid of St. Denis, whose relics reposed inside. "Just a few hairs, for that price," the metal-smith had told him. Jean-Michel could not afford a splinter of the true Cross. That would cost as much as a war horse—easily five years' pay as a cathedral guard.

Au nom du Pere, du Fils et du Saint-Esprit. He began reciting his morning office, which was not unlike that of the monks, but in French, a daily humbling reminder that he had no schooling and knew no Latin. The bell-ringing, longer than usual, paced his prayer until he heard scuffling from the stables. The nervous whinny of his own charger drew him up to his elbows. When the distant steeple bells of the Church of St. Mary joined the insistent chiming of the cathedral's, Jean-Michel smelled smoke.

The barracks door flew open with a bang, and a dark figure, haloed in an orange glow, beckoned frantically. "God help us," the man cried. "The church is on fire!"

Jean-Michel kicked off the covers and sprang from the straw. Other knights in the room rolled from their bunks, rubbing their eyes, punching awake those who snored in drunken stupors. Some praying, some cursing, they fumbled in the dim light, quickly covering their nakedness. Jean-Michel slipped into his riding breeches, shirt, and felt shoes, and elbowed his way out into the work yard.

Grooms and squires, who slept in the stables, were already leading horses outside. The frightened, skittish animals bucked, jerking at their tethers, but the handlers guided them toward the south gate. Jean-Michel saw Fidelity, his golden-maned charger, nose through the wooden doors, with Bobo, his groomsman, guiding her. Relieved, Jean-Michel crossed himself and turned toward the conflagration.

Flames danced like devils on the cathedral's timber roof, loosening tiles to slide and smash to the courtyard below. The scaffolding, made of rough-hewn poles lashed together by leather thongs, caught fire and slowly crumbled with a loud creak. Jean-Michel's eyes stung from tears that welled up from the stink of burnt pitch and the grief of seeing the church, the Ark of God, under siege. Like a galley assaulted by Byzantine firebombs, its crew having taken flight and its hull afire, the church's buttressing arches thrust outward and down like banks of mighty oars dipping in unison for a powerful stroke forward that would never come.

Outside the fenced yard, townspeople stirred and spilled into the streets, sounding the alarm. The frantic voices of overseers called for sand buckets.

Wooden shacks emptied as masons, mortarers, carpenters, stonecutters, plasterers, and penitents came to volunteer. Shouting and crying, they tripped over one another, while pulling on their breeches, and poured in a chaotic stream toward their church.

The bells weakened as a company of monks rushed from the building, coughing. They hugged books to their chests. The last two ran out with fire licking their cassocks. One rolled on the ground to snuff himself out. The other ran in circles screaming, his hood ablaze like a torch, before he dropped. Some of the workers left their bucket brigades to hurry to him, stripping off their cloaks to beat out the flames on the writhing monk.

Jean-Michel joined a line of men passing heavy sand buckets to the front. The rope handles bit into his palms as he hefted each one to the next man, a puffing, sweaty stonecutter.

"Who is strong enough," the man grunted, "to cast sand on the roof?"

"Or brave enough to get so close?" said the man next in line.

Those at the front could only spray sand on bits of tile and timber that had already fallen. The bitter smoke swirled around them, choking them, and they fell back, dropping the useless buckets.

The bells stopped ringing as fire raced up their ropes. The roof sagged and split, sending a fountain of sparks into the sullen sky. The thatched roofs of the closest houses smoldered and spit flames, which leapt from house to house. The men around Jean-Michel dropped their buckets and, raising their hands to heaven, begged their saints to shift the wind or send rain.

"The bell! The bell!" someone shouted, and men scrambled away from the tower. The untethered bells pulled from their moorings, like restless cows. Cracked blocks of stone tumbled down, and a shower of mortar pieces pelted the ground. Sounding a final, thunderous peal, the largest bell crashed straight into the shaft. Plank flooring splintered on its path before the bronze bell smashed into the limestone floor with a muffled clang. The earth trembled.

Jean-Michel's hands flew to his ears and he squeezed his eyes shut. When he opened them, he saw a canon of the cathedral, Anseau d'Auxonne, prostrate before him. At first, Jean-Michel thought the chief sacristan, keeper of the church's relics, had been struck down by a piece of falling debris. But Anseau clasped his bony hands in supplication and shook his hollow-cheeked head in despair.

"They are lost. Lost!" he groaned. He looked at the knight through tear-swollen eyes.

"Your men?" Jean-Michel asked. "Trapped inside?"

"The Holy Relics," Anseau sobbed. "Without them, there can be no cathedral."

Anseau dipped his head at the sound of rumbling. Jean-Michel saw it was an approaching handwagon, its iron wheels rattling through the gravel. Two men pulled it with long handles, while a third riding inside steadied sloshing water buckets. They followed the commands coming from the carpenters' shed. When they arrived, workers lifted out the buckets and splashed the walls and roof of the shed. The carpenters were determined not to lose their tools.

Face down and fingers entwined, Anseau moaned, "Saint Martin, forgive us for the loss of your most precious bones and holy sword."

Jean-Michel pressed his hand on Anseau's shoulder. "Your cape, Father," he said. "Give it to me."

"Can you be so cold while the flames of hell are so near?" Anseau scolded.

"For the Son of Saint Mary and for Saint Martin," Jean-Michel said, gripping the dark cloth. "I must have it to go inside."

"To go in . . . there?" Anseau glanced over his shoulder at the cathedral. The bell tower vomited black smoke like a blacksmith's chimney.

Jean-Michel yanked off the cape, and Anseau wrapped his hands around his own shoulders as though stripped naked. "You can't," he said, reaching out to grasp Jean-Michel's arm. "You'll never get out. Jean-Michel, wait!"

Jean-Michel slipped from Anseau's grasp and caught up to a second handcart headed for the master mason's shop where the wood frames used for cutting stones were stored.

The apprentice who bounced in the wagon, his hands on the pails, called, "Is God angry with us?"

"Only if we do not save His church," Jean-Michel said. He clamped his hands on the cart and pushed.

The cart braked. Before the lad inside could hand him a bucket, Jean-Michel hauled one out to the ground and plunged the bundled cape into the water.

"What are you doing?" the apprentice cried. He reached for the bucket, but Jean-Michel stiff-armed him backward. The boy fell on a pail, spilling it.

"Hurry it up; get the buckets out!" growled a man in front.

Jean-Michel shoved his way through the masons converging on the wagon. Clear of them, he raised the sopping cloth over his head and wrung it. The water chilled him and matted his hair over his eyes. He shook the hair away and snapped open the cloak. He raced toward the burning cathedral, swinging the cold cloth around his shoulders.

The front doors yawned open as if to swallow him. A warm breath of air passed over him. Above the entrance, the uncut blocks of limestone, soon to be carved into images of saints, flanked a single stone figure. Saint Martin, a bishop's staff in one hand and a sword in the other, seemed to urge him to enter. The lofty walls of the entryway and narthex glowed eerily. A haze thicker than the incense of High Mass hovered near the window gallery. Green glass winked in the firelight like dragons' eyes blinking away stinging smoke. Jean-Michel crouched on the cool flagstone floor and, spiderlike, crept past the first piers into the awesome sanctuary.

The clamor of falling wood echoed against the soaring ceiling of the nave where waves of sound battered the curved timber crossribs. The sanctuary's northeast corner sagged precariously where the bell tower joined it. Burning pieces littered the bare floor like crumbs fallen from the mouth of a hungry monster. The fire had consumed a major portion of the roof and was crawling its way down the maze of heavy crisscrossing beams supporting the work in progress on the first bay of the choir vault. The conflagration clawed its way with fiery fingers toward the helpless high-backed wooden seats in the chancel area around the altar.

Jean-Michel wiped his sweaty face with the wet cloak. It was already warm.

He ran down the middle of the pillared nave, crouching at the sound of stones crashing on either side in the flanking aisles. He shielded his nose and mouth against the hot dust with the cloak. A breeze from the unglassed windows, which looked arch-shaped in mimicry of the portals, fanned the flames above. The fiery monster harrumphed in glee. It crept toward the elegantly carved choir walls between the altar and the ambulatory, which circled behind, as though to intercept Jean-Michel. Beyond, a corridor led to the chapels and the repository of Saint Martin's blessed relics.

Jean-Michel reached the transept, the center of the cross-shaped building, and paused against the pillar to catch his breath. When he touched the stone, he realized how tender his skin had become in the baking heat. Ahead, the flames had beaten him to the entryway of the ambulatory, the corridor leading to the chapels. Rough-hewn timbers, shaggy with unshaven bark, crackled fiercely. The network of X's and V's, propping the crude arch of ashwood where most of the stone ribs had yet to be laid, would ignite quickly and collapse, sealing off his retreat. Jean-Michel glanced to the other side of the choirstalls, seeking an alternative route. Chained iron gates barred the other outlet. Next to the gates, on the first rise in front of the altar, stood the oak eagle lectern, its wings spread out as though straining to launch itself, but unable to escape. A polished beak shrieked silently in defiance and varnished eyes shone with fear. A streak of panic-stricken pigeons swooped through the piers past Jean-Michel's face. Sparrows screamed in the eaves where their nests became tinder for the fire. A flurry of bats fluttered from the wooden archway, like dark demons escaping a fire they had started.

As Jean-Michel spun to watch them, his face suddenly felt cracked and his throat parched. His eyes were no longer tear-filled, but hot and dry as if he were in a desert. The fiery monster hissed at him, daring him to pass, and the canon's cloak began to steam.

A dim voice called from the narthex. "Jean-Michel! Jean-Michel!" Anseau called. "It is no use! Save yourself!" Other frightened voices joined the pleading.

The cathedral answered with a roar, raining charred timbers and ripping a great hole in the roof. Clouds of smoke flowed to the new opening with the sound of rushing wind like the tongues of fire that were said to fill the Upper Room when the Holy Spirit descended on the apostles and the

Virgin Mother at Pentecost. The sound blotted out Anseau's cries, and Jean-Michel ran beneath the burning archway into the chapel corridor.

Bent low to where the air felt cooler, he counted the steps to the Chapel of Saint Martin by memory. When he lifted his eyes, his stomach knotted with fear.

The ornate iron gate, looking like a row of joined spears with bright bronze points, was chained shut.

In frustration Jean-Michel rattled the warm bars. Just steps away, beneath a long silken banner bearing the emblem of the Bishopric of Tours and the figure of Saint Martin in a gesture of welcome, lay the altar. The jeweled Tabernacle for the Host sat on the left, and on the right rested the narrow reliquary containing the sacred sword.

Jean-Michel dropped to one knee, his hands clamped together on the gate, not in genuflection but dejection. He shook the bars once, then composed himself. He wiped his brow with the cloak as he glanced down the corridor. The blaze was catching at the timbered entryway. He could hear the stones there shifting.

Drippings of hot pitch streaked the chapel walls. The fire dragon had reached the roof above, and black, gluey pitch stained the altar like dripping saliva. An ominous creaking set the banner aflutter. It made Saint Martin's outstretched hands on the banner look as if they were waving Jean-Michel away.

Disregarding the warning, Jean-Michel peeled off the cloak and stretched it taut. He flung one end to the top of the gate. It caught on one of the spear tips. He jerked it to test his weight on it. It slipped off. The ceiling moaned.

He tossed it again, in the same way he would sling a rope around a horse's head. A seam snagged on one of the bronze points. He pulled. The cloth ripped. He tugged. It ripped more. He knew it would not hold his weight. A thunderous crash resounded in the nave. The floor quaked. The wall nearest the nave showed cracks like branches of lightning. The topmost stones careened to the floor and exploded into jagged bits. Some cannoned into the gate, making the bars sing.

Jean-Michel coughed away the dust and swung the cape up again. The double seam around a sleeve opening held fast on a spear tip. He hoisted himself up. His wet shirt clung to him as though to pull him down. He found footing on one of the crossbars and pulled himself up hand over hand until he could grab the spear tip.

The crest of the chapel wall leaned in and toppled. Square stones pounded the altar with a deafening howl. The reliquary vanished beneath a billow of limestone dust. Jean-Michel lost his grip and went sprawling to the floor with a mouth full of chalk. Shattered glass from the high chevet windows fell around him like green hailstones. Chunks of stone jolted the gates as if to shoulder them open and crush Jean-Michel.

He dragged himself away, his bruised hip aching. He spat and coughed. His eyes were caked shut. Following the heat, he groped his way back to the ambulatory entry. He stumbled through the arch just as it surrendered to the weight of the stones, sealing the corridor with a crash of rubble and splintered timbers.

The nave felt like a bread oven. Jean-Michel shielded his face with his sleeve against the blast of heat coming from the mounds of smoking planks covering the left aisle. When he took away his arm, his face prickled with the heat, and he suddenly feared his hair would ignite. He heard a ghostly voice wail his name from the front of the church. *An angel*, he thought, *showing me the way out.*

He lowered his head between his elbows and moved dizzily toward the sound of his name. Shards of wood beat upon his back and arms and he wished for his shield. He stayed close to the stalwart compound columns standing—like the apostles upholding the church—unflinching before the flames. He felt for them, using them as guides through hell itself. He squinted against the scorching heat and pungent fumes. He fell once, scraping a knee, but he pushed on, his lungs burning and near to bursting. He heard gasps of surprise and calls for help as he emerged from the inferno. Grasping hands grabbed his arms and pulled him urgently into the open air. His knees buckled and dragged. Shaking like a man with palsy, he shivered in the outside air.

The monster inside bellowed as though enraged at his escape and ripped down half the roof. A tongue of fire darted from the front doors like a serpent's, searching for him. But he could not see it; nor could he see the crowd of awed spectators slowly clustering around him. Their pinched fingers flitted to their foreheads, chests, and shoulder to shoulder at the sight of his shirt. It was singed on the sleeve with a perfect cross.

2

Excellency Maurice Marie-Joseph Froissart DeBeauvais cursed his aching back. After each jolting step, he shifted in the engraved saddle, a lance of pain stabbing his spine. He bit his thin lip and adjusted his tilting miter, his headdress of authority. The silken headband had slipped sideways again.

He patted his silvery hair, hanging limp from the humidity like loose threads. The hunting forests felt much cooler than the valley, he mused. Longingly he wished for the comfort of his coach with its satin seats that cushioned bumpy rides along poor roads. But this path between his favorite hunting estate and the Commune of Auxonne could not even be called a road.

When the horse stepped around the rocks blocking the way, the bishop noticed how puddled and gullied the path had become. Mud sucked at the horse's hooves and spotted the hem of the bishop's velvet riding cape. He now regretted ripping up the smooth Roman stones that once paved this way. But he had needed them for the cathedral.

My cathedral, he moaned inwardly. Could something so large, that took a lifetime and more to build, be destroyed in one night? *It must be true,* he thought grimly. He heard no caroling of bells as was customary when he approached. He had christened them himself, anointing them with oil without and chrism within and praying over them that their sounds would summon men to prayer and rebuke demons and their works. But somehow the demons had silenced the bells, and the rain had come too late.

Behind him greyhounds yelped and pulled on their leads as the smells of Auxonne reached them. The hunting masters barked at the dogs, reining them in. Hooded falcons squawked in their cages, their ankle-bells tingling. Their keepers made kissing noises to calm them. The armed escort, their chain mail jingling, tightened ranks and lifted higher the bright pennants of the bishop's office. The leaden sky spit more rain over the patchwork fields surrounding Auxonne, and Bishop DeBeauvais felt relieved to be nearly there.

The bishop lifted himself up, standing slightly in the gold stirrups, for a brief respite from the pain. Settling back down and wincing, he saw the town walls ahead with the clutter of houses and spires behind them. The walls, built by Caesar's men for defense but now useless, had provided many good stones for the church.

The retinue clattered over the plank bridge, spanning the overgrown remains of an ancient moat, and escorted Bishop DeBeauvais onto the cobbled streets of Auxonne. Heralds cleared the way of shoppers, gawkers, and stray animals, except for a few mocking crows and a gang of cat-sized rats feeding on garbage in the gutters. The rodents scattered into holes at the yapping of the hounds and the pounding of hooves on stone. The merchants' stalls were closed and boarded, but above, from the overhanging second stories, curious eyes peeked through shutters.

The bishop kept his eyes fixed straight ahead on the work-yard gates of his cathedral. Already he could see the stomach-wrenching damage. Half the roof was gone, and parts of the walls near the chancel looked as if a giant had tried to kick them in, leaving holes and jagged gashes. He remembered the wall collapse ten years before, when he had been summoned to a similar scene to perform funerals. Nearly twoscore died that time. The masons had carved pieces of the fallen stones into grave markers. Miraculously there would be no funerals today. Still, the messengers had spoken with enthusiasm about another miracle, that of a survivor given a sign from God on his sleeve. The bishop tried to remember the man's name.

He approached the western doors through the muddy yard. Two trumpeters, flanking the entry, blared a high note to welcome the bishop and to alert the clerics waiting inside of his arrival.

Bishop DeBeauvais arched his thinning eyebrows in surprise at the stillness of the yard. The workmen's lean-tos, leather flaps down against the pattering rain, sat quietly like hooded monks at the feet of an abbot. The bishop pouted. Where were the saws singing on timber molds, the hammers drumming, the trowels tapping and the chisels chip-chipping on pier capitals and portal frieze borders? He shaded his eyes against the raindrops. Where were the creaking pulleys and the cursing men? Why weren't new blocks being lifted into place? Dismayed he noted the absence of scaffolding and the walls pockmarked by empty anchoring holes. *God's blood, did a little rain stop them?* he wondered.

Through the drizzle he saw only a few wagons, loaded with irregular stones, being pulled in procession toward a heap of stacked blocks guarded by mounted knights. The wagons stopped at the trill of trumpets. *It's been a week, yet the rubble-clearing is still underway?* he questioned. *They should be building again by now.* Shivering, he realized the damage exceeded his fears.

When the bishop reached the rise of stairs, he dismounted and knelt on a stool covered by gold-embroidered cloth. He hoped the trumpeters were finished.

The bronze doors opened. Nine canons emerged, clad in silken copes and bearing a jeweled cross with flickering tapers and smoky censers. The dean of the cathedral, a wizened man with a waxy face, presented a silver water sprinkler to the kneeling bishop. DeBeauvais aspersed himself, although his cape was already dotted with raindrops, then sprinkled the dean, who looked frightened. *The inside must look awful,* DeBeauvais thought, as he touched his lips to the cold cross.

He stood, masking a grunt, while the dean took his place on the right and the precentor, the choir director, on the left. In a fog of cloying incense, the bishop led the canons, all chanting, into the church.

DeBeauvais surveyed the sanctuary, cleared of the usual vendors, copyists-for-hire, beggars, and strumpets. The church would be packed the next day for the Feast of Peter and Paul with hundreds of people crowding for space on the charcoal-streaked floor. The bishop realized that the streaks were markings where the charred beams had been dragged out.

The interior, oddly bright without much of the roof, smelled of burnt wood, which even the burning incense could not disguise. The bishop kept watch on the chancel. The elegant chairs, carved choir stalls, ornate tables, and eagle lectern had all been ripped out. Only the canopied, tomb-like marble altar remained.

Stripped this way, the sanctuary looked as bare as the old crypt which stood originally on the spot where Saint Martin surrendered his sword to the prefect of Gaul. He had refused to fight against barbarian raiders, saying, "Hitherto have I served you as a soldier, but now I am a soldier of Christ." Prepared to stand unarmed in battle in Christ's name, he had dropped his gladius, a Roman shortsword.

Bishop DeBeauvais hoped that by now someone had found that precious sword. Otherwise, who would come to Auxonne for miracles or dubbing ceremonies? A patron of knights, Saint Martin had overseen many a young man's all-night vigil in his chapel in preparation for the bishop's blessing the next morning. What revenue would be lost! Why, even this Jean-Michel, yes, that was his name, had received his sword and spurs here.

The bishop recited a rote Mass, and then retired to the sacristy to change from riding apparel into longer garments. He stepped over puddles on the way and nearly slipped on the straw meant to soak up standing water. He looked toward the gaps in the ceiling. He clenched his fingers as if, reluctant to let them go, he were grasping fistfuls of silver *livres.* New timber for the roof would be costly. Without relics to attract pilgrims, how could the money be raised?

God's blood, the treasury is already stretched, he fretted, as he shook off his cape and held out his arms. Attendants draped him in brushed velvet robes decorated with silk-embroidered unicorns. The satin lining rustled on his hairy forearms. The pearls inlaid at the wrist openings clicked while he weighed the financial options.

He could raise taxes on his tenants again. But they would tolerate only so much before declaring war, and he could not muster and pay an armed force. Besides, in the event of fighting, Rome might investigate. And the Baroness would not support him. In fact, she might demand from him, her primary tenant, a higher tax in retaliation.

Very counterproductive, he thought. *I must have some relics.*

Then again, perhaps he could find some pretext to excommunicate a baron or two and then accept generous gifts to the cathedral for re-admission to the Mother Church. It was a short-term solution that had worked twice on Hughes DuVal. DuVal kept a roaring, whoring hall at his manor, and it was not hard for the bishop to find an excuse to humble the pompous overlord. A disgruntled tenant of DuVal's, Bishop DeBeauvais had hoped the gifts would be ruinous and would leave the baron with no option but to sign over his lands to the diocese. That would have turned the tables. But somehow the baron had raised the cash *(ransacked his own villages, no doubt)* and all the bishop had gotten was the chance to smite the baron on the back with a rod during his reinstatement in the cathedral chancel, calling, "Just are thy judgments, O Lord!"

DeBeauvais enjoyed the memory as he joined the dean for the brief walk to the Priory's refectory. A generous meal of excellent breads and clarets awaited him there. It made him think of the sumptuous fare at Hughes DuVal's chateau. Perhaps the Baroness DuVal would be open to a gift toward repairs, he hoped, now that her husband Hughes was away crusading in the Holy Land with His Majesty.

DeBeauvais smirked as he recalled Hughes, barefoot and barebacked, the welts hardly subsided from the beating, begging him to take the cross and grant indulgence for a pilgrimage to assist King Louis in Palestine. The bishop did not believe for a moment that Hughes meant to fulfill a penance by going there. Who did DuVal think he was fooling? Even though the king had indeed issued a call for men to join him at the Crusaders' capital at Acre, everyone knew Hughes only wanted to acquire land and wealth the church could not tax. He wanted to take out his humiliation on someone, and there was no one left to fight here; they had all been slaughtered in Egypt. No doubt, the bishop figured, Hughes stole enough in his raids on the local villages to pay for his passage to the Levant.

Such a venture was expensive, and this one was a major reason for the treasury's depletion. DeBeauvais thought of his last visit, when he had sealed agreements with nobles pledged to accompany Hughes to Palestine. The bishop had doled out huge sums for their lands, which were mortgaged to him and then entrusted to clerics who paid well for the privilege of running a fief. He held the lands as pledges, but he did not recall if the lands became his upon the deaths of the signatories or if they passed to next-of-kin. He inquired about it between bites of thick white bread, while he was tearing off the crusts.

"They do revert to you, my lord bishop, you recall it well," said Anseau, the pale-faced canon. "Baron Philippe and his two sons, Roger and Guillaume, drew up such charters with your excellency."

"He was not pleased with the sum, as others were," DeBeauvais said, frowning.

"You offered a generous sum, my lord," Anseau reassured him.

"I am not a Jewish usurer."

"Of course not, your excellency, and you saved many from having to deal with these thieves of the world. Besides you had several men to underwrite." He poured more wine, his hand shaking. "It's just that Philippe did not want to go at all. But when Hughes dared his vassals and castellans to join him on pilgrimage, Philippe could not refuse or he would appear weak."

The bishop swilled his wine and swallowed. "His sons seemed willing."

"More than willing, your excellency," Anseau said. "They were eager, eager as hounds on a hare's trail." He pushed a silver plate of sliced cheese nearer the bishop. "But there was another son who did not go."

The bishop grimaced. "Was he of age?"

"Yes. Newly knighted, but landless, being the youngest."

"He did not go to the Holy Land to take his own property from the infidel Saracens?"

Anseau shook his head.

The bishop patted the corners of his downturned mouth with the tablecloth. "The worthless, who love neither God nor glory, stay home," he said. "Who is this gutless son?"

"The man who took the cross from God Himself," Anseau said, his eyes shining with admiration. "Jean-Michel d'Anjou, son of Philippe."

Flat on the feather bed, facing Jerusalem with his arms outstretched like a cross, Jean-Michel recited God's favors to him. He used a litany taught him by Brother Hubert, the last injured monk to leave his company in the cramped, windowless infirmary. "I thank Thee for a foretaste of purgatory," the monk had prayed, his hairless, blistered head bowed earnestly.

When Jean-Michel finished, he lifted himself up to a kneel. His bruised hip cried out, and he pressed his lips together. Although alone in the room, he refused to make any noise that would betray the pain. He had learned this, while serving as squire to his older brothers, particularly on the day his horse stumbled in a swift stream and he tumbled headlong into the water. The current had thrashed him over the rocks and he came up choking. Roger and Guillaume laughed with donkey brays meant to imitate his crying. They had lifted him only to heave him into a deeper part. How strange, he thought as the memory rippled away, that to this day he feared water more than fire.

His chest still burned as if he'd swallowed hot cinders. He wondered if he would be released from bed rest to testify at chapter, the monk's daily meeting, where the bishop was conducting an inquest into the fire.

He drew a full draught of air and prayed aloud. "Let the blessed sword be found today, for the sake of Thy servant and soldier, Saint Mar—"

He stifled a cough. His stomach lurched and he dropped his chin to his chest to prevent a faint. He took shallow breaths and looked up to the wall over his bed where the singed tunic hung on a peg. The emblazoned cross looked like the Archangel's sword pointed down. It had a rich brown outline with a yellowish aura of irregular edges—a blade of flame as at Eden. To his brothers and father, the red linen crosses stitched onto their hauberks were little more than patches on coats of armor, token badges of pilgrimage. But the sword on his sleeve was a message from God.

As fascinated as ever with the divine design, he pondered what the message might be. Was it that he should join his father in the Holy Land even though he had been strictly ordered to remain at home? Could the Heavenly Father be overruling his earthly one, who said he would not pay the passage for one who was never to be his heir? Was the fire a Trial by Ordeal, meant to disprove his brothers' accusations that he lacked the fighting skill and stamina necessary in war? And who could tell him?

"Now, my true Father," he concluded under his breath, "Who desireth that all be saved, grant that

I may acquire Thy acceptance and love, even as have the holy angels and my namesake Michael, their prince, who all do Thy pleasure. Give us our daily bread for the body, what Thou causest to grow in the earth, and for the soul, the Holy Sacrament. Thus may I trust in the strength of my heart that which Thou hast bestowed, and in my good sword and my fleet horse—yet especially in Thee!"

After crossing himself, Jean-Michel rested his bandaged hands on his thighs and turned around. A lay brother in a chestnut habit stood in the doorway holding his breath, not daring to disturb Jean-Michel at prayer. The man gripped a tray of cheeses and breads left from the bishop's banquet.

Jean-Michel blinked as though awakening. Now that his stomach had stopped heaving, he felt ready for food. "And here is my daily bread already," he said. "Put it here, Brother Perrot."

Embarrassed to intrude, the novitiate nurse's face flushed. He set down the tray. His hands were rough from years spent in tenant farming. "Will I ever come to you when you are not in prayer? Are you trying to become a monk too?"

Jean-Michel laughed. As the youngest son, he had considered it, but he knew he was not studious enough. "My brothers always said I would be more comfortable in a hood than a helmet."

"Each is a hard life. How are you feeling?"

"I breathe and speak without pain." He inhaled, but caught himself up short and coughed. He beckoned to the wineskin slung over Perrot's shoulder.

Skeptical, the nurse eyed him. "I see. And your hands?" Perrot intercepted Jean-Michel's hand as he reached for the cheese. He inspected the gauze wrapped around the palms. Jean-Michel felt a tweak of tenderness as Perrot applied pressure.

"Good enough to throw a lance," Jean-Michel said, forcing away a wince.

Ignoring him, Perrot turned the hand. Pink scars lined Jean-Michel's arm where the barber had bled him. Perrot unwound the bandages. They smelled faintly of the mint poultice he'd mixed to cool the skin and prevent swelling.

"You seem well enough to receive the lord bishop," Perrot said. "He will come here after chapter. He desires an audience with you."

"An audience with me? It should be the other way around."

"Not so, for one so touched by God." Perrot pointed his small chin toward the shirt. "The crowds still gather outside after morning Mass, hoping to see you. The other hand, now."

Jean-Michel offered it while flexing the freed one.

"But they were fewer today," Perrot added. "Prior Francois is very strict about strangers coming to visit the infirmary. Of course, he is quite willing to allow family."

"My family is in the Holy Land," Jean-Michel said. "Except for Bobo, my groomsman, if he counts."

"Even your mother?"

Jean-Michel bowed his head. "Mother is dead. In childbirth, bearing me."

Perrot released the hand. "I am sorry."

"Mother Mary comforts and guides me."

Jean-Michel tried to ease Perrot's awkwardness with a winsome smile. But he found himself trying again to imagine what his mother looked like. He knew he resembled his father, who had eyes the color and sharpness of tempered steel, a high-bridged nose, charcoal hair, and stubby legs. He pictured his mother looking like the Virgin in the cathedral—tall and graceful as a doe, soft-skinned and soft-eyed. How many times he had gazed into that inviting face of infinite acceptance, hoping to see his mother there, forgiving him for causing her death. His father never had.

Perrot bundled the bandages and dropped them into a canvas bag by the door. *He will ask for the sheets next,* Jean-Michel thought. Perrot beat and bleached them every night, as though each stain were a sin on a soul. But there were some stains that could never be cleansed.

"When will the bishop come here?" the knight asked.

"It is hard to say. His excellency is questioning the brothers about the fire." He unplugged the wineskin and tipped it into a two-handed mug. "Refresh yourself now, please, before he arrives. This is a fine sauvignon, from Anjou. The bishop's favorite."

"I know it well." Jean-Michel lifted the bowl and sipped. He wondered if the wine came from his father's own cellars, which the bishop now controlled. They were cellars he would never call his own. The thought spoiled the taste. "Will the bishop question me about the fire's cause?" he asked hoarsely.

"It is not likely," Perrot answered. "Most are agreed that the devil did it."

"Yes, but by what means? He may incite someone to sin, or to be careless. A forgotten candle in the copying stalls, perhaps?"

Perrot looked offended. "Too far from the roof, where the fire caught so well. Lightning is ruled out also, as the night was calm. The blacksmith insists he kept watch on his fire. It was more likely a group of revelers, setting a fire like so many do to honor the feast of Saint John, as well as for warmth while they drank in the bell tower."

"Monks?"

"That is what his excellency is in chapter to find out."

"And the sword?"

Perrot sighed. "Saint Martin forgive us, it is still lost." Jean-Michel replaced the piece of barley bread he had chosen. Although more flavorful than the horse bread and porridge served in the barracks, it suddenly tasted like ashes.

"I see no need to wrap your hands again," Perrot said. "If the skin remains tender, apply the lotion in that jar."

Jean-Michel screwed up his nose at the thought. Out of curiosity he had already smelled it. The scent was not unlike the vinegary odor drifting through the doorway.

Bishop DeBeauvais entered the infirmary on slippered feet. Open-mouthed, he gaped at the shirt on the wall without lowering his eyes to Jean-Michel, who dropped to his knees. As his robed retinue entered the room, DeBeauvais lifted his ring absently for the knight to kiss. But his yellowed eyes remained on the shirt.

The canons, led by the dean, curtained the bed with their loose linen surplices and wide flowing sleeves. Beneath their amices, the flat-topped headdresses, they wore the smiles they usually reserved for royalty.

"Please, take your rest," DeBeauvais said, gesturing Jean-Michel back to bed. "And thank you,

Brother, for caring for this man of God's choosing."

Perrot genuflected to kiss the ring and then bowed his way out of the clerics' circle.

The bishop squinted, measuring Jean-Michel with the same scrutiny he might use prior to purchasing a hawk. "I come to thank you. I have heard of your prowess," he said.

Jean-Michel kept his eyes on the bishop's bejeweled finger. He remembered the sting of the same ring on his cheek at his dubbing, the last blow a warrior could allow without taking revenge. The bishop had called him *preudome* then, a man of prowess. The same admonition was delivered with a ceremonial slap to every newly-dubbed knight. Jean-Michel had blushed then, and he felt his color rising now. He was as warm as when he entered the burning cathedral.

"You braved the fires of the Fiend himself, who sought in his bitterness to destroy God's church," the bishop said. "So God has favored you with this wondrous sign of His blessing."

The canons bounced their chins in agreement.

"It reminds me of the sword I failed to save," Jean-Michel said. "I grieve for it."

The bishop's drawn face assumed a pained look. "We all do, for it is still lost. Giles, the master of the works, has found pieces of its container. I have ordered the search extended into the barracks and work sheds. Even the priory and the homes of hired workers."

Jean-Michel's stomach cramped. "Do you think one of our own took it?"

"A guard was posted, I am told, but there still may have been foragers." The bishop folded his knotty hands like a noose squeezing a thief's neck.

"But like the woman and the lost coin, we shall sweep every corner and search until it is found."

"Surely it will be," Jean-Michel said. "Why else would God burn the image of the blessed sword onto my sleeve, except to show His favor?"

The canons clucked in each others' ears, but hushed when the bishop raised his palm in rebuke. "Do you presume to know the message of the Eternal?"

Jean-Michel pinched his lips together and lowered his head repentantly. He swallowed to avoid a nervous cough.

"As the Scriptures of God are entrusted to the church to interpret," DeBeauvais said in a grave tone, "so are the signs of God. The brothers and I, after much prayer, have discerned the meaning of this one."

"Then I pray, tell me what it means, that I may be swift to obey my Lord."

The bishop lowered his palm to Jean-Michel's head, as in a commissioning. After he explained the sign of the sword, Jean-Michel thought the hidden message so plain and so pure that he nearly fainted for joy.

In the morning sunlight, Bishop DeBeauvais studied the stone harpies and satyrs gloating from their perches inside the cathedral. Their faces, as though hiding the secret of the fire, leered at the priestly procession below. They reminded the people assembled for Mass of hell's waiting horrors, though by the expressions on their upturned faces, the burnt roof reminded them even better.

The bishop marched behind a corps of priests and cantors draped in long cloaks embroidered with eagles and gryphons whose wings flapped with each stride. The canons' copes bore roses worked in pearls, which swayed as in a summer breeze. *If only the sanctuary smelled as sweet,* thought the bishop. The rabble stank of manure from the fields. Their chatter and prattle muddied the clergy's chant of *Venite Spiritu Sanctus.* Perturbed, Bishop DeBeauvais raised the volume of his voice.

Crossing the transept before the altar steps, the prelate passed between the benches where the burghers, masters of the guilds, and members of the Cathedral Chapter sat. Dressed in fine leathers and silks, the men dabbed at their foreheads with Flemish handkerchiefs. The bishop repressed a grin, knowing it was not the heat of late June that made them sweat, but the prospect of his sermon.

The bishop ascended the steps to the altar after performing the required genuflection. His red velvet vestments, patterned with gold and silk thread, snaked behind him on the steps. His gilded miter pointed heavenward. The concelebrants speaking with him, he intoned the introit to the Mystery.

The changing of bread and wine to body and blood was a great miracle. But without relics, the miracles most sought after by the faithful would be gone, along with their tithes. *When will we process into the church with a new relic?* he wondered while gathering the folds of his cape. He remembered wearing it for the procession of Saint Myrtella's remains into the Cathedral of Beauvais in his home district. The skeleton had worn finery nearly as splendid: It was dressed in the martyr's crimson and a gold crown of victory was fitted to the hairless skull. The festive parade of prelates, with thousands of cheering villagers and peasant villeins in tow, had carried the gorgeous glass casket to the altar for a glorious installation Mass.

He continued the Latin litany for the Feast of Peter and Paul. If only he could afford to go to Rome again, where the great apostles' precious bones lay! How rich in relics was the seat of Peter! In the Chapel of Ten Thousand Martyrs he had sung a Mass to release a departed friend from purgatory's torments. He had earned a twelve-thousand-year indulgence for himself by merely looking upon the Holy Napkin, on which an imprint of Christ's face appeared after St. Veronica wiped the Blessed Brow. In the city of a thousand churches, each claiming a treasure, he had only seen a few—the pillar on which Christ was whipped, Saint John's arm, Judas' pieces of silver, a strip of Christ's robe, Saint Joseph's tools, the skulls of the Holy Innocents, and Saint Martin's well, a gift to the pope from the bishop of Tours.

He could expect no gift from Tours, however. The bishop there, sure to profit from a diversion of pilgrims from Auxonne, would never part with even a hair of Saint Martin. Envious, the bishop frowned, and the deacons stepped back, afraid they'd offended him somehow.

Unless something is done, the bishop worried, his hands moving over the altar draperies, *the people here will go to Troyes.* Not an inconvenient distance away, it was where Bishop Gernier de Trainel, chaplain of the Latin army that had sacked Constantinople fifty years before, had brought many miraculous items. An arm of St.

James the Greater. The skull of St. Philip in a golden reliquary. Drops of Christ's blood set in a silver Byzantine cross. The basin in which Christ washed his disciples' feet. The long-sleeved surplice of Thomas of Canterbury with traces of his spilt brains. A foot of Saint Margaret. Some might even risk the robber-infested roads as far as Sainte-Croix de Provins, to see a fragment of the true cross Count Thibault had bequeathed upon his return from crusade ten years before.

No, the bishop could not afford to lose the people or the pilgrims, nor the support of the merchants whose trades depended on the cathedral. Neither could he lose the allegiance of the local abbeys, should he decide to relocate their relics to the cathedral by decree. To remove a rib from the cloister of Saint Amond or bits of Saint Bernard's robe from Poitelle or even a chip from the stone on which Christ stood when he ascended, kept at the priory of Remy-aux-Loire, would surely be cause for bitter resentment, even rebellion.

The bishop swiveled to hear the epistle and gospel read by a deacon, but he kept thinking about his one remaining option. He would reveal it in the sermon.

The deacon finished. The bishop kissed the upraised parchments, then signed the cross to the congregation. *Dominus vobiscum,* he intoned.

Et cum spiritu tuo, the clergy answered. The people shuffled in the straw, their whispering sounding like wind on a brittle autumn night.

Oremus. The bishop received his golden crosier from an attendant and eyed the men on the front benches. Though they looked anxious, at least they were listening.

He filled his lungs and in French, announced his theme from the prophet Haggai. *Ainsi parle l'Eternal des armees.* "These are the words of the Lord of Hosts: Go up into the hills, fetch timber, and build a house acceptable to me, where I can show my glory, says the Lord." He passed the crosier before him like a pike aimed at the crowd, and continued the scripture. "It is your fault that My house lies in ruins, while each of you has a house he can run to!"

He spoke as if the house in shambles were his own manor. His angry voice did not echo as it could before, but reached into the recesses of the narthex and quieted the crowd.

"The devil did not burn this house, as many say," DeBeauvais shouted. "You burned this house yourselves!"

The burghers mopped their brows as if feeling the fire.

"By your sloth! By your selfishness! By your manifold sins! For loving pleasure and not prayer! You kindled the Almighty Anger, and the fire of His judgment touched this house!"

Already he heard the whimpers of the repentants. Rene the Cobbler folded his arms, but beside him Etienne the Tanner fell to his knees, his dyed fingers interlocked in beseeching.

"Not even the prayers of Saint Martin could stop God's wrath," the bishop preached. "His sword could fight the demons who bring you diseases. But his sword could not fight against God Himself! It melted away in His presence!"

Knights covered their faces. Women began to sob. Their infants fussed. A contagious lament infected the people and their awe over the destruction transformed to shame-filled grief.

The bishop softened his hard face to a fatherly smile and opened his arms in a wide embrace. "But God is full of mercy. His anger does not burn forever. He has sent us a sign of His grace."

The whimpers changed to a rising murmur of assent. In expectation, the crowd called out blessings and vows. Standing in large groups, their voices sounded like rushing water.

The bishop stabbed his crosier toward the rear of the nave. "Behold the sign of God!"

Every head turned at the clanking of metaled feet on stone. The bishop's personal escort, in gleaming full-length mail and flowing surcoats, filed into the sanctuary by twos. Halfway down their shining lines, squeezed between them, marched Jean-Michel d'Anjou, dressed in the holy shirt.

The people cried out and pressed to touch him, but the soldiers closed ranks and pushed them away, carving an aisle through the crowd like a prow through the sea. The sanctuary shook from the people's excited shouting, joyous weeping, and frenzied clambering for a better view.

Once the burly guards had shoved their way to the steps, swinging their spear butts to clear a path, the bishop gestured a welcome. The guards bowed their helmeted heads briefly in respect, while Jean-Michel genuflected. The soldiers, still vigilant, beat back the over zealous.

The bishop raised the crosier in both hands, signaling for silence. He waited until the staff's authority overcame the restless rumbling and the swoons of the fainting. He called out, "God Himself has given the cross of pilgrimage to this brave knight. The seal of the lost sword is on his arm. The strength of the Lord is in his soul. The need of the church is in his hands. Jean-Michel, son of Philippe, Baron of Anjou, will you find a holy relic for us, that we may build a house acceptable to God?"

Jean-Michel touched his fist to his chest. His soft reply sounded against the highest remaining rib-vaults. "With God's help, I will!"

The throng cheered and surged again to touch the sacred shirt. The escort crossed their spears into a solid fence, grimacing from the strain as they pushed. A calm and lonely-looking man in the midst of a swirling maelstrom, Jean-Michel stayed on one knee with a circle of space around him.

The bishop pulled a silver pendant from his inner sleeve. He descended through the guards to Jean-Michel and hung a pilgrim's badge around the knight's bent neck. From a nearby deacon, DeBeauvais received a pilgrim's purse with a long strap. He draped it over the knight's bowed shoulder. Standing as straight as a pier, the bishop admonished Jean-Michel from the book of Romans. "I implore you by God's mercy to offer your very self to Him: a living sacrifice, dedicated and fit for His acceptance." DeBeauvais turned to the audience. "God gives His cross. The knight gives his heart. I give his scrip. What will you give?"

At this signal, the kettle-bearers emerged from the crannies and chapel corners. The pinging of pennies, rings, and bracelets in the iron pots was as beautiful to Bishop DeBeauvais as the chiming of his fallen bells.

3

He loved the feel of her flaxen hair when he combed it with one hand and smoothed it with the other. Her breathing deepened whenever he caressed her this way, praising her in her ear as he stroked. His hand passed down the slope of her back, and when he gave her a playful spank, she whinnied.

"It is early even for you, Fidelity," Jean-Michel whispered. "But the bishop says to leave by cockcrow."

The muscular horse, as high at the withers as Jean-Michel's chin, sighed a mild protest. She looked sleepy despite Bobo's vigorous brushing.

The stout groomsman, laden with bit and bridle, backed into the stall. He unloaded a rolled-up cape from his bowed shoulders and passed the harness to Jean-Michel.

The knight fit it to his charger. "Not even the sparrows are awake yet."

Bobo joined his hands at the fingertips to form a miter and raised them to his head. He bulged his eyes, then squinted.

"But the bishop is awake," Jean-Michel said to his mute servant. "His men, too?"

Bobo nodded, squat, and bounced with his fist at his chest as though holding reins.

"If they are already saddled, we must hurry."

They hoisted the high saddle in place. Bobo buckled it expertly while Jean-Michel held it tight, thinking it was bad to begin a day without Mass. Bobo tested the stirrups, and without request, bent to attach his liege's star-shaped spurs.

"We have a long ride today, Bobo," Jean-Michel said, tugging on his linen surcoat. The ivy-swathed crest of Anjou showed on the chest, a shield to deflect the fiery darts of the Evil One. "Le Chateau DuVal is in the hill country. It is not a good day to fast."

Bobo puffed out his cheeks, drew a circle on his head, and opened the end of the cape on the straw floor. He withdrew a dark loaf of barley bread.

Jean-Michel smiled. "So Brother Perrot thought of us. We'll have it later. Help with the saddlebags now."

After tying the bags to the seat, Jean-Michel mounted with a fluid swing of his leg, hardly clinking his mail shirt. The helmet and chain-mail lining in his bag rattled softly. He adjusted his thick leather belt below the horn, then patted Purity's hilt. The new ring on his hand clicked against the sword, and as he gathered the reins, he glanced at his finger. Saint Christopher, engraved in bronze, was smiling on his journey.

The bishop had fished the ring from one of the collection pots. "This cannot pay for a pilgrimage," he had confided to Jean-Michel. "Would you carry sacks of coppers to every hostel in Christendom? I have another way." The "way," he decided, led to the hall of Hughes DuVal. Judging from the number of hounds and hawks, Jean-Michel guessed the bishop felt as eager to seek game in DuVal's forested fiefs as he was eager to secure funding for a search for new relics.

He kneed his horse out of the stall, ducking the lintel of the stable door. Bobo pushed the door open, and Fidelity clip-clopped out. Bobo's tethered saddle horse, loaded with brushes, bits, and bundles of clothes, shied at the sight of the high war horse. Using kisses and clicks, Bobo calmed it, and took to saddle.

He speaks so well to the beasts, Jean-Michel thought. *If only he could speak to me.* His own father rarely did, and then only to criticize him. The old servant Philippe had left behind for his son seemed more of a father to Jean-Michel.

Together the men headed for the street where they could hear the stamp of impatient hooves. When the bishop saw Jean-Michel's horse nose into line, he ordered his men to advance.

With only a golden oriole's flute-like call for fanfare, the bishop's party left Auxonne. Jean-Michel had imagined leaving with a flourish, cheered by well-wishers and pretty girls offering him tokens from windows. Instead, he departed in the dark, riding between shuttered houses hunched shoulder to shoulder like sleeping bears. Webs of empty laundry lines crisscrossed overhead. Beyond them, Jean-Michel saw the ribboned clouds, spread like rose tourney banners against a lavender sky. A vanguard of ducks led the way.

When he passed the Roman walls and turned to bid farewell to the fog-robed rise of the distant cathedral, he knew he was leaving his old life behind with it. His spirit brightened like the horizon, and he would have joined the oriole's lilting song had it not turned into a catlike cry.

Far across the patchwork plain, Hughes DuVal's imposing manor crowned a verdant hill. Above the rush-lined riverbanks, it looked like a solid block of sandstone erupting from a wreath of trees. It commanded a fine position over the quilted plots of the peasants who toiled below. When they saw the bishop and his retinue passing, the workers dropped their scythes and watched in reverent silence. But the amber wheat waved in greeting, and the bitterns and warblers saluted from the reed-fringed pools.

The river stitched the low hills to the base of the fortress' mound, where it curled around like a glittering necklace, serving as a natural moat. At the toll bridge, the keepers let the bishop through without payment of the usual copper *obal* per traveler, and there was no need to ask if Jews were riding in the party.

The road steepened through the chalk cliffs on the other side into a long, winding climb through sloped pastures. Ranks of stately poplars stood as sentinels over plump sheep grazing among the regal irises and lowly buttercups. Jean-Michel realized the trees he had seen from afar formed an orchard, its trees heavy with apples. Quince and pear trees dotted the neat rows, but the perfume in the air did not come from the fruit. It came from the huge herb gardens sculpted into the terraced rise. Stooped women picked at parsley, mint, sage, lettuce, and fennel. As they genuflected at the bishop's presence, their skirts fanned, and Jean-Michel thought they looked as lovely and colorful as the swallowtail butterflies flickering around them.

Above them all loomed the menacing stone citadel. Round towers stood like grim giants. Turrets capped the crenellated ramparts like Norman helmets. The walls jutted outward at the bottom to propel rocks and hot oil upon besiegers. The high battlements showed streaks of pigeon guano and discolored patches of dried blood. Jean-Michel heard a herald's horn announcing the bishop from the central fort's watchtower.

With peacetime, the drawbridge was down and the gate raised for the noisy clutter of merchants and peasants—the villeins—stating their business to the porter. The grizzled doorkeeper, snarling at the peasants and beggars to make way, waved in the bishop. The horses clattered over the bridge, sending scores of frogs leaping from the scum-covered moat water into the baskets of waiting children. Jean-Michel winced at the sound of splashing water. He clutched Fidelity's reins and did not breathe until he had passed over the bridge.

The horses charged into the dark tunnel of the main gate with a deafening clangor of iron and spilled into the busy courtyard confusion of the outer bailey. Pigs and hens, competing for garbage, scattered with squeals and squawks. Dirty, naked children ran for their mothers in the thatched huts built into the walls. Ducks honked from puddles in the cobbled bailey and flapped up at the cry of the hounds. The falcons replied with ear-splitting shrieks from the mews where the hawkers fed them bits of freshly-killed rat. A startled donkey kicked over its cart, upsetting a load of cabbages. Jean-Michel ached for the grimacing serf who watched the green heads smash to the stones and roll beneath the crushing hooves. Growling curs rushed in for a tempting meal.

Jean-Michel turned toward the gate of the inner bailey, where a noble emerged on foot. From the man's shimmering silks and fur-trimmed cape, Jean-Michel guessed he was the first steward. Shod with smart boots, the greeter strode directly to the bishop's horse and took hold of the harness.

"Your Excellency," he intoned with a bow, "the Lady DuVal begs pardon for not greeting you in person. She sees to the details of the welcoming banquet, to provide you with every comfort." He fixed on Jean-Michel with beady rat eyes, examining him.

"Then peace upon her, and upon the house of DuVal," the bishop said, crossing himself. He surrendered the reins to the first steward, who led them all through the next gate.

They passed a thatched stable where horses champed their fodder. Nearby, a line of villeins waited to pay for the use of the oven house. Jean-Michel's stomach rumbled at the fragrance of freshly baked bread, and his nose twitched at the aroma from the roasting pit where a carcass turned on a spit. Jean-Michel guided Fidelity away from the tempting ricks of hay beside the stables and urged her ahead. "There will be dinner for us both soon," he whispered in her ear.

As they entered the inner ward, they left behind the bustle of men come to kennel the bishop's dogs and cage his screaming birds. No swine or fowl groveled underfoot on the clean pavement.

Two guard towers on the lofty, frowning fortress enforced the quiet. From narrow slits along the winding staircases inside, arbalesters could pick them off easily, had they been invaders breaching the outer walls. But the towers stood silent now, like two stern sergeants overseeing the pinnacled chapel to the right and the baron's handsome residence to the left.

Pages rushed forward to stable the horses and give them every attention. Jean-Michel patted Fidelity to reassure her in her reluctance to be led away by a stranger. The baron's stabler, holding his chin high, reluctantly deferred to Bobo, who led his own horse away, holding off the pages with a scowl.

Bishop DeBeauvais received the steward's ceremonial kisses on the shoulders and hand, and then turned toward Jean-Michel.

"This is the truly honored guest," he said.

The steward extended his palms in welcome, saying, "The noble son of Philippe's house." He kissed Jean-Michel's mouth and chin, the greeting for a man of rank. The steward clapped his hands and a bevy of maids scurried to his side. "Prepare our guest for the banquet," he instructed.

Two servant girls pulled Jean-Michel up the palace stairs to be bathed.

The bishop followed the steward to the barber's quarters where he would be bled for his refreshment.

At first Jean-Michel protested the fuss made over him. Content to splash his face, he wanted only to find a quiet place to pray. But the young handmaidens of the baroness, excited and expert, unhooked his mail, unbuckled his doeskin boots, and unlaced his tunic as quickly as squires. Giggling, they led him to an oak tub filled to the brim with warm water. Jean-Michel hesitated. A husky woman with a bellows was heating a new kettle over the stone hearth. She looked ready to fight him into the tub if necessary. He stepped in, linen foundations and all.

A young maid with ribbons offered Jean-Michel a golden goblet of wine. The other maidens, toying with their braids, stood by with towels at the ready, clutching them to their embroidered gowns.

A honey-haired maiden stood near the hearth with folded robes in her arms. Her narrow headband sparkled with tiny sapphires as blue as her eyes, and Jean-Michel guessed she was the baroness' eldest daughter. She had taken his tunic and carefully draped it over the arm of the high-backed chair beside her. She was watching him, like the others, her eyes cautious and curious.

The girl who had given him the goblet exchanged it for a pig-bristle brush. Jean-Michel held the brush awkwardly, as unaccustomed to it as to a baker's rolling pin. The only other bath he could remember had been a solemn event, a ritual washing away of his sins on the eve of his dubbing. But even then, scrubbing had been unnecessary.

"You are very . . . kind," Jean-Michel said with forced gratitude, his neck muscles tensed. The warm water of the tub stung his tender skin, and the level seemed to be rising to his neck. Jean-Michel fought for control of his breathing. "And your mistress, the Lady DuVal, is she kind as well?"

"She is kind to us," one of the girls said.

"And to strangers?"

"That depends on the mission of the stranger," the honey-haired maiden said in a strange accent.

"It is the same with His Excellency," Jean-Michel explained. His cheeks flushed to mention a cleric while in such a state before women, even if they were so young. Only the honey-haired maid seemed of marriageable age. "He comes to ask a favor of your lady," he said to her.

"She receives many requests, every day," the maiden replied. "The gates are crowded with seekers from dawn to sundown."

"But he is the bishop."

"To her he is a tenant, like the others," the maiden said.

"But surely she will not treat him like all the others?"

"Of course not. Each is treated differently. To the poor, she gives alms. To merchants, a market. To wandering minstrels, a place at dinner. To men on mysterious missions, a hearing."

"And a bath," Jean-Michel said.

The attendants giggled and whispered to each other.

"And am I so mysterious?" Jean-Michel asked.

"Not so much anymore," the maiden said with a glance toward his discarded clothing.

"We have heard of your shirt," a towel girl said. The beribboned servant next to her elbowed her.

"An awful fire," said another.

"Does His Excellency seek a donation for repairs?" the honey-haired girl asked.

"In a way," Jean-Michel said as the goblet-girl motioned for towels.

The attendants came forward, let the towels drop open and wrapped him as he stepped out onto the flagstones. He felt raw and skinny, like a chicken plucked and soaked for deboning.

As he took the robe from the honey-haired girl, she asked, "Your answer was interrupted, messire. Does the bishop seek money, or no?"

"I seek a relic in place of Saint Martin's sword," Jean-Michel said, "that the house of God may be rebuilt. His Excellency seeks the aid of your mistress in helping me find one."

"But the house of DuVal keeps no relics, although our lord permits minor ones for the women's prayer boxes and the swords of men-at-arms. Not even the chapel has any. Only a Host."

"I seek no relic here," Jean-Michel said as he tied the waist cord. "I seek the means to search for a relic on pilgrimage, if it pleases your lady."

The maiden's blue eyes measured his. "You will please her."

Jean-Michel entered the great hall for dinner dressed in a fresh shirt tucked into leather trousers. Purity swung at his side with a reassuring thump on his thigh. He made for the oak tables, set on trestles along the walls, where men and women of common rank jested and played with dice. His two female attendants, however, tugged him away toward a raised dais at the head of the hall. Before being steered away, Jean-Michel caught sight of Bobo shaking a handful of dice, and he frumped with disapproval.

On the platform sat several canopied chairs, elaborately carved and cushioned. The bishop occupied one as if it were his throne. His gorgeously patterned cape tumbled over the arms and gathered in folds on the stone floor. In velvet cap and satin slippers he looked more dressed for court than for supper. He spoke to officials of the baron's household seated beside him—the first steward, his rat eyes roving, a marshal, and an elderly noble cupping his ear to listen. On backless benches near them sat other knights and household charges, bragging and laughing.

The young girls guided Jean-Michel through a thick carpet of river rushes perfumed with dried roses and wildflowers toward one of the massive chairs, two seats away from the bishop. The central one, Jean-Michel guessed, was reserved for the Baroness DuVal, and he was to dine at her right hand. His stomach knotted in nervousness. What would she be like? If she was anything like Hughes, he had an evening to dread.

As he took his seat and the girls curtseyed and left him, he felt much too small for the chair. A scruffy dog nosing in the reeds for bones and bread crusts sniffed at him and barked. Sensing many eyes on him, he straightened and scanned the noisy hall.

At the opposite end, a long fireplace, where enormous logs on high andirons crackled with flame, thrust into the room. A loud-mouthed minstrel, surrounded by admiring females, tuned his lute by the fire light. His golden hair, tied back into a single braid down his neck, swung like a tail when he laughed. His chortling had a growl in it that set the ladies to swooning. Jean-Michel hoped the jongleur's lute sounded better than his laugh.

He recalled the honey-haired maiden's mention of itinerant jongleurs at the gates, seeking supper in exchange for songs. This was one of those vagrants, Jean-Michel surmised with a disapproving look. After the meal he would entertain the gluttonous guests and incite their wine-dulled minds to revelry—just like other minstrels in his father's hall.

Rich tapestries suspended from ribbed rafters reminded him of the songs of brave deeds, the *chansons de gestes*, recited in Philippe's hall. One wall hanging embroidered in dull reds and golds depicted the raising of the gauntlet to heaven by the hero of the Song of Roland pledging fealty to God. Others depicted hunting scenes, and Jean-Michel supposed that Hughes would bring back Arabian carpets to cover a few more drafty cracks in the stonework.

The old seneschal, the overseer of the estate, tottered to his feet to announce the arrival of the Baroness DuVal. He tapped his cane. The crowd's chattering ceased, and all rose to their feet with the screech of benches on stone and the clunk of mugs on table tops. As the bent man bowed in the direction of the baroness, Jean-Michel feared the seneschal would tumble over from weakness. But when he turned to see the baroness for himself, he nearly tumbled over with surprise.

The honey-haired maiden wearing the jeweled headband strode to the platform with a royal gait. Her flowing hair hung in two great braids entwined with gold thread. They swished on a white silk gown stitched with gold and edged with Flemish lace. Her high cheeks glowed with the blush of peaches and her rose-pink lips parted in a discrete smile. She was amused at his astonishment.

After she passed behind him and reached her chair, Jean-Michel bowed his head in courtesy. His gaze fell on her freckled hands. The same hands that held his robe before, he noticed, were hands that knew how to ride, hunt, and use a bow. They were calloused hands, tough and capable, and scratched from falcons' claws. He didn't recall the rings: a gold one with a sapphire to protect her from poisoning and a ten-beaded piece used for the rosary.

He raised his sights to her confident face; a smile played about the corners of her mouth. As she grasped the chair's arms and alighted on the cushion, the room burst into chatter again.

Squires pushed the tables closer to the dignitaries, while servers brought trenchers of sliced stag, platters of pork with prunes, and roast rabbit soup in small wooden bowls. Long pope's loaves, borne on bakers' shoulders, were laid on the tables and sliced.

Jean-Michel took a slab of the bread and used a squire's knife to cut away the crust. According to custom, he offered the soft part to the baroness to dip in her soup. She accepted it, dunked it, and bit it with pearly teeth. She chewed closed-mouthed, the ends of her lips curling in a mischievous smirk. She was pleased with the trick she had played on him.

"May I present Philippe d'Anjou's youngest son," the bishop said. He had gravy on his chin. "Jean-Michel, who has the love for God of Saint John and the courage of Saint Michael."

"So you are Jean-Michel?" she asked, as if they had never met. Jean-Michel stopped chewing and merely nodded, afraid he might choke.

"And the Baroness Blanche DuVal, formerly of the house of Etienne of Provence," the bishop said.

Jean-Michel gulped his venison. "I am so very, that is . . ."

"You wish to say 'pleased' or 'honored' but you mean to say 'surprised', *n'est-ce pas?*" She dabbed at her lip, wet and shiny, using a white embroidered napkin. "I was betrothed to Hughes at age fourteen. I have been in the north for only these last four years. You expected a wife of Hughes' own age."

The wine-pourers arrived. A sunny cabernet as bright as Blanche's smile flowed from the silver flagons.

"You did, did you not?" she said, sipping the wine. She made a face. "This is good, but the Sancere from Gascony in the South is better, do you not agree?" She raised her quizzical eyebrows and stroked the goblet's thick stem.

"My lady, it is surely as sweet and pure as you are," he said, trying to control his voice as her pink tongue tasted a lingering drop on the edge of the goblet.

"It is an excellent wine, and a tribute to your cellars," the bishop put in. "A testimony to your fine manners and foresight."

The bishop lauded Blanche throughout the second course. He praised her able management of the estate and her fairness to her tenants. He commended the pheasant with walnut dressing. He blessed her humility and courage to leave her home in Provence to marry Hughes, whom she had never met. He extolled the capon, mallard, and frog legs (fresh from the moat, Jean-Michel recalled). He acclaimed her gentility and generosity. He applauded the roast teal, pouring his compliments as thick as the saffron-spiced sauce.

The bishop's gushing did not distract Blanche from her meal. She took small bites, chewed quietly, and touched her puckered mouth often with a napkin. She nodded in the bishop's direction but looked past him, listening with a deferential distance. She directed the squires with discrete hand signals to slice bits of meat for her dogs, which sat, with perked ears and lively tails, before the table. She put aside her scraps for the beggars while the bishop mopped his plate clean with a fistful of bread.

"Is there news from your husband?" DeBeauvais asked, licking his sausagy fingers.

"Only that he is well," Blanche said, "and that he requires the monthly accounts, as always. I am pleased, on his behalf, that yours are in order."

"He always was an exact man," DeBeauvais said, a hint of displeasure in his tone. "Do you have a courier?"

Using two hands as though receiving a chalice, the baroness received a silver goblet from a cup-bearer. "There are many couriers on the king's business who pass by the river on their way to the Holy Land," she said. "The Queen Mother takes care to keep her son informed of matters of the realm while he sojourns among the Saracens." She dried her pouting lip, sipped from the cup, and handed it to Jean-Michel. "There are also those who go on pilgrimage."

Jean-Michel's heart bucked in his chest as he locked eyes with the young woman and accepted the cup. Their fingertips met, and a thrill raced up his arm. Reflections from the rim danced on her dress and cast a thin wreath of gold across her hair like a bridal crown. He tasted the wine, a light Muscadet, tart and teasing like her smile. It tingled on his tongue—like her kisses, he thought.

"It is on a matter of pilgrimage that we have come," the bishop said.

"Do you plan to go and take my ledgers?" she asked.

"Not at all," DeBeauvais said, shaking his head. "I speak of Jean-Michel."

"Oh?" She feigned surprise. "If you have come to invite me, I am honored, but unable. My duty is here."

Jean-Michel's mouth went cottony, and he sipped a second time before passing the cup to DeBeauvais as if it were a nuptial mass, when the chalice passes between the betrothed. He wondered how Blanche had felt when she handed the wedding cup to Hughes, a man surely as old as her own father. What would she have felt if his own hands had entwined hers at the altar instead of Hughes'? If they had exchanged the rings of union and the blessing had been given and the banquet enjoyed and the tourney enjoined by all the nobles of Philippe's allegiances, would she have smiled as she was smiling now? After his father's drunken hugs of congratulations, when the guests curled up on their cloaks on the floors, would they have stolen away to the chamber with the scented candles. Then the braids would be unwound and she would coo and coax him with wine-sweet kisses.

"This is not what you came here to do," Blanche said.

Her real voice jerked Jean-Michel back to the banquet. He felt his cheeks blooming and stuffed his mouth with stag.

"No, indeed," the bishop said, leaning closer. "God has called this man through a miraculous sign to a holy quest."

Blanche smoothed her gown in her lap and folded her hands there, demure and defensive. "So I have heard of it."

"And soon you shall see it for yourself," the bishop said.

The baroness looked like she wanted to smile, but she primmed her mouth.

"By it," the bishop continued, "God has shown favor on His church. So in thanksgiving we pledge to send forth His chosen one, fully supplied, to find such relics as God will provide for the restoration of His house in Auxonne. We urge all to participate in this blessing, unaffected by covetousness. As you know so well by managing the fields, one who sows sparingly shall also reap sparingly and one who sows bountifully shall also reap bountifully. As God is able to make all grace abound to you such that you have all sufficiency in everything, you also have an abundance for sowing good deeds unto a harvest of righteousness in the world to come."

While the bishop droned, the baroness studied Jean-Michel's face. She looked at him as keenly as a cellarer examining bottles. Entranced, Jean-Michel searched her sapphire eyes for a sparkle of empathy for his quest. But her eyes had become cold gems, calculating and practical, the playfulness blown away by the bishop's windy words.

"Thus will you be further enriched in largesse," DeBeauvais concluded.

The banqueters applauded. The bishop smiled in appreciation. But the claps and cries of approval rose for the cooks, who were wheeling in a flat cart with a peacock resting on grass-green pastry. The bird's plumage fanned in a bright display of aqua, as if the bird were alive and primping. Behind the cart, two squires tugged an enormous pasty. The filling bubbled against the crust.

The crowd hushed expectantly as Blanche rose, rounded the table, and descended from the dais. Ceremoniously she took a dagger from a squire and poised it over the crust. With a deft stroke, she sliced open the pie.

A score of little birds flew out and darted about the room with a noisy flutter. The anteroom doors were flung open and the baroness' falconers entered. They unhooded their hawks, which soared from their gloves to the kill. The feasters ducked and hooted with delight, cheering the predators. The terrified prey trilled over the tables as peregrines and goshawks swooped upon them with deadly efficiency, sinking needle-sharp talons into their backs in midair. The prey crashed onto the tables and tumbled in the rushes, their wings spread out to brake. The bells on the falcons' leg jesses jingled as they drove in their claws.

The dogs growled in scattered fights for the slain sparrows and snipe, but the hawks slashed with hooked beaks and gashed a snout or two. With raw meat on their gloves, the hawkers spread out in the hall to reclaim their birds. They covered the dead woodcock and thrushes with their leather-wrapped hands and pressed on the hawks' legs, coaxing them to step up to the offered meat. Some birds flew back to their masters at the sound of a whistle.

Amid the falcons' screams of victory and the laughter of guests and the snarls of dogs denied, the dead birds were gathered into sacks and whisked into the kitchen. Servers passed bowls of walnuts for dessert, and spiced wine in clinking glass cups. The bishop received his gladly, but Jean-Michel ignored his.

Instead he watched Blanche congratulating the head falconer, a dark man with narrow eyes and a sneer for a smile. The man stroked the bloody breast feathers of his white gyrfalcon, a huge bird in a hood of tooled leather capped by fluffy white plumes. Jean-Michel regarded both Blanche and the bird. Each was regal, beautifully colored, and independent, though bound by obligations.

When she returned to the platform, her gown furled like flying wings, she took her chair as gracefully as a gyrfalcon takes its perch. The bishop, his robes spread in peacock fashion, gave thanks and bade the guests to rise and wash in time for the entertainment. His mouth looked like the thin slit in the pasty. And Jean-Michel thought the bishop's many words, like the little birds, would come to no good end. Sitting beside Blanche, he felt like one of the birds himself—plain, powerless, and in her grasp.

While the guests splashed their faces at the basins and the trestles were kicked away and the tables carried off, the jongleur skipped to the platform and bowed before Blanche. His braid flipped up and his brief tunic, a lurid purple, hiked up to expose his garish blue and magenta striped hosen. His gaudy green silk shirt, open to the navel, showed a hairless chest.

"I fly to the fist / With one that you missed," he crooned. He snapped erect and thrust his hands ceilingward. A white dove flew up from his palms to the rafters.

Blanche applauded with surprise and pleasure. "Renard," she laughed, "you are full of tricks."

He is full of pride and foolishness. Jean-Michel frowned, distrusting the singer's cockeyed grin.

"Will you please us with a song?" Blanche asked. "As I please you every night," Renard said, winking.

Does this jester dare to defile this dove? Jean-Michel was burning. He felt for Purity's hilt and measured the distance to the jongleur's jugular. *An easy reach*, he thought.

"Cousin, what song have you tonight?" Blanche asked.

"A song of pilgrimage—for relics and for royal honor," Renard answered, his impish eyes switching to Jean-Michel and reading his expression of surprise.

"Then play on," Blanche said. She sat, her palms together, poised for applause, and her face aglow with anticipation. "I know which one he will sing," she whispered to Jean-Michel. "He sang it while we were yet children, and father once thrashed him for it."

"Children?"

"Did you not hear? He is my cousin, from Languedoc in the South."

So that is where you learned your pranks. It also explained her subtle, exotic speech, which pleased his ear.

"But he disguises his accent quite well, *n'est-ce pas*? Another of his tricks, the fox."

Le renard, Jean-Michel thought. A stage name, no doubt, borrowed from the Beast Epic bearing the name of its chief rascal, the fox. *Is that his specialty*? But jongleurs knew dozens of tales with thousands of lines. Jean-Michel searched his own mind in vain for the memory of Renard the Fox on pilgrimage. *He would only do such a thing as a trick to escape a well-deserved hanging.*

Renard the Jongleur hugged the pear-shaped belly of the lute close to his lap and tickled its blonde strings with a lover's playfulness. Even the rowdiest men were stilled by the opening notes of his lusty baritone voice, and the little snarl in it encouraged prickles on ladies' necks.

Once Charles Le Magne gird on his sword and crown,
both wrought of gold,
And with his dame he faced his lords and barons,
rightly bold
And said, "Is there another king of whom it may be told,
'He conquered many cities! There are none he
cannot hold?'"

The Empress, she (foolhardily) replied, "But yea,
my king,
There is a one, far in the East, to whom not any thing
Is e'er denied. As for his wealth, each finger bears a ring
As symbols of the provinces which tribute to him bring."

The king was wroth, and shouted forth, "If thou hast
lied to me
Then you will feel the bite of steel on thy neck, speedily."
"For love of God, I am thy wife, and I thought but to jest!
I'll make amends; I'll cast me down from heights, at your
behest!"

Renard's falsetto voice and fluttering eyes drew chuckles from the crowd. He strummed and then sang on.

"Nay, do not that," quoth Charles, "but straitway only say
his name."
And on her knees, in hopes to please her lord, the answer
came,
"Hugon the Strong, who ruleth Greece, from
Constantine's great throne,
And Cappadocia, Antioch, and Persia are his own.
There is no baronage like his, excepting thine alone."

So Charles Le Magne, at Saint Denis, made offerings at Mass,
And laid his head upon his bed to let the anger pass.
But thrice a dream befell him there,
wherein he went across
The distant sands to worship at the Sepulchre and Cross.

Renard regarded Jean-Michel while picking at the string. The young knight's hand went to his shoulder where the fire had left its sting. He wondered if he'd find himself in what the fool would sing.

Enthralled like the others in the hall, he heard Charles call the names: Dukes William, Gerin, Berenger, and Ogier the Dane; Naymes the Hard, Aimer, Bertram, and Bernard De Brisbane, with Roland and fair Oliver, two knights of hero's fame.

Nodding to the bishop, Renard rounded off the list with Archbishop Turpin, making twelve companions in all, in imitation of Christ. The jongleur repeated the grandiloquent speech in which Charles bade them to journey with him to the Holy Places to seek a king of great wealth, and to vow to never return until they found him.

Bringing a train of mules and sumpter horses laden with gold, supplies, and tents of silk, the king passed through Saint Denis for the Archbishop's blessing and to receive a pilgrim wallet at the cathedral. Jean-Michel thought of his own scrip, which was stored in his chamber. Would this story move Blanche to supply his need and put a few *derniers* into his pilgrim's purse? By her glassy look, she was not thinking of him, but of the king of the Franks and his army, eighty thousand strong, trooping over Lorraine, Bavaria, and Hungary and through the forests of Croatia and Greece into the hills of Romany and the mountains of the Turks and all their hated enemies beyond to the Holy City where Christ trod and died. Renard's description transported them all, so each banqueter imagined himself in the company of France's great king.

He entered first that church where wine and bread were first
transformed,
A room with twelve Apostles' chairs, and one more in their
midst,
He sat upon the central seat. Each other noble warmed The
rest.
And how their faces glowed with heaven's very bliss!

A Jew came in and saw the king, and thus began to tremble
For so exalted was Charles' countenance that he resembled
Christ Himself, come back to reign, with His twelve
Apostles assembled!
The Jew fled to the Patriarch, and up the stairs he stumbled,
"Baptize me now, for I have seen the One of whom ye
preach!
The same is in the minster with His barons!"
he beseeched.
The Patriarch begowned himself in vestments white and
bleached,
And with a grand procession, chanting hymns, the bishop
reached
The room. He bowed to Charles; he took his hands, and
kisseth each.

Renard spun around and fell to his knee in fealty to a suzerain before a startled Jean-Michel. "Sire, where is the land of thy birth?" Renard recited in the whiney voice of the Patriarch. "Ere this time, no man dared enter this vault except at my command or by my counsel."

The guests laughed at Jean-Michel's sudden role as Charles the Great.

"I am Charles," Renard boomed, as if prompting Jean-Michel, "and France is the land that bore me! Twelve kings have I conquered, and a thirteenth I seek, and I am come to worship at the Sepulcher and Rood."

"A worthy knight thou art," Renard continued as the Patriarch, "for thou sittest in that same seat as God Himself sat, and Charles the Great thou truly art."

Jean-Michel resisted shifting in his chair, which felt harder than before. He dared not display his discomfort.

"God thank thee five hundred-fold!" Renard replied in Charlemagne's lion-like voice. "If it please thee, give me of thy holy relics to bear back to France, to glorify there in a cathedral."

Jean-Michel's palms dampened. He controlled his expression, although his stomach knotted with uncertainty. Was he being mocked, or honored, or tested? Blanche was covering her mouth to hide her amusement, but he resolved not to become resentful in her presence. Instead, he listened with renewed interest as Renard assumed the Patriarch's part again.

Thou hast done well in coming here
To find God and His treasure.
I give thee relics, none better
On earth, rich beyond measure—

The head of twice-dead Lazarus,
The arm of Simon Martyr,
The blood that Jesu spilled for us,
The milk of Virgin Mother,
The nail that pierced Jesu's feet,
The chalice that He blessed,
The knife that Jesu held at meat,
All these have I possessed.

"And right virtuous they were," Renard added in a resonant contralto, turning to the rapt audience. "For when the Patriarch caused them to be brought, a cripple lying hard by, who had not moved in years for his cracked bones, leaped up with a shout! So the Patriarch caused the city bells to resound, and the king caused a reliquary to be made. A thousand marks of the finest gold of Araby were melted for its mold, and the Archbishop Turpin was charged with its protection." He gestured to DeBeauvais, who grinned broadly.

What relic will God entrust to me, and where will He lead me to find it? Jean-Michel wondered while Renard continued the tale of Charlemagne's chivalric deeds. The story gave him no comfort; instead it tempted him to envy. He was no king like Charlemagne, now departing with a hundred mules via Jericho. He had no Patriarch to guide him in search of Hugon the Strong.

"I have met all requests of thine," Renard said in the Patriarch-voice. "Knowest thou what I would fain ask of thee?" He looked deeply into Jean-Michel's eyes. "Destroy the Saracens, who hold us in contempt."

Does he accuse me, that I did not go with father? The jongleur's gibe bit like a basilard into Jean-Michel's chest. His bicep itched where the cross was stitched with flame. *Perhaps I am to go,* he thought. *God did speak through a mule to Balaam, so can He speak through this ass as well.*

Renard recounted Charles' promise to go to Spain: "And so he did, later. He kept his faith, in which time Roland met his death."

To Spain? To the shrine of Saint Jacques Compostelle? That was a pilgrimage yearned for by thousands, second only to ones to Rome. But did not God plan to direct him to a place not so, well, so trampled? Was there not a relic to be found in France?

He quickly rebuked himself for being so haughty and close-minded to whatever message lay in the story for him, even if it did come from the mouth of Renard.

> Thus Charles Le Magne rode on with relics strong through
> God's own might,
> Their virtue healed the cripple, and the blind received their
> sight,
> They opened up the rivers so like Israel they could reach
> The other side all dry. The deaf could hear; the mute had
> speech.

Jean-Michel glanced at Bobo. Though hearing these words, the groomsman did not seem to brighten. Like the company around him, he sat entranced at Renard's description of Constantinople's belfries and bridges, gardens and great knights clad in ermine, their fair ladies beside them in gleaming gold embroidery. Even grander was the palace, veined with azure, lit by diamond windows, adorned by silver statues of beasts and birds, upheld by marble pillars plaited with crystal and ivory. Charles looked upon it all in awe and remembered his Dame, whom he had threatened, just as Hugon entered with his Empress and fair daughter.

> Her hair was spun gold, her face like a dove,
> As Oliver gazed, his heart turned with love.
> "O may it please God to call her my own,
> to take all my pleasure in this one alone."

Renard looked at Blanche once he said it. Jean-Michel again felt the blood rush into his cheeks. His temples tensed. He missed most of Renard's description of the banquet which Hugon gifted to Charles, featuring venison and peppered peacock, fountains of wine and clever jongleurs. The guests applauded, complimenting the baroness for providing a feast equally as sumptuous. Renard took his bows as well, catching his breath as he plucked at the lute.

> The Franks are in chamber and well-filled with wine,
> And each has taken to his own broad bed
> With pillows of samite and covers of ermine,
> Without knowing a servant of Hugon is hid
> Within the hollowed wall, his ears big as thine.

Renard pinched a squire's ear, and continued singing.

> "Look well on this splendor," Charles thus began,
> "And upon the fine knights! Yet take any man
> And let him be armed with two helms, on a courser,
> And let me smite with my sword where the helmet shines bright;
> It would cut through helm, head, and horse
> Into the earth and go its own way to a lance's height,
> That no mortal man could pull it up again."

The audience cheered for each of the twelve outlandish boasts that followed from the king's drunken men.

Roland declared he would blow Hugon's ivory horn so hard that every palace door, no matter how heavy, would fly from its hinges.

Ogier, Duke of Denmark, claimed he could grasp the central pillar of the palace and spin it upside-down. The winter-white Naymes bragged that though bow-legged, he could leap the city's awesome bulwarks. Count Berenger dared that he could leap from the same walls upon all the up-turned swords in Hugon's army and smash every one without a scratch on himself. So each in turn, with blustery boldness, outdid one another in exaggerating their strengths and skills, prompting cheers from the banqueters, until Oliver's.

> "Boast thou, Sir Oliver," quoth the king.
> "Gladly," saith the knight, "if to thee it be pleasing.
> If Hugon took his daughter with hair so fine,
> And brought her to me that mayhaps we would wed,
> With only one kiss she would beg to be mine,
> Else, by my oath, I should lose my own head."

The men guffawed. The women cupped their mouths and whispered giggles. But Jean-Michel, embarrassed, stitched his lips and looked down, thinking of how much warmer the room had become.

> "By my faith," quoth the spy, his face turning red,
> "How foolish of Hugon to give them their beds.
> They show neither shame, nor regard for their heads!"

"So he visited Hugon in his chamber," Renard narrated, "who inquired in haste, 'Tell me, what doth this proud Charles? Does he plan to remain with me?'

"'By my faith,' quoth the spy, 'they gave no thought to it. This night they boasted a plenty at thine expense, and mocked thine house and daughter.'"

"And King Hugon waxed angry with each reported boasting as the spy remembered them. 'By the Lord,' saith the king, 'This is great folly! If they do not fulfill their boasts, I shall cut off their heads with Excelsior my sword and display them on pikes at the gates!'"

A hundred thousand of his men he summoned to gird on armor and polished swords, to attend him in the morning. So when Mass was sung, and Charles and his twelve bold peers came from the church, Hugon closed his mighty ranks around him and spoke to Charles reproachfully.

> "For what reason didst thou boast
> At my expense upon thy beds?
> Is this the way you treat your hosts?
> Now I shall have your heads!
> Unless you can fulfill your most
> Outrageous boast, instead!"
> A hundred thousand swords were drawn, the sound of steely thunder,
> And Charles did fear on one command they'd all be cut asunder.

The audience and even the pages, who stopped tending the wall torches, waited with bated breath.

Renard softened his voice. "The Emperor of the Franks looked upon his brave men, distressed. 'Methinks the king had a spy in our chamber while we were overcome by wine and our own pride.' Then to the king, he quoth, 'Sire, it is our custom, when we have had enow of wine and our hearts are merry, to go to bed with games and boasts of both wisdom and folly. If, perchance, we have wronged thee, let me speak aside to my bold barons, to seek a recompense, by my pledge.'

"'By my pledge,' quoth Hugon, 'too great is the shame! Speak if you must, but by my white beard, when you depart from me you will never boast again!' "

> So Charles Le Magne took counsel with his men beneath the shade,
> "Seigneurs," quoth he, "Evil hath befallen us! We have bade
> It come on ourselves, from foolish talk and too much wine and mead."

He called for the relics, and they smote their breasts to pray
A tearful penance, asking God for King Hugon to stay
His wroth. Behold, an angel came, shining like a star
Who lifted Charles. "Be not dismayed," quoth she,
"Thy boastings are
Indeed great folly! Christ thy King bids thee never
do the same
To any man again. But now, fulfill any Hugon names,
For none of them shall fail." The king rejoices,
like his men.
They cross themselves, come out, and speak to Hugon
once again.

"Sire," quoth Charles, "If you are offended as a host, then we are likewise offended as guests, for you left us with a spy, a great felony in our homeland. We shall, therefore, for a proof of God's favor, fulfill any boasting ye choose."

And Hugon did not hesitate, nor did the king mischoose.
"Here standeth Oliver, the foolish knave who vowed to lose
His head, else with a single kiss he could persuade to wed
My only daughter! Should he fail, then ye shall all be dead!"

Renard picked at the lute to indicate the passage of time.

"And when quiet night had come, the guards took Oliver to the daughter's chamber of silken curtains. And she herself, her skin as white as roses in summer, waited in a gown of finest weave, like a mist on a swan. Her flower-fresh mouth spoke from behind a veil a courteous and seemly word: 'Sir, have you left France to slay the women of the East?'

"'Fear not, fair one,' quoth Oliver, 'for you have already slain me.' He took his place beside her, and saith, 'Lady, thou art fair, full of virtue and loveliness, and therefore, though I have spoken a boast, I will not fulfill it against thy desire.'

"'Sir,' quoth the maiden, 'have pity on me. I shall never have joy again if you deny me now and put me to shame. For 'twas I who urged the king to choose your boast from among the others as the one boast not possible to do, even with an angel's help, and so save my father's honor.'

"'Dear damsel,' quoth Oliver, 'then let us kiss, not to acquit a boast, but to seal a vow that I will love thee forever and boast only of your fairness.'

"And thus, while sealing, Hugon burst in upon them and pried them apart. He demanded of his daughter, 'Will you have this boaster?'

"'Yea, my lord,' she answereth. 'To him I forever pledge my troth.'

"No need to ask if the king was wroth."

When the laughter had subsided, Renard wrapped up the story, strumming happily.

"Our queen did speak a wrong when praising this king," quoth the Franks,
and nothing now they wish for is denied. Thus, giving thanks
unto their God, they have enow of venison and geese,
and crane, and Hugon offers as much treasure as they please
to bear away, but Charles didst say, 'Alas, they cannot carry
it, already they have all my wealth, and may not tarry
here. The mules and sumpter beasts were ready for their mounts
when Hugon's daughter ran to Oliver. She hugged the Count.
"To thee I've given all my love and friendship, that perchance
you bear me in thine arms anon and carry me to France."
Quoth Oliver, "Of all the riches Charles on me doth bestow,
thou art the greatest treasure! Sit beside me, let us go."
Right glad was Charles, that doughty knight, what need to stretch the tale?
They passed through foreign realms and came to Paris, where the grail

> **and all the other relics were paraded for display.**
> **Charles sent them severally throughout his kingdom, where today**
> **A traveler may find a one, if God show him the way.**

Renard bowed to Jean-Michel at the last line, sweeping his arm as if pointing the way to go.

The guests burst into applause. Like Blanche, many jumped to their feet, their cheeks shining with happy tears. The women flung themselves at the singer, mad with love for him, and smothered him with kisses. He broke free and left his lute at Blanche's feet, a sign of surrender to her. Twirling, he raced to the door and waved goodnight to his cheering admirers, winking at the disappointed maidens left behind as a promise for another time.

The guests, in a lowering murmur, claimed their customary corners in the rushes and huddled in pairs. The torchbearers removed the tapers from their brackets to light the way throughout the hall. Bobo followed the squires to their appointed places in the stables.

The bishop stood to leave. Blanche dipped her knee to kiss the bishop's ring when he passed, and Jean-Michel did likewise. After DeBeauvais departed, Jean-Michel found himself face to face with Blanche, each on their knees as if they had just received the bishop's nuptial blessing.

In the hearthlight, Blanche's taffeta gown glowed like a beacon, drawing Jean-Michel forward toward the harbor of her embrace.

"Good morrow," she said curtly, standing and spinning away from him. Attended by her maidens, she disappeared from the hall, the swoosh-swoosh of her silken dress lost in the rustling of guests bedding themselves for the night. In the dim light, Jean-Michel retained the image of her prim face, its golden hue no longer soft like peach but hard like the sandstone walls of her fortress.

His two attendants from before escorted him to his room.

"Good night, sisters," he said, sending them away, "and please God, who never slumbers."

When his eyes adjusted to the pale moonlight, he rubbed away the image of Blanche's brassy braids. How could he have imagined she would ever be his lady? He hung Purity over the bed post where he could reach it for strength. How could he have believed Blanche would fund a stranger's pilgrimage? *Perhaps I am not meant to go at all*, he thought despondently as he dropped into bed. Like Charles Le Magne, it was the King, Louis IX, who was on pilgrimage, chosen by God to return relics to the realm. But would Auxonne, a backwater parish, receive one of them? *Unlikely*. His stomach rumbled with discouragement. What was the meaning of the shirt? And of the song? He implored the Mother of God, whose presence always calmed his troubled stomach and turbulent heart. As he drifted into a dream in the solace of her embrace, he heard Renard's voice again. It was distant, but not in his imagination. The playful snarl came through the flue of his hearth, followed by a woman's giggle.

In the predawn darkness, Blanche marched through the castle corridors, her huge silver key ring, used to unlock cupboards and closets, swinging at her side. She cast long shadows in the light of the torches behind her, as the sleepy bearers struggled to match her brisk pace.

Perhaps if she kept busy she would not think of him.

She doled out the daily supplies to the maids and cooks, who had been hurriedly roused from their beds, earlier than usual. She received the steward's drowsy report while inspecting the castle's complex honeycomb of linked halls, chambers, bastions, annexes, stables, and gardens. All would soon be abuzz from footsteps running up and down stairs, kettles clanking in the larders and barrels bumping in the wine cellars, hooves stamping in the stalls, javelins jingling in the armory, and falcons screaming in the aviary.

Gascon the Falconer was already up and training young birds to pounce on the prey—pheasant wings tied to a stick. He slept with them so they would get used to his human smell, though Blanche believed he had taken on the odor of their guano instead.

The night began to fold away like the purple curtains on her canopied bed. Blanche hastened to the chapel ahead of her torchbearers, their fires spewing a stupefying smell of resin. It was nearly as stifling as the stink of refuse drifting from the gully outside the manor walls, walls that daily seemed higher, thicker, and closer together. Even her clothes felt constrictive and ill-fitting, and she strained against them when she crossed the claustrophobic courtyard, trying not to appear eager.

She saw the knight at Mass. His eyes were closed and his soft mouth moved in prayer. His slender fingers joined at the ends like a spear tip on the lance of his strong arm. His hands looked agile and gentle, unlike Hughes' rough, stubby hands. She remembered how raw and soiled she felt when Hughes groped at her on their wedding night and how afterward he had no need for her. Instead, according to custom, he had "sampled" the peasant men's fiancées, and hanged any who resisted him. How often she had lain alone on the vast feather bed, cold and curled up, thinking of the seigneury children in her care as baronness, but knowing none of them as mother.

But she had known no other man.

She sighted Jean-Michel across the chasm of the aisle. His eyes were still closed. No, they were squeezed, fervent in petition, not flagged in fatigue like those of the others. She faced forward, hoping no one had seen her staring so rudely.

Had he looked up as she looked down? She had the feeling they were stealing glances. She tugged at her trailing sleeves to straighten them and to line up the mother-of-pearl set in the seams. She fretted over her uneven barbette, the stiff linen hat wrapped under her chin and over her braided hair. It felt lumpy. Her hair had been plaited in a hurry by dim candlelight. How she wished she could wear her hair free and flowered as in Provence. But here it must be bound and restricted, like her heart.

At the bishop's dismissal, she departed first while the congregation stood. She resisted the temptation to peek over her shoulder to see if the knight's steel-gray eyes were upon her. Somehow, she knew they were.

Stepping outside, she enjoyed the clear summer sky, blue as the banner of Saint Denis. The soft breeze that caressed her cheek and the sunbeam that kissed her chin lightened her spirit. *A good day for the chase*, she thought.

Seated on her bed of state, richly made up with cushions and counterpane, she ordered her braids re-tied. The serving girls unwound them and began to twist and weave while Blanche breakfasted on weak wine and bread. After the silk ribbons were tied and she satisfied herself in a looking glass, she moved to a high, heavy chair and gave audience to a parade of inquirers.

Marcel the bailiff complained as usual about unruly peasants.

"We caught two with dead hares from your grace's fields," he gruffed. He twitched his pepper-black mustache indignantly. "What punishment do you order?" he asked.

Hares, she mused, *an easy catch for Regina.* "They killed them, or found them dead?"

"Of course, they killed them."

"They confessed?"

"No villein confesses to poaching." The bailiff's lips curled with disgust.

"Stocks 'til sundown."

"Hughes hung poachers," Marcel huffed.

Blanche crossed her chamois-gloved hands on her lap. "'Til sundown," she repeated firmly.

"Hughes will hear of it," the bailiff threatened, stamping out.

Blanche recalled a time when she sat beside Hughes as he casually ordered the hanging of peasants. They had killed a wild boar for uprooting their meager crops. "Keep the gallows busy," Hughes had said, "to keep the villeins busy."

The chamberlain, a neckless man with a perpetual shrug, brushed his sleeve and bowed. "The hunt is prepared, my lady," he said. "The Master of the Hawks awaits your word."

"If you are the last to see me, I am almost ready," she replied. "And the others?"

"His Excellency the bishop is at the stable preparing his mount with his escort. Payens, Provost de Bracieux, and Raoul La Boucher are also saddled."

"No one else?" she asked, hopefully.

"Your cousin Renard."

Her heart drooped.

"And Messire d'Anjou requests the honor of serving your house in the hunt."

She felt her face brighten, but she suppressed a smile. "Very well," she said, sounding very official. "See that he is properly equipped."

She ordered her favorite white cape, the ermine-trimmed one, to spite the heat and bespeak her station. The serving girls rolled her braids into tight buns and fit them into gilded nets. A page brought her the black boots fixed with silver star-shaped spurs. Once she pulled on the white felt hat with the pointed brim and flowing plume and blushed her cheekbones with a soft brush, she felt ready for the chase.

The horses crashed over fences, leaped brooks, and vaulted hedges of yellow broom. The trampling hooves and the trilling hounds stirred up the fragrances of white campion, ragged robin, speedwell and dog daisy. The wild orchids matched Blanche's stunning cape, and the flamboyant purple-rose flowers of the Judas tree resembled Renard's costume. The jongleur, without a lance or even a womanly bow, bounced in the saddle of his prancing stallion.

So why must he come along and slow us all? Jean-Michel complained to himself. Balancing a borrowed hawk on one arm, he wondered, *to amuse the falcon master?*

Gascon, dressed in a festive forest green, looked like a parrot. He even sounded like one when he squawked at Renard's jokes. But when he threw back his head to laugh, his squinting eyes scanned the treetops for nests. The June eggs would soon be ready to hatch and provide him with prize eaglets to raise.

The pale sky was empty of other birds, but Jean-Michel heard them twittering in the trees, warning each other of the hunters' coming. In acknowledgment, the hoopoes answered with their hollow hoo-poo-poo notes.

The sound excited Gascon's hawk, a glorious Great Northern blindfolded by a hood adorned with gold thread and opal. The feathers of a former kill flared from the cap, and bits of dried meat clung to its steel-like claws.

"Over there," Gascon said, pointing with his beaked nose.

"But my dogs are over that way," DeBeauvais answered, pointing in the opposite direction. The bishop's bird, a nervous merlin, jingled on his bejeweled glove.

"They smell an old trail," Gascon said.

Jean-Michel's temperamental sparrow hawk dug into his gauntlet and twitched its hooded head in the direction of Gascon's voice. Jean-Michel gripped the hawk's leg jesses more tightly with his fingers. He would not allow it to take off again, seeking Gascon's familiar hand, without permission.

"You are right, messire," Jean-Michel said. "There is movement where you say."

"I am always right," Gascon said. He eyed Jean-Michel, inspecting his posture and the positioning of his borrowed hawk. Looking satisfied, Gascon called, "My lady, call your hounds."

Blanche wheeled her handsome bay, keeping her hand perfectly level for Regina's perch. The gyrfalcon fanned her feathers as if helping to complete the graceful turn. Blanche secured the ornamented reins to the saddle and swung her hunting horn up from her shoulder. She raised the ivory oliphant to the length of its silken cord and blew a rich note. The dogs dashed toward her.

"Up, seigniors!" she shouted, spurring forward.

"Fidelity!" Jean-Michel called.

"By Saint Germaine!" DeBeauvais exclaimed.

Renard barked like the sleek greyhounds racing past to flush out the game.

The nobles, Payens and Raoul, kicked their horses into action. Cheering, they pounded through field and fallow. A peasant family working the wheat rushed away in a panic, dropping their tools.

"Was that your prey, Gascon?" Renard taunted. The nobles doubled over in laughter.

Gascon, his hawk screeching an insult, pulled up and glared at Renard. "Look there, fool," he said.

A covey of quail, fleeing the dogs, scurried out of the wheat stalks. Their round, blue-gray bodies bobbed in unison as they ran. They scattered, some taking wing, with plaintive cries.

"Hoods off!" Gascon commanded.

As one, the hawkers stripped the hawks of their cowls. But Jean-Michel fumbled with the sparrow hawk, and the bird pecked at his fingers.

Gascon scowled at him. "You know how to call it back?"

"My father taught me."

"This is not his bird," Gascon said with disdain.

"Let fly," Jean-Michel challenged.

The hunters threw their falcons into the air. Like bolts from crossbows, the birds shot skyward, and the nobles and the bishop shouted their wagers.

Blanche's gyrfalcon soared in a spiral, rising to its pitch where it dived. It picked its airborne quarry and banked with perfect timing. Both talons struck, trussing the game in mid-air. The quail cried out as Regina sank in her needle-like claws. The birds hit the grass together and Regina squeezed the life out of her prey. When the struggle had ended, she began to rip away the quail's breast, shaking her head to fling off the downy feathers sticking to her bloody beak.

Blanche blasted her horn to regroup her dogs at her side. The bishop's attendants reined in his hounds. Restless, they pulled on their long leads. The attendants angrily yanked them into submission.

Blanche sounded the recall again, but the dogs, barking and yipping, ran in confused circles at the forest's edge. "They usually come the first time," she said as a few returned, whining and yearning for the forest.

"Stray quail," Payens said. "Let them be. Fetch your birds."

Jean-Michel was already swinging the lure. He whirred the feathered decoy overhead, and the feisty sparrow hawk landed faultlessly on his glove, releasing its catch into his hand.

Blanche noticed and nodded in approval. But Gascon's eyes, instead of showing pleasure at the safe recovery of his bird, showed a glint of jealousy.

Payens and Raoul galloped to where their falcons fed and coaxed them back to the gloves. Gascon's Great Northern circled high above him, screeching. The falcon master, troubled, puffed his cheeks and pierced the wind with a whistle that sounded like the scream of his falcon's mate. The bird swooped in a low arc and landed on Gascon's gold-embroidered gauntlet, staining it with dark, coagulated blood. Gascon hooded the bird quickly to calm it.

Regina, still on the ground with her kill, scolded the crazed dogs growling near her. But there were too many for her. With a series of quick wing beats, she lifted herself to a dizzying height, leaving her prey on the ground, and then glided away from the hunting party and over the wood.

"First the dogs, now this," Blanche said. She stuffed her lure in the leather pouch hanging from her belt and urged her horse forward in pursuit of the bird.

Gascon sounded two sharp whistles but the gyrfalcon only replied with a defiant cry.

Jean-Michel turned Fidelity to follow Blanche.

"Wait here," Gascon said to him hotly. "I'll handle this." And he ran his horse through the pack of dogs that had broken free of the bishops' handlers and were running behind Blanche.

The baroness kept track of her bird, a dark, screeching speck, doubling back overhead. Blanche jerked the reins to bring her horse about but, skittish from so many dogs underfoot, the beast resisted and kicked. The hounds yapped uncontrollably and rushed headlong into the bushes. The frightened horse neighed and reared. Gascon pulled alongside and reached for Blanche's reins, letting go of his own. His bird shrieked and beat its powerful wings; the force nearly pulled Gascon from his mount and he cursed.

Then they heard a growl.

An enormous black bear slashed through the hawthorn and launched itself upright, a tower of fur and fury. Its claws gleaming, it punched the air with massive arms and growled again. The roar rumbled and rolled like summer thunder through its bared fangs.

Blanche's horse bucked in terror and bolted. Blanche lost her grip and crashed to the ground.

In a frenzy, the dogs ran out from behind the bear and snapped and snarled at it. The bear swung its huge pitchfork paw and caught a hound, tossing it into the air. The dog yelped and landed limp.

Gascon's falcon leaped from his glove and soared upward, screaming. Its leg jesses snapped taut at the full length of the straps and the bird frantically whipped its wings in Gascon's face. Gascon's panicked horse spun helplessly in a circle.

With lumbering steps, the bear advanced on the dazed Blanche. Her hair net had ripped and unravelled hair covered her face in a tangle. Her left leg was bent beneath her and she cried out as she struggled to raise herself on a bloody elbow. The dogs jumped between her and the bear but the beast swatted two away, opening one's snout and gutting the other.

"My bow!" Payens gasped, fighting to control his horse.

Jean-Michel checked Payens' saddle, then Raoul's. It had been a cry of regret. No real man used a bow.

Jean-Michel released the sparrow hawk. He jabbed his spurs into Fidelity and the horse charged forward with a snort. As Fidelity's golden mane fanned his face, Jean-Michel crouched tightly against the horse and pulled his lance up from its saddlestrap. He leveled it in the crook of his arm, his heart drumming to the beat of the hooves.

The bear dropped to all fours, suddenly a smaller target. It shook its shaggy head and roared, dispersing the dogs. Fidelity flinched but Jean-Michel drove in the spurs. The bear reared up again, bushy arms spread and its teeth glinting like two rows of daggers. For a moment Jean-Michel saw only the wooden quintain Bobo had used to teach him the lance. The turbaned head and round Saracen shield were the targets. Once he hit it and passed he had to duck, or the spinning dummy would smack his skull with a chained mace. The bear's claws, curved like scimitars, awaited him now.

He pounded past the bear, releasing his lance at the last moment. The spear sliced through the bear's throat. An angry swipe of paw caught his boot and tore it from the stirrup. Jean-Michel nearly fell, but Fidelity, feeling the weight shift, made a sharp turn and he regained his seating. He heard Blanche scream.

He pivoted the horse and drew Purity ringing from the scabbard. He was ready to charge again. But the tottering bear flailed its furry arms and grasped in vain for the lance. A muffled roar of pain became a desperate gurgling as blood jetted from its mouth. Toppling with a thud and a gargling sigh, it kicked briefly and lay still.

The dogs moved in and bit at the matted body, but Jean-Michel trotted among them and chased them away with his sword and Fidelity's stamping hooves. He dismounted and sheathed Purity, while Payens pulled up with Blanche's horse in tow.

Gascon controlled his hawk at last. He alternately stroked it and patted his panting horse. His face was scratched and bloody and his jacket was smeared with gray excrement.

Jean-Michel felt the falconer's hot stare as he bent down to Blanche. "Dear lady," the knight said, "let me help you."

She refused to accept his hand. "I am all right."

"You are bleeding."

"It is the bear's blood."

Her spattered dress bloomed crimson at the elbow. She pushed herself up, her jaw clenched against the pain.

"Your horse, may I . . ."

"I can mount myself."

"But your leg . . ."

"Come here, Alix."

The dutiful horse scuffed to her side. Blanche wiped her cheek with her knuckle, smudging it. She brushed by Jean-Michel and gave Alix's nose an affectionate pat.

Jean-Michel, wounded by this rebuff, wanted at least a grateful glance. He did not know what to do with his hands. They fidgeted by his sides. He spied her cap and stooped to retrieve it. He swept off the dry grass, straightened the plume, and offered it to Blanche. He held it there for an awkward moment before Blanche, busy soothing her horse, took notice.

Pinch-lipped and pink-cheeked, she snatched it from him and limped to the side of the horse where she could use her good leg to swing up to the saddle. She kept her shoulders squared and her chin high with each step.

Raoul rode to her side. "My lady, we are so glad you are safe."

"Thank you, messire," she responded.

She does not thank me, Jean-Michel thought dejectedly.

Blanche remounted, biting her lip, and composed herself in the saddle. She turned away from Jean-Michel and looking into the sky, pulled the lure from her bag, which was still secure on her belt. She spun the lure with her left hand. Accustomed to using the right, her motion was a bit awkward.

The gyrfalcon descended and flapped onto Blanche's upraised glove. It pecked at the spots of blood.

"*Mais non*," Blanche said, as if correcting a child. Her other hand dug in the pouch for the hood. She found it and fit it over Regina's face. Wincing, she steadied her horse with her knees. Her right elbow dripped blood. "You are all well?" she asked evenly, nonchalantly swinging her loose braid.

"His Excellency is calming his hounds over there," said Raoul.

"And Gascon?"

"Here, Ma Dame."

"And Renard?"

The trees rustled at the forest edge. *The bear's mate*, Jean-Michel thought, forgetting his disappointment and swiftly drawing his sword.

A splash of purple-pink silk appeared above a tree branch. "Up here," called a cheery voice. Renard swung down in a somersault, making a springy two-point landing.

Jean-Michel squeezed the hilt of his sword indignantly. "You ran away up a tree?"

"*Au contraire*," Renard said. "I was trying to coax the bear back to its natural habitat."

Blanche and the nobles shared a laugh of nervous relief, but Jean-Michel firmed his mouth. He could see by Gascon's stern look that he, as well, did not find cowardice amusing. Then the falconer's fierce eyes focused on Jean-Michel, like those of a hawk spotting a quail. For a moment Jean-Michel thought Gascon might order his hawk to attack and mar his face beyond looking upon or loving.

The sparrow hawk, he remembered. *I've lost his sparrow hawk.*

He remounted and recalled it to lure and fist. But Gascon still wore the frustrated frown of a hunter who has just lost a prize doe to another man.

The company feasted on bear that night.

Renard worked the tables, singing of the hunt and composing ditties that included the diners' names. When the bishop retired early, the wine flowed as freely as the spring that fed the moats, and Renard relaxed. DeBeauvais had not recognized his face or his name, and he felt assured of a warm bed for at least one more night.

When the tipsy guests began to clap in rhythm, demanding a dance, he leaped upon a trestle. Tapping his felt-covered feet, he whirled, a blurry spin of color, singing,

Wine sets the spirit afire,
And wine brings passionate ardor;
When there is plenty of wine,
Sorrow and worry take wing.

Don't, at any such time,
Put too much faith in the lamplight.
Judgment of beauty can err,
What with the wine and the dark.

Flaws are hidden at night,
And every flaw is forgiven,
When the cats are all gray,
Then are all the women fair.

The diners were up, choosing dance partners. Grasping hands, they twirled in dizzying circles. Some dropped to the rushes, exhausted but laughing. Others reeled into benches, falling to the cheers of fellow revelers. With Blanche's chair empty, the hall became rowdy.

While the crowd took up a drunken song, Renard made his way to Jean-Michel. The long-faced knight still picked at his meager portion, his sad eyes wandering. Renard lounged in Blanche's seat beside him.

"You have a song of the chase for me as well?" Jean-Michel said without looking up.

"Not I, but Ovid does," Renard replied. He leaned closer to Jean-Michel's chair and in a melodic minor he sang:

Be a confident soul, and spread your nets with assurance.
Women can always be caught; that's the first rule of the game.
Sooner would birds in the spring be silent, or locusts in August,
Sooner would hounds run away when the fierce rabbits pursue,
Than would a woman, well-wooed, refuse to succumb to a lover.
She'll make you think she means No! while she is planning her Yes!

Jean-Michel looked blankly at Renard. "What are you saying, fool? Speak plainly."

"Are things not plain enough to see?"

Jean-Michel shook his head, looking confused and irritated.

"There is no need to return to Auxonne," Renard said. "You will be on pilgrimage within the week."

Now the jongleur had Jean-Michel's full attention. "The baroness has told you this?"

"No, but women have a way of speaking without using words," Renard answered.

When Jean-Michel failed to respond with the anticipated chuckle, Renard rubbed his chin and spoke more evenly. "Your money will come, one way or the other. But even if it does not, I have a proposal for your pilgrimage, if you'll permit me."

Jean-Michel's eyes took on a suspicious look. "Speak on," he said.

"My business in your fair country is finished. My cousin is well-settled in her duties and my services are no longer needed. So I have decided to return to Provence." He paused, noting Jean-Michel's sudden interest, and then continued. "I know every shrine along the route—well," he laughed, "I know the taverns near them better. But the roads can be hazardous for a lone traveler. I could use an armed escort."

The knight looked thoughtful, mulling over the possibility of traveling with Renard. Not wanting to risk another day under the bishop's scrutiny, Renard pressed him. "And you could use a guide."

Renard paused and smiled kindly at Jean-Michel, trying to project the sense of safety he wanted the young knight to feel he would have traveling in the company of an expert guide. "So, it is settled?"

"But how shall I pay . . ."

"Fret not," Renard interrupted. "It is I who should pay you. For a few songs and stories in the inns, I could earn us both our beds and some bread."

"I suppose . . ."

Standing as if a pact had been sealed, Renard said, "Good. I will ask Gascon to have my horse prepared immediately." He bent nearer to Jean-Michel and added an urgent coda to his statements. "I should not delay, if I were you. Gascon is not pleased with you and, like his hawks, he is able to do swift harm."

He bounced away to the solar for the next order of business. He was encouraged by Jean-Michel's hopeful face, but he hid his own, so that the fear of what awaited him in the Midi would not show.

"To dinner! All of you! Shoo!" With a broom-like gesture, Blanche swept the serving girls out the door.

"But Ma Dame . . ."

"You must eat . . ."

"Your strength . . ."

"Enough!" she shushed them. "I will come when I am hungry and not before."

When the bolt clicked and the echoing voices faded, she eased herself onto the feather bed as gingerly as she had dipped herself into the steaming tub. The heat and herbal perfumes had melted away much of the soreness, but had done nothing to restore her self-respect. Her hip and leg still throbbed from the painful olive-green bruises. The physician had offered his best leeches, but Blanche had demanded a strong wine to dull the pain.

She reached for the wine goblet on the nightstand, and her bending elbow stung from the wine used to cleanse her abrasions. But the rich burgundy hue reminded her of the bear's blood, and she withdrew her hand. *It is for the better*, she thought. *The wine would only worsen the headache.* Besides, it would do nothing for the ache in her heart.

Was she so vain that she could not accept Jean-Michel's hand, or give him a seemly *merci?* Or was she afraid that she would be unable to let go once she took his hand? She agonized over the scene in her mind: she, sprawled on the ground and close to sobbing in embarrassment and fear, but refusing to cry; he, his face aglow from the heat of combat and his sword aflame in the sunlight, standing over her like a guardian angel. She had fought back the tears then, but now a free flow of them welled up in her eyes and warmed her cheeks.

Regina shifted from foot to foot on her tall T-shaped perch and cocked her head. The tinkling of the gyrfalcon's bells caused Blanche to lift her wet chin.

"You tried to save me, too, Regina," she said, sniffling. "You tried to warn me. I have no better friend."

The bird made a throaty sound.

"Though he could be my friend . . . if I allowed it."

The bird blinked questioningly.

"Did I treat him too harshly?" she asked aloud, regret in her voice. *Mais non*, she thought. The rebuff did not disguise her attraction to him at all—it called attention to it. She was fooling no one, least of all herself. She'd been pretending that acting rudely could somehow overcome her feelings and at the same time prevent others from sensing her yearning for him. He saved her from the bear, but he could not save her from her brute husband; it was sinful to even think of it. Her wedding band seemed to squeeze her finger like a chainless manacle.

She lifted herself up slowly, unable to use the arm with the bruised elbow, and huddled near the brazier as the evening chill embraced her. She stirred the crimson coals and saw her own heart in the iron grill. It was glowing softly but coated with ash to conceal her discontent and desire. The burning behind her eyes came again, but it was not from the smoke. Her crystal teardrops darkened the stone floor, just as condensed water beaded on the walls and trickled between the tapestries.

Blanche tried to rub away the goosebumps raised by the drafts. Her loose flaxen blouse was not warm enough, but its softness comforted her. She eyed the strands of her own hair, woven into it and glittering like gold threads in the torchlight.

It would be a fine token, she mused, to belatedly express a proper lady's gratitude. She enjoyed the feel of the flax between her fingers, and imagined him stroking her in the same way. She caught herself, felt her throat constrict, and sulked.

She considered doing penance on the prayer stool while facing the ivory triptych she had brought from Provence. The middle panel was Christ, peaceful and pale hanging on the cross, and on each side panel the women faced Him. The Magdalene bent forward in a pose of anguish and adoration. Blanche felt she finally understood that impossible longing.

She fingered the flaxen sleeve again. As a gift, it would assuage her gnawing guilt, and it would recognize his bravery. Who would object to that? Why should it spawn rumors? It would represent the thanks she could never say properly, that is all. It is an acceptable prize for the victor in a duel for her honor against a bear. *That is all.*

Would anyone believe it?

To test the idea, she would suggest it in passing to her servers. The elbow complaining, she piled her hair atop her head, and wrapped the linen barbette under her chin and over her head to cover herself modestly. She rouged her cheeks to mask the pinkish blotches caused by crying. Dabbing her eyes, she strode to the door, opened it smartly, and called for a torchbearer.

"The Great Hall," she said.

Leaving the men to their raucous games of chance, the ladies retired from the dining hall. Sequestered in the solar, they convened a court of love to debate the limits of an abandoned wife's fidelity and appointed an expert to arbitrate the opposing views.

Renard, in a gold-lined cape, presided like a baron over a dispute of his vassals. He listened, feigning gravity, while representatives from each side gave their speeches. Each sought to impress him. When each finished, he traded secret smiles with her and blew her kisses.

The majority held the opinion that an abandoned wife, given no guarantee of her husband's safe return from a long and dangerous journey—say, for the sake of argument to Palestine—had the right to consort with another man so long as they both remained discrete.

The other side disagreed, declaring that passion easily overcomes love. A lonely wife could offer her lips to be kissed in friendship, but nothing more. They asked for Renard's decision.

His ego was aroused by the earnestness of their pleas, and Renard strutted among them like a coxcomb among hens. "If their love is so rare, so warm as ever touched this cold earth, so much finer than the cuckolded husband's who touched her as he would his horse, or cow—his own property to be used and stabled for another time—what would she offer her friend to show her gratitude that because of him she could feel love again? What token would she give to show that her wayward tenderness had returned? What proof could she provide that her broken heart was mended and she had hope once again of loving?"

"A peck on the lips?" He pouted.

The women shook their heads and shivered with anticipation.

"Such a heartless, merciless deed," Renard said, rolling his eyes, "to lead her lover to the fortress of her heart, and then leave him at the outer gate."

He looked over his shoulder and ducked affectedly, as if he were checking for eavesdropping husbands. He lowered his voice to a stage whisper and added the little growl that he knew made their pretty arms prickle.

"But suppose, dear ladies—if this will not make you blush too much or spoil your fair faces—that she is filled with thanksgiving for her newlyfound affection; would she not allow him to approach the inner gate behind which her heart is kept prisoner?"

They listened, breathless, their knuckles to their teeth.

"Would she not permit his hand to pass the portcullis of her skirt to caress her foot and rub away the soreness of her household chores—running to and fro from chef to chamberlain but reluctant to run to him?

"And what if she says nothing with words but everything with a sigh as he slides his hand up the silk to encircle her knee that coaxes her horse forward for the chase, but has yet to coax herself into his arms?"

One of the girls gasped.

"That is quite enough," said a voice that froze them all.

The ladies scattered to the walls like finches caught in the open field by a falcon. They huddled in pairs for protection, their faces lowered and their cheeks pinking.

Renard gave a courtly bow. "Ah," he said, "but we make way for one more witness before this court renders its judgment."

"I will give the judgment," Blanche said, her fingers curled into fists. Renard could not tell if her face was red from anger or embarrassment or restraint. Her breathing came in short puffs, the way it did before a tirade or a tear-letting.

"Out! To your rooms," she ordered the girls. "You have jobs to do. You have no time for this. I will inspect the apartments tonight."

Shamed into silence, the women shuffled through the door, making a wide path around Blanche. She followed them with an intense stare as if to push them out faster. When the last one had disappeared, she turned her icy blue eyes on Renard.

He flashed his most disarming smile. "The court awaits your judgment, my lady," he said with a low bow.

"How could you?" Blanche's voice was tight and her lower lip trembled. "How dare you try me this way?"

"It is love that is on trial," Renard replied.

"Am I deaf?" she cried. "You speak of me and the Angevin, Jean-Michel."

"If you say so."

"*You* said so!"

"So you deny it? You do not love him?"

"I did not say that."

"Then you do?"

"I am bound to Hughes."

"But you do not love Hughes."

"What is that to you?"

"That is why you love the Angevin."

"Say no more about love."

"What, then, shall we call it?"

Her eyes moistening, Blanche restrained herself. "I think you should leave the manor."

"I think you should tell him," Renard countered.

"What does he care if you leave?"

"He already knows I am leaving," he said softly. "Tell him how you feel before you lose him forever."

Blanche's anger turned to alarm. "What do you mean?"

"He is leaving on his quest. I am to be his guide."

Blanche's face fell. "When will this be?"

"The morrow, 'God willing and providing,' as he says."

"He has no money for it," Blanche said. "He will become a beggar, or starve!"

"Yes," Renard replied, "unless he can sing in the taverns, as I do. Even the abbeys require a fee."

"They will still be looking for you."

"Speak no more, cousin. I have packing to do." He gathered his cape. "One more thing. Please do not tell your ladies of my leaving until the deed is done. We simply cannot take them along."

Blanche lay awake, listening. The soft breathing of the sleeping maidens rose and fell. The wind fluted in the windowpanes like Pan calling her to love.

The noise is keeping me awake. But immediately she knew she was fooling herself. Half-formed dreams of the young knight caused her restlessness—of the Angevin, whose dreamy eyes were closed even now in sleep.

Perhaps. Or was he awake, too, thinking of her?

Not good thoughts, most likely, she pondered, turning. The flaxen chemise she wore to bed was twisted. She pulled it straight with her good arm; the other arm ached.

She knew she had brought this on herself. She had teased him; then for the sake of her own pride she had spurned him. She had not done it for the sake of her marriage. Her ring felt heavy and thick as she rubbed it between her knuckles. It prompted ugly images of Hughes and thoughts of his beery breath and the utter silence when he turned his hairy back to her each night, the perfume of another woman often mingled with the stink of his sweat. She shut her eyes tightly to squeeze out the memories. *Think of something else,* she told herself. *Something else, think of—Jean-Michel.*

A warm sensation spread through her and she smiled. *He will awaken soon. And then I shall see him again.*

Or would she?

The warmth cooled with her sudden concern. What if he should leave early? What if he should depart immediately after morning Mass? How could she ever explain, ever apologize, ever tell him that she—Could she say it?—wanted to love him? Wanted to be accepted by him? Wanted to be loved by him? What did she want to say?

"Tell him how you feel before you lose him forever," Renard's words echoed in her mind. She remembered how he had looked when he said it, his cocky mouth serious.

She held her breath. What if he had left already? What if, fearing more rejection, he had stolen out into the night to avoid another meeting with her? *Mais non, non. May it not be so.*

Her dressing gown hung in the oak wardrobe with the creaky doors. She could not fetch it without awakening her gossipy servants, but she could not go out barefoot, unbraided, and bloused only to her knees. She did, after all, have the dignity of a noble upbringing in an honorable house of Provence. *He will be there tomorrow*, she assured herself in the dark, *if it was meant to be. Sleep now. Try to sleep.*

She pulled up the fox-pelt cover. The fur felt soft on her neck like her hunting cape. It was about the same size.

Why not?

She gathered the corners to her shoulders and slipped through the curtains. Careful not to let the coverlet drag over any of them, she stepped through the sleeping servants. From near the entry she took the candle that was lit each night to keep the pixies away. Then, praying it would not squeak, she slipped through the door.

It didn't.

Though she cupped the candle while she ran, the little light shuddered and struggled. Blanche thought she knew the corridors well, but the jumping shadows played tricks on her eyes. With her bare feet she could feel how cold and wet the stone floors were, but she shook off the chill and hurried down the steps to the guest quarters. She heard only the sound of her own quick breathing. She realized with a pang that she did not have her keys and that the door might be bolted for the night. Could she knock? *Mais non*, she thought. *It will awaken someone.* She could not bear the humiliation of being caught in the corridors, skulking in the dark before the door of a virtual stranger, shaking from cold and apprehension and, yes, the hope that perhaps he might take her in his arms.

Stop it. Stop it. She cleared her head; she had come to apologize, to explain, to make amends, to . . . God forgive her, she was justifying herself again.

Her fingers atremble, she reached for the door latch. How could she know his reaction? He could easily refuse her, shaming her, but did it matter? He would be gone in the morning. Then he would be only a memory. It must be a good one, without regret for what could have happened. They could talk, and she could wish him well, and offer a kiss of goodwill.

She felt a peculiar tingle in her arms as she pressed on the latch.

It clicked open.

The draft snuffed out her candle. She drew a startled breath and squinted in the lavender moonlight that spilled through the open window. She could not see him.

"*Mon Dieu*, he is gone," she whispered.

The bedcovers rustled where Jean-Michel tossed in a troubled dream.

Once Blanche's eyes adjusted to the dimness, she could make out his prostrate form. His hands were stretched sideways as if in entreaty. He moaned and thrashed, twisting the bed's marten-skin covers.

Short of breath and chilled, Blanche tugged her coverlet tighter around her. The window draft flared her cape and rustled the hem so that she looked as if she were hovering over the floor.

Jean-Michel sat up with a start and stared at her as at a ghostly apparition.

Blanche bit into her bedcover cape. She stood rigid, like a rabbit, her heart thumping.

"Mother Mary," Jean-Michel said softly. "Come to my aid, and turn not away a poor humble knight and servant of your Son."

Blanche dared not reply, nor retreat, nor reach out to his upraised arms. *Are his eyes open?* she wondered. *Does he see me?*

"I have His seal upon my arm," Jean-Michel said, "and I must fulfill His call. Woman most pure, do not deny me the means."

He does not see me at all, but Mother Mary, Blanche thought. Her heart fluttered with the thought that a man could look at her and see virtue. The hardness encrusted on her spirit by Hughes' rejection seemed to melt away with Jean-Michel's innocent, adoring gaze.

"Fairest of women," he continued, "consider me with favor and accept me, weak and foolish though I am. Do for me what I have asked."

Blanche touched her forefinger to her quivering lip. Should she answer him, and perhaps dispel his vision? Tentatively, she raised a hand of blessing. She ached to touch his extended fingers, to draw them to her cheek and ease her loneliness for just a little while, but she could not. "Rest, dear heart," she said. "You are mine."

Contentment filled his face, and he relaxed into the feather pillows.

Blanche relit her candle from a glowing ember in the nearby brazier. Her hands and her soul warmed. She began to think of ways that she might juggle the accounts to inconspicuously transfer a generous amount of silver *livres Tournois* to him.

To cover for her absence, when she returned to her chamber, she roused the maids and set them to their morning chores.

Gascon lay awake too. His face itched where his hawk had gouged him, but his pride hurt more, and his stomach stung from the bile of jealousy. *If the Angevin only knew*, he fumed.

He listened to the scratching of claws on a perch. *The hunger will wake that one soon*, just as his own hunger for revenge had kept him awake all night. The image of the passing glance of admiration Blanche had given the young knight burned in Gascon's mind. It was a look he longed for and meant to have for himself. Had he not risked enough for the baron that for his reward he might enjoy the pleasures of Hughes' forsaken wife? Hadn't he suggested that Gascon try to tame her? And what was she to Hughes but security on a good property in Provence? The baron had more love for his grapes than he ever would for this girl.

It wasn't because of Blanche's looks that Hughes spurned her, thought Gascon as he pictured her taut skin and heart-shaped lips; nor was it her imposing height. She was simply too independent for Hughes. That was it, and she was not worth the trouble, when there were so many other eager wenches with good connections vying for his favors. But not she. *She would put up a fight,* he smiled, *like a good hawk. But they all can be trained.*

Still, she had paid more attention to the bow-kneed, stump-legged Angevin in two days than she had paid to Gascon in two years of his trying to please her. Well, soon enough Jean-Michel would be gone, and Renard, the buffoon, too.

And the sword.

Gascon's stomach knotted again from the gnawing fear of discovery. It had troubled him ever since he had gone to the cathedral under Hughes' orders to set it afire. The church had burned like the flames of hell Gascon knew he deserved. But no one had thought of questioning him during the bishop's inquest. He was after all a familiar figure, freely permitted to search the heights for eagles' eggs. He left by a different door each time so that on the one day he remained, the lazy sentries assumed he'd gone.

It was while sleeping with the bats in the crawl space above the chapels that the idea struck him. He secured to a beam the rope he usually brought for ascending parapets to the nests. Then he lowered himself into the Chapel of Saint Martin. By the flickering light of the votive candles, he easily snapped the fragile lock of the ancient reliquary.

At first he was surprised that there really was a sword inside. Pitted and chipped by time and perhaps a few Visigoths, the dull bronze blade was streaked with turquoise discoloring. The length of a man's forearm and hand, and having hardly a hilt atop the handle, it looked more like a dagger than a modern sword. Gascon half expected to feel a tingle when he touched it. He hovered his hand over it a long time. When he finally grasped the sword, he thought he heard angels flapping down to arrest him. But the sound was only bats rustling in the rafters. He closed the reliquary, slid the blade into his belt, and shimmied back to his hiding place, chuckling to himself for daring a saint and surviving.

Then all he had to do was torch the tallow-soaked nests and tip a few candles on the way out. The freshly-pitched roof would flare in a hurry, but he knew he could get out in time before the stink and the smoke overcame him. *No one knows the passageways better than I do,* he congratulated himself, excepting Tomas the Master Builder, Giles the Mortarer, and perhaps Anseau, the nosy sacristan.

Hughes will be pleased when he gets the news, Gascon thought. He would return in a few weeks, if there are no storms at sea. From so far away, Hughes would be blameless, though it was he who had said, "Burn it to hell, and see that it cannot be rebuilt." No one would be beaten on the behind by the bishop in there again.

Gascon rubbed his bottom, rolled up from his mat, and shook off the straw. He crawled in the dark to the brine barrel, where he pickled rats. Though accustomed to the stench of the mews, he screwed up his nose in disgust. He heaved his shoulder against the barrel and, ignoring the sick sloshing sound, reached beneath the recessed bottom. He slid out a canvas sack. Then he let down the barrel, sat against it, untied the sack, and drew out the sword of Saint Martin.

In the dark it was only a black silhouette, but he knew that by daylight it shown like a late September sunset. Since he had rubbed it with resins and oiled it, the weapon looked wieldable again. But its Roman design was too distinctive. He had to be rid of it. He could not conceal it forever in the manor.

He rehearsed his options again, as he had a thousand times before. He had thought of burying it in the fields, but he had no occasion to be in them, except when he was out with the birds. Someone was always with him then. He could hide it in the garden, but some peasant's plow was bound to unearth it and a miracle would be proclaimed. He could throw it in the river. What if a miracle occurred and, like Elijah's axe, the sword drifted to shore?

No, it had to be carried away—far away. And Renard was leaving at daybreak.

On the way back from the hunt, the jongleur had asked Gascon to prepare his finicky horse Sylvester for a long journey. *Back to Provence, finally*, Gascon thought. The singer complained of the bumpy ride and how his piles would ache on the long trip south. He asked for a specially cushioned saddle blanket. Renard gave no reason for leaving. These vagrants and their viols come; then they go after they've had their fill of food and females, Gascon concluded.

The Angevin would be leaving as well, returning to his duty of guarding the Cathedral d'Auxonne, or what was left of it. *A fine job he did.* Without money from the baroness, and without finding a relic, the knight would return in failure and disgrace. *Serves him right for showing off,* Gascon thought, rubbing the sword's blade.

The jongleur would not discover the sword if it was hidden well, until he was well into the journey. And even if he did and he knew what it was, the scoundrel would not be likely to return it. Although he might try to sell it.

The falcons began to scratch and peck at their cages. Gascon stashed the sword in its hiding place and exercised the birds. As the stable hands passed by on their way to the oven to fetch their morning bread, he counted them to be sure all had gone. The Angevin's mute valet gave him a long, inquisitive look when he went by.

Then, cloaked in the shadows of dawn, Gascon crept to the stables with the sword in his shirt. He found Renard's horse and his saddle blanket hanging on the peg. He slit a seam and slid in the blade. It was a snug fit. He lifted the blanket to see if the added weight would be telling. The difference was not too obvious. A stable hand might notice but likely would think only a dagger was concealed, a wise precaution against road brigands.

Farewell, Saint Martin. Gascon sneered. *See to it that Renard has a long, safe journey . . . to the edge of the world if possible.*

Let him never return.

The horses despised each other.

In the stables Bobo could tell by their nervous chuffing. They nickered and nipped at each other in the manor's narrow gate. They competed for the lead on the trail, and Fidelity kicked at Sylvester each time the saucy stallion nosed her tail.

Renard lightly rebuked his steed, saying it was not seemly behavior for one named after a saint. Noticing Jean-Michel's grimace, Bobo maneuvered his mellow mount between them. He was pulling a dappled packhorse behind him by a rope. That separated them, and Bobo hoped that would end the trouble. And it did, until they reached the first village.

Renard led the way past the corncribs and cottages, scraping his viol and singing hey-nonny-nonnies to announce his arrival. By the time Jean-Michel, Bobo, and a few pilgrims from Le Chateau DuVal caught up to him, Renard had gathered an eager audience at the well. Children in rags ran to him from the wattle huts and cattle sheds. Grandmothers, wives, and widows dropped their kettles and milk buckets to come and catch the latest gossip. Most men were away for the day, working their fenced parcels. But a few in the nearby barleyfield came in with their clumsy mattocks balanced on their backs.

While Bobo watered the horses and set them to graze among the goldenrod, Renard enchanted the villagers with the tale of the knight's mission. In a most excellent vision, he declared, the Virgin had praised Jean-Michel for singlehandedly putting out the fire in Her cathedral. She had given the brave knight a wondrous token—a woman's bliaut, woven of gold and embroidered with the Virgin's own hair, filled with silver and gems.

The crowd marveled aloud and turned to see such a great knight. But Jean-Michel had slipped behind the kitchen shed to use the privy ditch.

Inspecting the pack horse's bags, Bobo chuckled to himself. The tale was getting taller at every stop. Why not tell the truth, which was just as amazing? After his dream of the Virgin's blessing, Jean-Michel had found Blanche's own blouse inside his door. It was tied in a bundle with silver *livres* and hastily-drawn letters of passage inside. Packs of salted strip pork, strings of skinny Arles sausages, dried peas, and hard biscuits appeared in the stables overnight. And why not tell of the shimmering tears in Blanche's eyes when Jean-Michel parted, or of the simmering anger in Gascon's beet-red face when he saw Blanche's token in Jean-Michel's pack?

Instead, Renard sang a hymn of homage to the Queen of Heaven, or Lady Love. It was always hard to tell which. For that matter, it might have been a song for Blanche. Bobo had not failed to notice Jean-Michel's starry eyes and shaking knees whenever he was near the brassy baroness. Renard's sentimental adagio rose in the Langue d'Oc, an elegant troubadour tongue,

> *Et am del mon la bellazor,*
> *Dompne, e la plus prezada,*
> I love the most beautiful lady in the world,
> And the most prized.
> And I believe that she has a good inclination toward me
>
> According to my judgment.
> Of my beloved I make Lady and Lord,
> Whatever may be my destiny.
>
> Above all men I shall have great success
> If such a shirt is given to me
> As Iseult gave to her lover,
> For it was never worn again.

Bobo refilled the water skins. He was touched by the resonance of Renard's lyrical voice and troubled by his own inability to repeat the tune to himself. The strings on Renard's viol hummed, but the chords in Bobo's throat were silent. Even the mouths of the water bottles could bubble merrily. But Bobo's voice had been stolen long ago, and he could only try to remember what his own singing once sounded like.

Capping the canteens, he realized that Jean-Michel was not listening. He had wearied of Renard's singing early in the trip. The knight reclined in the shade of an oak, a wet cloth over his eyes and a pinch of mint in his mouth to calm a queasy stomach brought on by the humidity.

Bobo felt like dozing himself, but the snort of the horses shook him alert.

Hooves high, Fidelity reared and pawed at Sylvester. Sylvester neighed angrily and bit back. The shy pack horse whinnied in fear and snapped away from the tether fence. It pounded away, spilling some of its load to the dirt. The sacks burst open, spewing out peas and cooking pots. The loud rattle frightened the horse even more and he bucked the rest of his load.

Bobo smacked his bald forehead in dismay and bounded after the panicked horse. Jean-Michel clambered to his feet and whistled. Stamping and indignant, Fidelity backed off. Sylvester stared stupidly, champing a mouthful of geraniums.

A weather-beaten woman in the crowd cried out. Her orderly flower garden had become Sylvester's dinner. Like a robin rushing to its endangered nest, she flew to her little plot. She bunched her spotty hands into tight hammers to defend the few remaining petals. She cursed the horses and scolded an embarrassed Jean-Michel, who stood between her and his charger.

The village women restrained the upset matron and, trying to comfort her, offered their shoulders for her tears of fury and grief. Sylvester sauntered off. Renard bounced up and steered his horse away from the fracas. He pulled wet flower stems from Sylvester's teeth. "Pay her a copper," he called to Jean-Michel over the peasants' heads.

"It was your horse!" Jean-Michel said.

"I haven't passed around the bowl yet."

"You were going to take a payment from the poor?"

"A man must make a living!"

"We stopped only for water!"

"That is not all we shall get!"

Unshouldering their heavy hoes like battle-axes, the burley farmers turned from the tearful woman to the strangers. None dared take on an armed knight singly, but in a group they could hurt him badly. Worse still, they could cripple his horse. One of the men growled at Renard.

"The copper, now, if you please," the jongleur trilled to Jean-Michel.

"Madame," Jean-Michel pleaded apologetically, "find it in your gentle heart to forgive our rude animals and us. Brutes though they are, we are no better for failing to control them."

The peasants lowered their pick hoes.

"And if you please," Jean-Michel added, digging into Fidelity's saddlebag, "accept this small gift. It's not as precious as your flowers, but is a fair price to ransom ourselves from your anger."

The curious villeins leaned in for a closer look at the leather satchel. Jean-Michel pulled out the soft linen edge of a woman's blouse. Sunlight glinted on the golden strands in its fine weave. The women whispered while the men muttered quick prayers. The jongleur's story was true, after all.

Jean-Michel drew out a silver *livre Tournois*, stamped with the *fleur-de-lys* of the French crown. It had been freshly minted at Tours for the expenses of Louis's crusade. The woman's eyes shone as brightly as the palm-sized coin. Jean-Michel placed it in her trembling hand, and she looked at it disbelievingly as if a priest had just given her a consecrated Host.

Bobo and the pilgrim men successfully reined in the frightened horse, soothed it, reloaded, and cinched its baggage. One pilgrim, a baker, rubbed a kettle clean on his sleeve, while another retied the pea sacks.

Jean-Michel called to them, "Brothers! We move on!"

The peasants regarded the knight respectfully as he swung up to the saddle. "*Adieu*," he saluted.

"Go with God," the old woman answered, crossing herself with the coin, "and with His Mother."

Under a sky as blue as the Virgin's veil, a dazzling company assembled in the broad emerald pasture. From manors in the surrounding hill country, from castles standing guard over the Loire and Saône rivers, from the wealthy abbeys of Saint Ober and Saint Bruges, clerics and nobles gathered to do homage to the new Count of Anjou.

One by one, in an order determined by rank and family, the men unbelted their swords, uncovered their heads, and knelt before the count.

He asked each one the same question. "Do you wish, willfully and without reservation, to be my man?"

"I so wish," they answered in turn.

The count then clasped the hands of the kneeling vassal between his own and confirmed the compact with a kiss on the lips. He bade his servant bring a jewel-encrusted case holding the relics of saints, vassals themselves to the King of Heaven. The men placed their palms on the engraved cover, near the fragments of bone and ringlets of hair upon which the nobles swore their holy oaths:

"By my faith, I do promise from this time forward I will maintain my homage and be faithful to Count Jean-Michel of Anjou."

Amid the festive cheers Renard's hee-haw of derision brayed. "You fools pledge fealty to a man who murdered his own mother? He should be a hermit, not a noble! Hee-haw! Hee-haw!"

Jean-Michel grasped his sword and swung it high, and found himself sitting up on a bedroll, his fist in the air empty. Fidelity, standing watch above him, chuffed. Renard snored nearby. "Hee-haw. Hee-haw."

Jean-Michel ran his fingers through his knotted hair and wiped the perspiration from his neck. His skin had chilled in the night's coolness; he shook his head free of the flickering images in his troublesome dream. *Count of Anjou, indeed.* That title belonged to the king's own brother, Charles. That was one way to keep the province out of English hands, and to tie the Angevin barons like his father to King Louis's central authority.

How could he have dozed on his watch? *Ah, but Fidelity, you were taking my turn.* Tomorrow, they would be in a proper hostel and stable.

He leaned back on his elbows. He looked for patterns in the stars. They were like a splash of crystals on a black velvet cape, like the one his mother probably wore in death. There was so much he wanted to tell her. How sorry he was not to have known her. How sorry he was that Philippe did not accept him. How sorry he was. How sorry.

He told the Virgin Mother instead, and soon the sky began to brighten with Her royal blue presence and the songs of sparrows.

Gascon watched the silhouettes of sparrows carrying crumbs up to their nests in the palace corbels. He would have let fly his shrieking tercels just to see a little blood, but it was too early in the morning to loose them, and too dark yet to enjoy the spectacle. He would feed the hawks by hand.

He wiped the caked yellow sleep from his eyes and thought of his night brooding in the castle cellars while collecting mice from his traps. A few, dead from starvation, had been partly eaten by the ones still squeaking in the little trip-latch cages. The sackful of his squirming victims roused his birds to a frenzy.

Gascon pulled on his glove. If only he could retrieve Jean-Michel and Renard the way a falcon did its finches, or capture them the way he did these miserable mice. He hauled the sack into place before the feeding trays. It was the same sack that had hidden the sword.

He ground his teeth. How was he to know the two men would be traveling together? He should have guessed the coward Renard would want a guard, and that this poor excuse for a knight would want an older man to show him where the road was. He spat. How could he have believed the Angevin would return to Auxonne empty-handed? These regretful thoughts tumbled in his mind like the mice in the sack.

Gascon plunged his hand into the bag and seized a mouse. It bit the glove but the studded leather, tough enough for a hawk's talons, easily withstood a rodent's gnaw. He flung the mouse into the feed drawer and kicked it shut. A rush of feathers, a squeak, and it was over.

By now the baroness would be receiving reports from her staff, if she hadn't cried herself to sleep too late and delayed the meeting to tend to her puffy eyes and blotchy cheeks. They would look like bruises against her creamy skin, and no one would be fooled by her powders and dusts—not her maids, not the chamberlain, not the bailiff .

He shifted his eyes this way and that. *But wait, now.* Perhaps there was a killer eager to snag these birds in flight. Marcel, the bailiff, loved to catch poachers as much as his birds loved to catch hares and quail. Gascon could tempt him with the prospect of a thief on a noose in the same way he might use a swinging, baited lure to tempt a hawk. *Of course.*

He chuckled at his cleverness, then snatched another mouse and swung it once by the tail before whipping it into the feed drawer and slamming it home. He laughed as the hawks fell on it.

The bailiff, suspicious but interested, folded his arms. "How do you know of this?" he asked Gascon.

"I cannot say for sure," Gascon said. His eyebrows busy, he worked on his troubled look. "It is like finding eagles' eggs. Sometimes your guess is good, sometimes not. But I am usually right."

"What makes you think you are right this time?"

"He seemed too eager to leave," replied Gascon. "And his groomsman, the mute, would not let anyone near his gear. It was as though he were . . . ah, hiding something."

"Why did you not accuse him before he left?" The bailiff chewed impatiently on his mustache. Gascon could see his ruse wasn't working. "If wrong, I did not want to appear to be a fool in public."

"Or appear jealous?"

The personal jab hurt, but Gascon pressed ahead. "So you do not believe the story of the Virgin's visit, either?"

The bailiff smiled lewdly. "We both know who he really saw in the night. Like you, I do not believe the bishop. And I do not believe you, either. You have no proof."

"Of course not; he is carrying it." Gascon regretted raising his voice, and he tried to steady it. "Not only has he taken the sword, Marcel. But by saying the sword is lost, and pretending to go on pilgrimage, and by pretending to love the baroness, he has taken Hughes' money." Ah, now he had Marcel's full attention. "You know that Blanche will fix the accounts so Hughes will never know about it," Gascon continued. He swung the lure of words more enthusiastically. "I tell you, this Angevin is a fraud and a thief. He has stolen from both our bishop and our baron, and Hughes will not be happy if he finds out that you let him slip away from under your nose with such a large sum."

The bailiff yanked on his mustache. "I will be the fool if I ride out with a troop of sergeants and then find he does not have the sword. If that happens, mayhaps I will hang you instead."

"He is clever, Marcel. He could hide it in someone else's pack, or he may be rid of it along the road. Renard might convince him to sell it for even more silver. So you must hurry."

The mention of Renard made Marcel pause. "The baroness will never let me chase her own cousin as a criminal."

"Why say anything to her?" Gascon asked, taking advantage of the bailiff's bad mood. "Say you are on patrol for poachers. If you find nothing, we say nothing and save face. But if you find the sword, there will be a hanging in it for you and she cannot object."

"And for you?" asked Marcel.

"Only our baroness's favor," Gascon replied, "and a blessing from His Excellency. His church will be rebuilt, with many places for eagles' nests."

The bailiff smirked. "Always you think of your birds."

"I think only of the ones who are now in flight from you. You remember where they flew?"

The bailiff remembered. The bishop had announced it in his benediction. He went as hastily as a hawk flies off a glove.

Gascon walked down to the bailey to watch him go. The horses were saddled and bridled and the sergeants mustered and armored. The gates opened in a great commotion, and the posse, armed with pikes, thundered out.

Blanche called down from a balcony. "Is there danger, Gascon?"

Silently cursing the bailiff for not being quieter about this, Gascon composed himself and turned. "Only poachers, my lady," he said.

By midmorning Jean-Michel's party reached the broad pilgrim path leading to Saint Mary Magdala de Vezelay. The baker, the fuller, and others who had enjoyed Jean-Michel's protection up to this point parted company to make their way to the mountaintop basilica. They joined a rowdy band of travelers on the uphill route to one of Christendom's most sacred sites, the reputed resting-place of the Magdalene, who with Lazarus first brought the Holy Faith to France's shores.

"Imagine a twist of her hair for Auxonne," the fuller said.

"Or Lazarus' burial cloths!" the baker said.

"They belong to Vezelay," Jean-Michel said. The holy items had been miraculously spared in the Great Fire of 1170, which had consumed a thousand trapped worshipers. It was strange to think that at Auxonne lives were spared and the relics lost. "God fare you well, brothers," Jean-Michel said, saluting cheerfully to disguise his regret. The rebuilt basilica of the Magdalene was exquisite, he knew. Its pilgrim hostel well-spoken of and its objects of veneration powerful aids for prayer. "But I have a letter from His Excellency for Prior Pierre of Notre Dame d'Espere."

"May the shrine fulfill its name of 'hope' for you, messire," blessed the baker.

"And may you reach it before sundown," the fuller said.

"If we hurry," Renard said, rolling his eyes, "we might make it in time for Vespers."

As he neared the Saône, Jean-Michel reached back to his pack, looking for the bill of passage from Blanche. It would allow him to cross the bridge without paying the exorbitant toll. Bobo's bald head bobbed on his chest sleepily while

Renard sang a *ballade* of Rudel to the rhythm of Sylvester's clopping iron hooves:

> *Je mais d'amor no.m jauziray*
> Never ever will I take joy in love
> If I do not rejoice in this, my distant love.
> So high and elevated is her worth
> That there in the kingdom of the Saracens
> I would for her sake be called a captive.

"That is enough, messire," Jean-Michel said sternly.

"Do the lyrics grieve you?" Renard asked.

"The noise will alert robbers to our approach," Jean-Michel said.

"The only robbers on this road are the ones who run the inn near the shrine. Their fees are much too high, but I think I can bargain them down. And they fill their false-bottomed tankards with watered ale." Renard scratched his smooth chest. "At least the beds are free of fleas. That is, when they keep the Sicilians away."

Bobo, awakened by Jean-Michel's rebuke, whistled pertly and pointed at the dirt. Two long, rusty streaks of blood stained the path, as if a body had been dragged along it.

"Don't bother smelling it, Bobo," Jean-Michel said. "It is fresh." He sat taller, looking left and right. Robbers preferred early dusk, when colors blended, and even a jongleur's garish silks had begun to dim.

Bobo's face lost color. *He is remembering his family,* Jean-Michel thought, feeling a cramp of sadness in his belly. *Had it been this time of day?* The English hoodlums, remnants of a rebel army in Anjou escaping the troops of the French crown, had overrun Bobo's village in search of food. The people did not resist. Still, the rebels put Bobo's young son to the sword and took turns with his wife, Kaara, until they speared her before his eyes. They held him, screaming, until his voice was gone. It had never returned.

Why his father took Bobo into his manor after that was a mystery to Jean-Michel, even though the incident had occured within his seigniory. He did not think of his father as a kind man. Perhaps Bobo's experience as an equerry in the commandery of the Templars had impressed his father and made Bobo useful. Perhaps it was because Jean-Michel was close to the age of Bobo's slain son. Since Philippe would not send Jean-Michel away for training as a proper squire, he left the job to this man associated with the Knights Templar. Bobo taught him to ride, to charge, to race. The old stable master had seen enough of Templar fieldwork to drill Jean-Michel in the broadsword and lance. Bobo became more of a father to him than Philippe and more of a mentor than any gold-spurred knight. He was almost Bobo's son—the son Bobo swore would be able to defend himself.

Jean-Michel rested his hand on Purity's pommel while kicking Fidelity to a canter. He examined the bloody trail again. Why had the bandits not dragged their victim into the woods? Why had they stayed on the stony path for so long?

He did not have to wait long for an answer. Around a steep bend a party of pilgrims was just reaching the bridge ahead. Dressed in hooded gowns with a heavily-laden donkey in tow, they approached the toll taker on bare feet. One member lagged behind, shuffling forward on bloodied knees and leaving a double streak behind him. Jean-Michel relaxed his guard.

"There are your robbers," Renard chortled. "More robbed than robbers, and proud of it."

The journeyers' cowls and broad-brimmed hats were covered by metal badges and brooches, sacred souvenirs from various shrines: shells from Saint James Compostella; little brass heads of John the Baptizer from Amiens; charms of the Three Magi from Cologne; and silver images of the Virgin from Rocamadour. The man on his knees held a droopy, dry palm branch, the sign of one who has been to Jerusalem.

Stopped by the mail-shirted tolltaker, the pilgrims' clinking quieted and their chattering began. The guard waved them away brusquely. The rabble fell to their knees as if a great wind had resulted from the swing of his arm, and they intoned a prayer in unison. They lifted their hands, and, with medallions jingling, cried, "Hail, Mary, full of grace, the Lord is with Thee . . .". The prayer was a new one the Dominicans were trying to popularize. Likely the pilgrims had learned it at Rocamadour.

"Begone!" the guard scowled, pulling one petitioner up by his hood. "Away, you vagrants! An *obal* apiece, like everyone else!"

Jean-Michel clicked his tongue to urge Fidelity to a trot. Just before he pulled up to the bridge, two other soldiers bustled from the timber guardhouse. Pressing on their conical helmets, they took hold of the kneeling pilgrims, but released them when the huge golden charger approached.

"What is the matter here, messires?" Jean-Michel demanded.

"Are you their escort?" the guard retorted. "Is your scrip empty as well?"

"Let the good sire pass," said a silky voice. "He is not with us." A woman pulled back her hood; a tumble of midnight-black hair fell against her snowy skin. Her eyes were so blue that to Jean-Michel they seemed to be windows to heaven. Her neck looked so white next to her coal-dark curls that he thought he might be able to see wine flow down her throat when she swallowed. It seemed so brazen for a woman to go with hair uncovered, but Jean-Michel dismissed his discomfort. She faced Jean-Michel, and her cherry lips drew up into a full, admiring smile.

"Good lady, if you are on the way to visit Our Lady of Hope, then surely I am with you," he said.

"But it is Our Lady who has visited me, first," she replied. "She sought me, a runaway from the Sisters of Hope, for two years. Now I am coming back." She fingered her luxurious curls. "You see this hair, messire? To mark me as a nun, it would not grow while I was gone. But after I repented, it grew long and beautiful. I have testified to this miracle in many shrines, as I was commanded to do. And I have come here finally to willingly present my hair on the altar and to take the veil again. If," she paused and looked toward the guards, "we are able to cross the bridge."

Her companions nodded vigorously to add weight to her story.

"For two years?" Jean-Michel said. "Were you not missed by your abbess?"

The pilgrims laughed. "Have you not heard, messire?" one of them exclaimed. "This tale is all over France! Our Lady herself took on this sister's visage and performed her chores for those two years! It is no wonder the abbey awaits her eagerly."

The woman addressed Jean-Michel, her eyes cast down. "But since we have traveled to every shrine as commanded, we find we are now unable to meet the meager toll necessary to complete our mission. Still," she turned a radiant face toward heaven, "Our Lady will provide a way."

Jean-Michel drew a silver *livre* from his saddlebag. "Let them pass," he said, tossing the heavy coin to the guard's feet, where it landed with a dusty thud. "And by order of His Excellency, the Bishop of Auxonne, and Her Grace, the Baroness DuVal, we beg to pass." He flipped the sealed parchment roll into the startled guard's hand. The flustered man did not bother to break the soldered lead seal. He glanced at the imprint, and then used the parchment like a baton to wave them through.

Jean-Michel nudged Fidelity forward. He set his jaw and locked his eyes straight ahead as her hooves thumped onto the planking of the bridge. The rushing waters below swished in his ears and swirled in his brain. He clamped his lips and held his breath as if he'd been dunked under the eddies gurgling on the rocks below. If thrown, even without armor, he knew he would sink like a stone. Sweat dripped into his eyes and itched under his clothes.

"*Merci*, good sire," called the woman. "May you find what you seek."

He did not look back. Acknowledging her would mean risking a glimpse over the edge, and his gallant demeanor would be lost. They would all see his panic and laugh.

Once the horse had crossed to solid ground, Jean-Michel released his breath. His lungs burned in protest, and his heart seemed to knock at his ribs like a prisoner rapping on dungeon bars. He fought back a cough and breathed in deliberately, sitting taller in his squeaking saddle.

Renard, wearing a condescending smirk, turned to Jean-Michel; Jean-Michel smiled back, pretending nonchalance. Had the jongleur noticed this fear? What a ribbing he was in for. . . .

"I do not believe you fell for that," Renard said laughing.

"Pardon?"

"Those tricksters at the toll. They had enough coins to smelt for a dozen saints' statues! Their wallets were ringing like tambourines!"

"I believe that you would not part with a worthless English penny to help someone in need," Jean-Michel countered.

Renard shrugged. "It is good they had only a story to sell, and not a relic."

At the crossroads, beneath the customary crucifixes, they encountered the first vendors. Hawking their wares to passersby heading from the inn to the abbey, the sellers called and cajoled from their colorful tents and tables.

"Mutton pie!"

"Fresh ale!"

"Cherry cakes! Honey bread!"

Ragged beggars, smelling like old fish, camped beside the vendors. They rattled their clackdishes and showed their revolting sores and stumps, some the result of punishments, some self-inflicted either for penance or pity. Jean-

Michel gulped, hoping there were no lepers among them, but he did not hear any hand bells.

"Alms, alms," the invalids cried, lifting their bowls and cupped hands to his high stirrups. It pained him to ignore them and press on, knowing the wealth in his saddlebag.

They blended into the parade of pilgrims and penitents traveling toward the abbey for the sundown service. Some chanted psalms, some argued or joked, but all their chatter was punctuated by the hacking coughs and low groans of the sick. Buckets clanked, pottery jugs clicked, and goatskins swayed on the pilgrims' backs. These were vessels to bear away water from the shrine's healing springs.

Nearly all were on foot. Some were borne on wheeled litters. Jean-Michel and his mounted companions towered above them. Clumps of worshipers preceded them on their way to the nearest hill, a verdant mound ringed by trees but cleared at the top, like a Dominican's tonsure. There sat a stout compound, walled by sandstone that glowed golden in the slanting sunrays. It looked like a little crown, with its pointed turrets and a central dome over the shrine it enclosed.

"Tears of the Virgin!" rang a seller's voice to the left. The words pulled Jean-Michel's head like the bit in Fidelity's mouth steered her.

"Shed for her Son, and saved for the church by the apostle Jesu loved," intoned the seller, a gaunt man with gloomy eyes. He clasped a tiny cruet to his tattered tunic. Certain of Jean-Michel's attention, he continued. "And a splinter of the true Cross. All I have brought back from the Holy Land, and these wounds which I gladly bear for Christ."

He displayed his misshapen hand, with the two smaller fingers missing. It seemed to perpetually sign the Trinity. "Help a fellow knight," he said. "This is all I have left. But for a fair price, I may continue my journey home."

"And what would you consider a fair pri . . ." Jean-Michel began.

"Gaspard! You old weasel!" Renard called. He trotted up from where he had lagged behind, meeting maidens who were likely guests at the inn. "Still selling the river, I see." He laughed.

Gaspard paled and shook off the remark. "Master Renard, you . . . you are at the Boar's Tooth again?" The vendor tried to smile, but his thin mouth twitched. "Give me leave, while I bestow a blessing on this gentle knight."

"Take no blessing from this thief," Renard said to Jean-Michel, who had already unbuckled his money bag, "and give him none in return. He has sold enough tears of the Virgin to make a waterfall, and enough splinters of the Cross to make a forest."

Jean-Michel's eyes narrowed; he moved his hand across his lap to Purity's polished hilt.

"Messire, n-no, I b-beg you," Gaspard stammered, raising his three-digit hand. "I only work to b-bless others, to give them what they seek, t-to . . ."

With a singing flash of steel, Jean-Michel drew Purity from its sheath. Fidelity reared and crashed her hooves on Gaspard's little table. The water jug underneath shattered and little bottles flew in the air. Gaspard ran off, head down, into the crowd.

"It is no use chasing him," Renard said, eyeballing the raised sword. "Put that thing away."

"The abbey should know of this," Jean-Michel said.

Fidelity snorted.

"Mayhaps they do; if so, they take a percentage, just as from the other sellers," Renard said. "Come now, don't look so surprised." He reined Sylvester about. "I go to the inn, to secure rooms and a place in the stables. My credit there is good. You may go on to the abbey." He wagged a finger. "But be mindful of who you talk to."

Jean-Michel leaned forward and strained to hear the service being sung behind the black wrought iron gates. The nave was a frenzy of piercing cries and prayers of excited pilgrims. They were stumbling over one another to reach a little pool bubbling in the center of the puddled flagstone floor. They competed for space at the edge to dip their hands, buckets, and bottles into the healing waters. The pool hissed, not from heat, but from natural carbonation. The screams of fettered madmen, the moans of the diseased, and the clacking of crutches echoed wildly in the Romanesque dome over the sacred spring. A limestone Mary looked down at the press benevolently and patiently, her twelve star crown aglow in the light of the swaying oil lamps and offering candles. A flat crescent moon at her feet glistened from the wet kisses of the faithful. Piles of bent silver pennies, tossed there for penances or favors, glittered around her pedestal. A scraggly man, pretending to kiss the moon, surreptitiously caught up a few pennies.

Jean-Michel noticed pickpockets nimbly working the crowd. He gripped his saddlebags more firmly. They were getting heavier on his back, perhaps from absorbing the virtue of the shrine, and he hoped he could soon sit down somewhere. But every crevice and column base was already occupied by wax votives in the shapes of various limbs and organs, each pleading for a particular healing. Jean-Michel remembered the busy booth outside where the ready-made figurines were sold.

He leaned against a pier, where the sweet smoke of a burning trindle helped to alleviate the stench of pus and poverty. By the length of the coiled hemp, Jean-Michel could tell the taper had measured a tall person in some faraway village who could not endure the trip.

As Jean-Michel breathed a brief prayer for the unknown patient, the crowded crypt was quieted by the high-pitched praises of a little girl. Her skinny arms were raised and her smiling face was upturned to the stone Virgin. The girl's mother, dressed in black like a nun, gesticulated crazily. She pulled her shouting daughter to a high oak desk where a cowled custodian sat ready to record cures in the *liber miraculorum.* The monk's hand crawled from his sleeve like a sleepy badger emerging from its burrow. He dipped a goose quill in an ink pot and scratched the girl's name and the nature of her miracle on the parchment. The sheet was nearly full of entries.

Dutifully, the dour priest signed a certificate for the girl and her ecstatic mother, ignoring the rush of others to the exact spot in the pool where the child had dipped. The altar bells rang to end the service and the tower chimes gonged in reply to announce the close of the nave for the night. The bored custodian began to hand out signed certificates to pilgrims who required verification of their visit. He accepted bags of coins and jewels in payment of penances, and then jotted the amounts in his leather-bound ledger, while armed attendants carried the treasures away.

Jean-Michel joined a line of waiting penitents. A barefoot man in front of him was not wearing the usual robe and cross patch, but a smelly hair shirt alive with lice. The supplicant turned, and seeing Jean-Michel's thick saddlebags weighing heavily across his shoulders as though across a pack animal, he signed the cross to such an obviously wicked sinner. Embarrassed, Jean-Michel turned away.

Most of the people cleared the church obediently, but a few needed to be pried off the piers, bound, and carried back to the monastery's hostel. There, they would sleep head-to-toe on straw. Each hoped to be healed by being so near the springs. Jean-Michel thought gratefully of the wide, warm bed awaiting him at the tavern. He hoped Renard would spend the night elsewhere, and he would not have to share his bed.

"What is the sum?"

The priest's sharp voice sliced through his thoughts. Jean-Michel stood dumb, forgetting what to say.

"The sum of your penance, if you please," the priest said testily. He rubbed his weary eyes and left an ink smudge on his dark brow.

"I have not come for penance," Jean-Michel said.

"You want a certificate, then?"

"No."

The priest blinked and examined Jean-Michel with an inquisitor's stare. "What is it you want? What are the bags for?"

"I must see the sacristan, and deliver this to him," Jean-Michel said, drawing a rolled parchment from his belt like a dagger. He passed it to the priest.

"I am he," the custodian said. He punctured the seal and unrolled the letter on his desk. His fatigued face gradually brightened as his finger traced the Latin script. He rolled it up, looked about, and seeing no more certificate-seekers, dismissed his attendants and said quietly, "Come this way."

Behind closed doors, the sacristan read the letter again, and then rerolled the crisp parchment. He studied Jean-Michel with steely eyes that bored into the knight's soul. The sacristan's keen nose looked like an axe head planted in his face. His words were chopped and direct. "You seek a holy relic?"

"I do, Father, God helping me." Jean-Michel felt his palms dampen. *I smell of horses and dirt*, he chastened himself. *I should have waited until morning.*

The priest steepled his long fingers, and his spiked elbows dug into the table. "His Excellency DeBeauvais is my old teacher, you know," he said. His breath caused the flame to flicker on its wick. The priest's creviced eyes darkened, as if he had donned a dramatist's mask. "How is His Excellency's health?"

"God preserves him, Father, but his heart is sick from grief over his church."

"Of course," the priest said. He tapped the parchment, thinking. "I cannot sell a relic," he said. "It is a most improper act, fit only for thieves."

Jean-Michel bent his bowed legs and hoisted the saddlebags to the tabletop. At the loud chink and the clinking of settling coins, the priest drew back, open-mouthed, like a man either startled by an unexpected sound or repulsed by the thought of a bribe.

Jean-Michel opened the bag. He untwisted its linen lining and felt warmed by its softness and the thought of Blanche wearing it. He spilled the coins into a gleaming pile. The *livres* tinkled like hand bells at Vespers.

The sacristan licked his bloodless lips. "However, for a generous donation, a relic may be offered in gratitude for your favor."

"Then you will take me to the abbot?"

The sacristan's smile looked like a gash. "There will be no need for that. Has not His Excellency sent you directly to me?"

Jean-Michel nodded.

"I am permitted to act under my own authority in such circumstances. If you feel you must see the abbot, you must wait until the morrow, since he retires after Vespers."

"I see no need to disturb him."

"Why, just today at chapter," the priest said breathlessly, "Father told us of the urgent need for funds to maintain our devotion and hospitality to the faithful. The basilica at Vezelay, of course, receives the greater endowments from the local lords. The resting place of the Magdalene overshadows the springs and the remains of Saint Germaine."

The name chimed like a consecration bell in Jean-Michel's ear. "That is why His Excellency sent us here," he said, looking up at the rib vaults. "He invokes that name on the hunt."

"Saint Germaine was always one of his favorite saints," the priest said. "A frequent hunting companion of Saint Martin himself."

Jean-Michel felt a brief rush of excitement, but soon settled into a sober realization. "But surely the abbot would not permit such a relic to leave his care. I can see how many people come to honor such a champion of heaven's hosts."

The priest shook his axe-head nose. "Few, if any, know of Saint Germaine's presence here. They come for the spring water."

"But if Saint Germaine is removed, will the blessing on the water remain?"

"The spring is dedicated to Our Lady, and she will remain. So the faithful will always return. They must. By the time they get the water home, the bubbles are gone and so is the water's healing power."

"Then I would not impoverish the abbey?"

"Not at all. Rather, you would enrich us by giving us the opportunity to be generous."

"Then take what you need, Father, and do not be shy in claiming God's blessing."

The sacristan, his eyes bulging, began to form his hands into a scoop, but then withdrew them into his sleeves. "I will fetch the holy bones at once," he said, "that you may be on your way before dark. Wait here."

He rose and spun away through the door into the shadows. The eager scuff of his sandals faded in the stone cloister.

Jean-Michel clapped his hands in triumph and raised them in thanks. The echo seemed like angels applauding. Surely God guided the faithful, and worked all things together for the good of those who loved Him. The candlelight sparkled on the silver coins; Jean-Michel longed to see the same twinkling in Blanche's bright eyes and the shine of her approving smile when he returned successful. His travel-weariness left him, and he felt lightheaded. *When Bobo sees this,* he thought gladly, *how proud he will be of me. If only Father could know. He would be proud of me too, for the first time in his life. And Renard—ha!* he tapped his foot. *He will have to go on alone*! Jean-Michel enjoyed the prospect of no longer enduring the braggart's crude songs. Relieved, he knew he would easily reach the Boar's Tooth over the knoll by dark, and be ready to celebrate.

He calmed himself when he heard the shuffle of the sacristan's returning steps. As the priest entered the room and shut the door, a cold breeze swept over Jean-Michel. His fingers trembled, not from the brief chill, but from anticipation.

The priest glanced over his shoulder and whispered, "Has anyone else been here since I left?"

"No one, Father."

"It is well that none be tempted beyond their means and fall to covetousness," the priest said. He pulled a dark velvet purse from his broad sleeve and set it on the table. Loosening the yellow silk drawstrings, he slid out a polished brass case. He opened a pearled latch and lifted the lid a crack to reveal a pile of fine white powder inside.

Jean-Michel nearly fainted at being so near the radiating blessedness.

"Mustn't let any of it blow away," the priest said, snapping the box shut. "The ashes of Saint Germaine were not meant to be scattered in Burgundy. He belongs near the woods where he and his beloved companion hunted." He noticed the slight disappointment on Jean-Michel's face.

"You expected fragments of bone, I can tell. Do you recall that Saint Germaine perished in a forest fire?"

Ashamed at knowing so little, Jean-Michel shook his head.

"It seems fitting," said the priest, "that Saint Germaine assist his friend Saint Martin in rebuilding his church harmed by fire." Returning the bright box to its bag, the priest pushed it across the table to Jean-Michel and snatched two fistfuls of coins from the pile.

Jean-Michel thought the amount too modest for so valuable a relic and was about to urge the priest to take more. But the priest held his hands out to Jean-Michel. "Take these for your journey home," he said. "The inn is not free, and there are tolls to pay. And give my richest greetings to my old teacher."

A glint of silver reflected in his black-rimmed eyes.

8

The old woman, her knotty fingers atremble, drew a little pouch from inside her collar. The bailiff snatched it away, snapping the string. He pulled out a silver *livre* and shook it in her terrified face.

"This is stolen from Her Grace, the Baroness DuVal," he growled.

"I . . . I did not know," the woman whimpered. Her nervous eyes flitted to the lowered pikes of the mounted sergeants. Her pig grunted at them.

The bailiff held up the string and let the purse dangle. "I could have you hanged."

"O messire, I beg you . . ."

The menfolk shuffled forward.

"Back!" The bailiff barked. "I would burn down this miserable place if I did not need it for the night."

"He gave it to me because of the horses . . ." the woman pleaded.

"Enough," the bailiff barked. *Villeins will say anything to save their necks.* He stuck the coin in his belt. He had what he needed—confirmation of their speed, direction, and destination. But he could not traverse the forests at night, especially with the dull moon veiled in clouds. He would billet here until predawn, and fall upon his prey in the morning.

"Kill that pig," he ordered. "Fresh pork for all."

Jean-Michel paid the tavern owner in advance. The round, ruddy man showed him to the back. "Horses there," the innkeeper said, pointing. "And you're up there." He indicated a second-level corner room in the stone tavern house, accessible by a flight of wooden stairs entwined in ivy. "Le Renard likes to have two ways in," the man chuckled, his beer belly bouncing. "I think it is so one woman can get out as the next one comes in."

When Jean-Michel did not respond, the man stopped laughing. "Carp stew tonight. Bread and apples at sunrise," he said.

They stabled their own horses, well away from Sylvester, who stamped a welcome, and carried their goods up the creaking stairs. Bobo hauled the armor, and, as usual, Jean-Michel carried the saddlebags, but not over his shoulder. Without the money, the bags were light and flat. The left pocket showed a slight bulge from the brass reliquary, which was wrapped snugly in Blanche's blouse.

Through the inside door they could hear muffled laughter and the chinking of mugs from the dining area below the mezzanine.

"You stay with our things," Jean-Michel said, unfastening his sword. "I will fetch food from downstairs."

Bobo took the weapon and posted himself on a stool beside the oversized, overstuffed bed. Accustomed to straw and horse blankets, Bobo admired the lumpy down mattress and quilted covers. There was even a clay pot in the corner for passing water.

"Bolt the door," Jean-Michel said, sliding the saddlebags under the bed frame. "Let in no one but me. If Renard comes, refuse to leave. He will need to go elsewhere with his guests."

When he opened the door leading to the balcony, he was greeted by the twang of Renard's lute from below. The jongleur was warming up for the night.

On the way downstairs, he passed two harlots on their way to the lofts, luring their first customer of the evening. The blonde brushed Jean-Michel against the banister and whispered through thick berry-red lips, "Just a copper for you." Jean-Michel tightened his jaw and averted his eyes. He noticed that the scent of perfume came from the pudgy customer, a balding, fifty-ish merchant wearing an embroidered jacket with lace sleeves.

In the tavern, the merchant's companions sang around a table. They swayed their ale mugs to the beat of a Flemish ditty, while Renard tried to pick up the tune on his lute. At the end of each rowdy chorus, they touched cups and splashed foam on the floor. They washed down their bread and mutton and ordered another round.

"And one for the brave knight!" Renard said, springing up. He clapped Jean-Michel on the shoulder and steered him to the table.

"Messire, join our company, if it pleases you," a mustachioed merchant said. He beckoned with fingers full of rings and slick from gravy. The others tipped their floppy felt hats in greeting or raised their mugs. Their patterned sleeves hung like pennons attached to tourney trumpets.

Renard kicked a chair into place and sat Jean-Michel in it. A full stein was pushed in front of him. "A noble quest," the big merchant said, "worthy of your courage."

"May Our Lady grant you success," said another. He was slurring already, and the evening was young.

"She already has," Jean-Michel said, trying to conceal his pride.

Renard stopped strumming. "How so?"

The news bubbled from Jean-Michel's mouth like the fizz bubbling from the abbey spring. "I received a relic from the abbey tonight."

"From who?"

"What is it?"

"Praise be!"

"Imagine!"

"From who?" Renard asked, insistent.

"Not some vendor, if you fear that. From the sacristan himself."

Renard did not look at all relieved. "For how much?"

"All of it," Jean-Michel said.

Renard slapped his forehead in disbelief. His braid flapped. "You gave him the entire sack of silver for some bones?" He said it loudly enough to turn heads. "I kept enough to pay the bill and get us back, if that worries you."

"They must be bones turned to ivory," Renard said.

"The ashes of Saint Germaine himself in a case," the knight said.

"Not a very good bargain," the big merchant said. "Unless you intend to drive up the value for resale."

"Messire," Jean-Michel retorted, "the holy relics of Saint Germaine will be given to the people of Auxonne for their cathedral." He coughed and wet his throat with ale.

"But of course," the trader apologized, "and they will be grateful to you for such a valuable gift."

"But who can put a price on a saint?" asked a jowled seller of silks.

"It has perceived value and can be traded," argued a curly man.

"Perceived by whom?"

"The buyer."

"I say the seller, for he paid the last price for it."

Other men in the tavern, leather-vested and heavily bearded, moved closer to the discussion. Liking the attention, Jean-Michel drained his ale and took another. The burly merchant leaned toward him. "How did you manage to get it at all? What abbey lets go of its treasure so lightly?"

"Just as the fox took the cheese from the raven," Renard said, his jovial voice returning.

Jean-Michel, his nose in another stein, thought: He has noticed the gathering crowd and cannot help himself.

Renard bounced atop a table and positioned his lute. "Do you remember?" he asked.

> Renard the Fox, his nose to the breeze,
> Wanders the woodland afar, 'til he sees

Karak the Raven a perched in the trees
Primping his feathers and clutching some cheese.
(Ah, the smell of it!)

"I knew it was you, I could not be wrong,"
Says the fox with a smile. "I could tell by your song!
To whom else in these woods, so wide and so long,
Could such a beautifully pure voice belong?"
(Let me tell of it!)

"Do you mean me?" says the bird with delight.
"Of course," quoth the fox. "From morning's first light
Your music has made every heart ever bright."
Karak puffs taller, but the cheese he holds tight.
(Will he fall for it?)

"Oh, sing it again," pleads the fox, feigning glee,
"And pray, raise your voice to a much higher key
So all of the creatures about heareth thee,
Since most of them have not keen ears, such as me."
(Oh, the gall of it!)

The raven obliges, and out of its throat
Comes a cackling croak like the bleat of a goat
That has fallen headlong into a deep moat
And in desperate straits does not know how to float!
(Hear the call of it!)

Renard put his elbows to his ribs like wings and cawed a few sour notes. The guests bellowed in laughter.

"That's what the priest sounded like, God's blood," Jean-Michel said, unlacing his tunic at the collar. Why was it getting so warm? "And he had a nose like a beak." He wiped sweat from his lip and tried to cool himself with a draught of ale. *Watered down, as Renard said; I can hardly taste it.* "Just like that, the priest's voice, it was." *And gullible as the raven*, he crowed to himself. He drained his drink. Had he hit his lip with the mug? It felt numb.

The merchants guffawed and called for another round.

"How lovely, how fair," lies the fox. "If you please,
I'll hear it again, in the highest of keys."
So the bird, at his word, shuts his eyes with a squeeze,
And croaks his loudest, thus dropping the cheese.
(That's not all of it!)

Renard cries in pain and drops to the ground.
"The cheese broke my knees! Did you not hear the sound
Of the bones cracking? O bird, I bid you fly down
And lift me away, 'ere I'm mangled by hounds."
(Ah, he falls for it!)

The raven takes pity. He sees that the prize
Piece of cheese is untouched, and trusting, he flies
To Renard's aid, who leaps up and tries
To add to his dinner! But Karak shrieks, "Lies!"
And flaps up to safety, unwounded and wise
To Renard's tricks. The fox eats and sighs,
Thinking of blackbird and robin's egg pies.

The audience applauded and banged their mugs on the tables. Renard bowed. Jean-Michel scratched his head but couldn't feel it. *Pies.* Of course. He had come down for food, for himself and for Bobo, left behind in the room. *How could I have forgotten?*

Renard was picking another tune and singing of a Christian knight, held prisoner in a Saracen palace, given food by an infidel princess.

Food. I promised Bobo food. Jean-Michel pushed his chair back and tried to stand. The room spun, and he tottered.

"Easy, friend," came a stranger's voice. Jean-Michel felt two meaty hands steadying him. The stranger's breath stank of fish and ale, but the stench did not clear his head.

"Fish," Jean-Michel said. "Where is the fish?"

"You need some carp stew, do you?" the stranger said in a croak like Renard's raven. "I've a bowl right here."

Renard had already reached the stanzas where the princess, converted to the true faith, frees the knight and hides him in her chambers. But the jongleur shouldered his lute, grabbed an empty stein and passed it. "No jingles, no tingles," he goaded. The men flipped *obals* and silver pennies into the mug to have the story continue.

"You're a man of morals," the stranger said to Jean-Michel. "No need to hear this filth."

"I left my servant in the room hungry."

"We'll take the stew to him, and you can rest."

"God be kind to you, messire, as you are to me."

The song had barely resumed before Jean-Michel rapped on the upstairs door. "Bobo, I have fish for you. I am sorry I took so long."

The bolt was thrown. The stranger jammed Jean-Michel into the door. His nose began to spurt blood, and he felt himself tumbling like a shot pheasant to the planking. He heard several men force their way in and step over him, men whom he'd not noticed at all on the way upstairs. Dully he heard the sound of his helpless, voiceless valet being pummeled. Purity clanked beside him. He tried to roll and reach out for it, but his body did not respond and his eyes refused to focus. He called out once but the ensuing rapid kicks in his ribs and temples made him curl up and cover his face. As dizziness turned to darkness, he discerned the raspy voice of the stranger crowing, "Get away! I have it!"

Robbers, like roaches, run in all directions when surprised.

These will be no different, Marcel, the bailiff, thought. He ordered three sergeants around to the back of the tavern to prevent any escape.

He dropped from his saddle to the gravel, drew his sword, and pounded the hilt so hard on the front door the blade hummed. Above the cries of women and curses of men roused from slumber came the innkeeper's call, the jangle of keys, and the jolt of the night bolt.

The bailiff burst in, his sword point up, forcing back the fat, flustered innkeeper.

"What do you want?" the proprietor demanded. He was wrapped in a bedsheet. "What is the meaning of this?"

"The jongleur, Renard, and his escort, a young knight. Where are the thieves? Speak!" The bailiff poked his sword into the man's fat midriff.

"You are looking for the thieves?"

"The knight and the jongleur—they stayed here?"

"I gave them the corner room, up there . . ."

The bailiff jerked his chin and his men raced behind him up the stairs. Guests bedded along the walls pulled up their cloaks for protection. The sergeants shouldered the door.

"Wait, I have a key." The owner fumbled, trying to find it while holding up his sheet. "But the robbers went out the back way . . ."

The door cracked off its rusty hinges. The bailiff rushed to the lumpy bed and ripped off the quilt with his sword. A cloud of downy feathers puffed into his face from a torn pillow. The bailiff cursed. He stomped to the mezzanine. "Where did they go?" he bellowed, holding his blade menacingly.

The innkeeper shivered. "After they beat him, they ran out the back. They carried his precious relic into the night. Who could tell with all the noise down here?"

The bailiff arched an eyebrow. "Who are you talking about?"

"The thieves, messire. You have come for them much too late, I am afraid. They beat the knight and his groomsman and escaped before any of us knew of it. They took his sword—everything. Le Renard found the knight in a faint. He said it was from drinking . . ."

"They took the sword?"

"And whatever money he had. An awful loss, messire. The poor knight was sick over it."

Gascon was right, Marcel marveled. But the idiot knight, his tongue loosened from ale, had probably boasted of it. Now it was gone. "The knight? And the jongleur?"

"Gone as well as you see," the innkeeper huffed, throwing a corner of the sheet over his hairy shoulder. He looked more offended than frightened now.

The bailiff scowled. Did it matter where they went? Without the evidence, he could not arrest the Angevin.

"Mayhaps you will find him at the church, repenting of his drunkenness," offered the owner. "Or mayhaps he is on the way to Dijon, with the merchants."

"Merchants?"

"They lodged here, on their way to the fair of Saint Ramoul."

Marcel pulled on his mustache. So that was the Angevin's game. Sell the sword at the fair, out of his seigniory's jurisdiction. *But now the robber has been robbed.*

He sent his men downstairs. There was no sense in chasing his quarry to Dijon. A foray into the next fiefs could incite a brawl with the neighboring baron. He did not wish to provoke a war, what with Hughes gone and a mere woman left in charge of the defenses. That would certainly be worse than letting a thief get away.

"We will take a meal, and provisions for our horses," he growled to the innkeeper.

Two days of riding for nothing. No sword. No thief. No hanging. Marcel chewed on his mustache. He would burn that village on the way back to make the trip worthwhile.

Jean-Michel stopped to wretch up bile, for nothing else was left in his twisted stomach. When his guts settled and he rinsed his mouth

with watered wine, he resumed his place alongside the heavily laden mules of the merchants. His swollen head pounded with every trot of his charger. He doubted his ability to beat off brigands in this condition. Pain shot through his ribs where the thieves had kicked him. The light hurt his eyes. Squinting, he prayed he would not doze. A borrowed sword rubbed his thigh, and he wished he could hold Purity's familiar handle to ask Saint Denis for aid.

The fair at Dijon was only a few hours away. The predawn start would enable them to meet other traders en route—Englishmen with hounds and furs, Spaniards with swords and shields, Italians with alum and dyes needed for Flemish cloth. In numbers, the danger would be diminished. The merchants bore arms also, but they were accustomed to needles and scissors, not swords.

For the few days of the fair, he would stand guard over the merchants' bolts of cloth, just as he had guarded the cathedral stoneyard. But could they trust him after his humiliation at the hands of robbers? Somehow Renard had convinced them. Perhaps it was Renard they really wanted along. The jongleur sang merrily up in front, his voice irritatingly loud.

Ailas, com mor! Alas, how I die!
Quez as, amis? What is the matter, my friend?
I am betrayed!
For what reason?
Because one day I set my affections on her
 who gave me an encouraging glance.
And is your heart sorrowing because of that?
Indeed it is.
Is your heart thus set on her?
I have set it so, very strongly.
Are you therefore so close to death?
I am indeed, more completely than I can tell you.

Jean-Michel's stomach rolled again and he leaned over the ditch. Nothing came out but tears for Blanche's lost treasure. He stroked the blouse, tied to his saddle like a token in a tournament. In the darkness, the thieves had tossed it aside like a rag. He rested his hands in its tender folds, one moment soothed by the memory of Blanche's apple-sweet breath and honey-flecked hair, and the next moment despairing at the thought of returning to her empty-handed and ashamed. How could he ever return now at all?

> What course, sir, should be taken?
> A good and courtly one.
> Tell it to me at once.
> You will come before her quickly and ask her for her
> love.
> And if she takes it as an affront?
> Do not disturb yourself!
> And if she answers me dismissively or angrily?
> Be patient, because patience is always triumphant.
> And if the jealous one finds out about it?
> Then you will both act more stealthily.
> Both of us?
> Of course, yes.
> If only she wished that!

Jean-Michel sighed. His throat burned, his chest cramped, his heart ached. Even if the kind men of Flanders paid him handsomely, out of pity, it would not approach the sum Blanche had entrusted to him. What honor did he have left? What had he left in Auxonne? Neither family, nor fortune, nor future. Who would miss him? Only Blanche. But she would forever take him for a philanderer and a fraud, and despise his memory. The thought stabbed him deeply. If he'd ever had hope for her attention and favor, it was gone now, like the sword. Like the saint. Like the silver.

> You despair?
> I do indeed, so that I am certain of nothing.
> All those who are in despair because of love feel thus.
> Certainly love has brought me to this,
> because everyone knows that the man who dies yearning
> dies badly, so I cannot mourn for my heart.
> Go friend, toward your delight before everyone
> knows about it, so that you do not lose your determination.
> Because one loses easily what one hesitates over.

Must he be so loud? Jean-Michel grumped.

The raucous noise at the fair pressed upon Jean-Michel like a carpenter's vise. From pennoned pavilions and gaudy booths, sellers advertised their goods and struck deals. Tenant workers who had slipped away from their overseers for the day gaped at rich silks and engraved leathers, cages of pet monkeys, and cases of sweetmeats shaped like cats and cows. A crowd of villeins cheered a game of blind-man's bluff, in which four men swinging clubs in a muddy ring bashed each other while trying to kill a squealing pig set loose among them.

Money-changers at long trestles chatted with interpreters and traders while weighing and counting French *deniers*, royal *livres*, Venetian *zechins*, German *groats*, and English shillings. Scribes wrote on tally boards, reading the audits aloud for their fur-draped nobles. An argument erupted near the striped tents where the Jews made discrete loans. Armed sergeants-at-arms broke it up, and the Flemish merchants cheered them.

Arriving in midafternoon, the travelers missed the grand procession of Saint Ramoul's relics which opened the fair. But silver commemorative pins and threads of the saint's cloak were still on sale, as well as a few remaining flowers which had bedecked the parade casket. Near the souvenir stand, a juggler and his dancing bear attracted a circle of villeins. All scattered at the approach of the high-stepping horses of the Knights Templar, as they pounded past on their way to the stalls where they held the monopoly on wool-weighing.

Jean-Michel admired the knights' confident bearing, rhythmic riding, shining mail coifs, and flowing white mantles signifying their Cistercian vows. Their bushy beards were as black as the half-field on their *beauseant* banner, the square standard that led them in battle against the infidels.

Now there is a proper guard and escort, Jean-Michel thought as the attendants bearing the tourney lances trotted by.

He had once carried his brothers' lances to the tournament at Troyes. Spindly at fifteen, his hands as big as his clumsy feet, he had been thrilled at the prospect of squiring in the lists, of preparing his brothers for mock combat, and of seeing His Most Christian Majesty, King Louis himself, in attendance, mustering interest among the barons for his crusade.

Jean-Michel had stayed up half the night polishing their shields and helms. Then he eagerly stacked the ashwood shafts in racks beside their pavilion. Bobo had outfitted their stallions with fringed caparisons and inspected the new shoes and silvered bridles. He looked so solemn. He could not warn Jean-Michel about what awaited him inside the tent.

Jean-Michel ducked inside where his brothers were already fitted into ninety-pound suits of mail. Two young boys in feathered caps were adjusting and pulling the armor to the brothers' knees. Philippe stood to one side, stroking his severe chin and evaluating their progress.

"Be sure that is buckled," he said to the young boys. Then he noticed Jean-Michel. "The helms are oiled?" he asked sternly. But Jean-Michel did not hear it. He had expected to dress his brothers. He stood woodenly, watching the two strangers, both younger than he, folding down the final clasps.

"What are you staring at, runt?" Guillaume muttered.

"The helms," Philippe repeated.

"Oiled and ready, Father," Jean-Michel said weakly, winded with disappointment. "Do you not smell them?"

"Do not talk back to me," Philippe said, jutting his chin. "Show me the lances."

Jean-Michel led Philippe outside where, looking critical, he re-stacked the lances in a different order. The young squires came out, whispering between themselves. They took hold of the horses from Bobo. Roger and Guillaume emerged, blinking in the sudden sunlight, their mail flashing and their emblazoned surcoats flapping in a gust of wind. It blew dust into Jean-Michel's face and his eyes began to tear, but he did not wipe any of it away for fear they would think he was crying.

"Get to the stables," Philippe ordered him. "See that the pack horses are cleaned."

Jean-Michel slumped. He would miss the action in the lists. How could he be denied it after so much anticipation? Could he not prepare the sommiers after the tourney?

"Do it now," Philippe said, as if hearing Jean-Michel's cry of objection.

Bobo guided the sulking boy away. No word of comfort was possible, only a sympathetic companionship while they brushed the bays and combed their tails. The cheers of the crowd and the crash of metal was but a distant din. Perhaps it was God's will after all, because the host's pregnant mare went into labor that afternoon, and Jean-Michel assisted in delivering a sunny colt.

"Yellow," the baron frowned. "A worthless mare." Generous from wine and a win in the lists, he gave the colt to Jean-Michel. From then on, the horse rarely left his side. As her hide darkened to a glowing gold, Fidelity had became closer to him than his brothers ever would.

Now she jerked ahead to follow the Flemish merchants off the main thoroughfare. For a moment Jean-Michel feared Sylvester was nosing her in the tail again. But the jongleur's beast was nowhere to be seen. Both singer and steed had melted into the crowd. They proceeded to a set of wooden stalls already piled with bolts of cloth and rolls of lace. A companion party, which had arrived earlier to construct the stands, greeted the newcomers with slaps on their backs. Some men tended the horses, while others in German mail hoods stood watch over the merchandise. Instinctively, Jean-Michel knew what was coming next.

"You have served us well," the burly merchant said, extending a leather purse. "Take this, and buy a proper sword. Return me the other when you have found one. There are many fine armorers at this fair."

Jean-Michel thanked him with a measured courtesy, accepted water and feed for Fidelity, but declined lodging at the inn. The merchant understood, and suggested the hostel of the nearby Abbey Saint Claude.

Thus dismissed, Jean-Michel set off for the blacksmiths' lane. He peeked into the purse. It contained a gold *florin* with a pleasing design. He showed the coin to Bobo, who let out an admiring whistle. Jean-Michel flipped it in his palm and prayed for a fitting replacement for Purity. Dear Purity, she was now being handled by a thief's sin-stained hand. The thought, mingled with a spicer's odors of ginger, clove, and cinnamon, made him nauseous.

To avoid the smell, he directed Fidelity down a different lane and past the tents of fortune tellers and luck peddlers. Ruffians were throwing dice, wagering their futures. Charms and readings were offered at each stop. A few women with unbraided, flowered hair offered themselves.

"Treasures of the Holy Land," one seller chanted, his booth bedecked with brittle palms. "Straw from the manger!"

From the stables, most likely, Jean-Michel thought.

"Feathers of Gabriel!"

Pigeons, probably.

"The stones that martyred Saint Stephen!" cried another. "See the blood on them, messire."

His own, no doubt.

"The sword of Saint Martin!"

Jean-Michel halted his horse.

A hooded seller hunched cross-legged on a blanket. His hand gestured to a stack of swords beside him. Some bore fine enamel, English leather handles, and Castillian etching.

"And his mail mittens," the man whispered, "which might fit you, Jean-Michel."

That voice.

"Renard?"

"Shh, not so loud." Renard peered up from the hood, a roguish twinkle in his eye. "Have they let you go so soon? The fair lasts for a week."

Jean-Michel recovered from his surprise. "These swords that you sell, where have they come from?"

"Oh, I do not sell them." Renard was chuckling. "They were given to me in payment for some of these." He drew a cloth from his sleeve and unrolled it, revealing a row of bones.

"Mutton chops? From the Boar's Tooth?"

"To you, perhaps. But to seekers of good luck and miracles, these are the bones of Saints Cyrilla and Anastis of Constantinople. Cures headaches and hangovers, you know."

Jean-Michel's head throbbed anew from indignation. "How dare you," he said. "You are worse than the thieves."

Renard produced a pigskin pouch. "That may be, but I have earned back all they stole." The bag looked heavy. Looking this way and that, he jiggled loose the drawstring and then discretely showed Jean-Michel the gold pieces inside. "*Bezants*," he said. "The money changers will love them."

"The Lord drove men such as you out of the Temple with a whip!"

"This is no temple," Renard retorted. "And how much did the cloth makers give you?"

Jean-Michel dismounted, any pride in the little gold florin evaporated by the heat of his anger.

"Not much," Renard said. "I thought not."

"You are the one exploiting the wishes of honest men."

"Not at all. I am fulfilling yours. Here, choose a decent sword and be rid of that one. Personally I like the one with the wing-shaped hilt. Come now, before anyone sees you. Wait. Here come more customers."

A boisterous band of mounted knights, their laughing squires close behind, crunched over the straw-covered street. The warriors whooped as whores flitted to them like moths to lights. The joy-women flaunted their assets. A few were chosen and scooped up to the saddles. The knight's coursers, spattering manure and straw, galloped past Jean-Michel in a wild rush.

"Get away!" the leader snarled, spurring his chestnut stallion. He charged close by, forcing Bobo to leap aside and Jean-Michel to skip back, his hand to his face. The rider snapped his reins with one hand, squeezed his woman with the other, and pounded down the lane. His curved shield, carrying the emblem of a blood-red gryphon in flight, bounced on his back.

Jean-Michel stepped into the alleyway and wiped dust from his brow. He knew that face, fearless and seamed with scars; those eyes, proud and cunning; and that voice.

"It is the thief," he said, his stomach somersaulting. He pointed his finger at the receding rider like a bowman taking aim. "He's the one, Bobo, I know it."

Bobo tucked his right fist under his ribs.

"Yes, the one who beat you," Jean-Michel said.

Bobo shook his head. Jean-Michel had misunderstood his sign. Bobo thrust his fist forward in jabs and raised his other elbow in a shielding position.

"He has come for the tournament? You could tell by the shield?"

Bobo beamed and nodded.

"He has come to sell the relic," Renard said. "At least, if I had a real one, that's what I would do. There will be important people at the tourney who would want it."

"He will not be able," Jean-Michel said, his spirits rising. "If he has come for the tilt, I will challenge him. And as God gives me strength, I will unseat him and demand Purity and Saint Germaine for the ransom prize." Propelled by hope, he vaulted into the saddle. "To the carpenters," he cried to Bobo, "for lances."

"Lances are expensive," Renard sang out. "More than you have, I would wager." He jingled his pigskin purse gently, as though it were an altar boy's bell.

Regretfully, Renard was right. Jean-Michel eyed his offer with suspicion. "And in return?"

"Win or lose, you continue with me to the Midi."

"That is more than I want to pay."

"That is what you will say to the lance makers, also."

Jean-Michel looked toward Bobo for advice, but he got only a shrug of resignation.

"Very well," he said, his exhilaration gone. "Take it, Bobo."

"You won't be sorry," Renard said with a shopkeeper's smile.

But Jean-Michel did not hear him. He was already galloping toward the woodsheds.

Renard gathered the swords to sell to the armorers. He patted his hip and felt the outline of the only sword he planned to keep—the bronzed hunting dagger he had found in the seam of Gascon's saddle blanket. *He forgot it in his haste to be rid of me,* he grinned. *He will probably miss it.* It was an odd size and shape, but just right for prying away nests and poking into holes. Gascon had probed a good many, too, by the look of it.

Renard headed toward the smoke of the smithy's fire. He chuckled to himself to think he might have convinced Jean-Michel that the dagger really was the sword of Saint Martin, flown to the fair by an angel.

10

When the equerries pulled back the gates, Jean-Michel's heart began to gallop. He trotted Fidelity to the middle of the field to face the nobles' gallery.

He rode along the lists, a rough-hewn log fence about chest-high which divided the dusty arena. A squad of sergeants were clearing the track of broken lances and loose armor. They moved off once he reached the center. Amid the odors of oiled steel, sweaty horses, and crushed grass, Jean-Michel saluted the canopied grandstand. He prayed that his potted helmet, balanced back on his leather cap, would not fall over his face.

Jean-Michel could hear the nobles in their bright shirts asking about him. Who was this knight in the colors of Anjou? Why weren't his crest and name displayed the day before? The merchants waved at him. The ladies, dressed in their finery of sendal, samite, and pearl, wondered aloud whose token was tied to his right arm.

The golden threads in Blanche's blouse put a sparkle in his eye and strength in his arm. The cross on his tunic, pressed to his shoulder by the weight of his mail, steadied his heart. Yet his still sensitive stomach churned with misgivings.

He had watched the thief, Galbert Le Marichal, defeat a dozen knights in a row that morning. He had admired the splendid German armor and superlative Spanish plating this man wore, as well as his huge plumed helmets and painted lances and tooled saddles and golden harnesses of fresh, spirited chargers. All were booty of those conquered in the jousts and taken "prisoner." The conquered were subject to ransom by the forfeit of their horses and equipment. He had seen those very men fallen on the field, and physicians and armorers running to them carrying frightful saws and hooks to cut open their shirts and chests.

Anxious, he shifted his gaze to the forest of brilliant banners fluttering over the pavilions of visiting contestants. Among the emblazoned shields and heraldry hanging at each tent, a red gryphon stood out. Under their shields, surcoated knights leaned on the fences, tended by their squires and servants while awaiting a challenge. Behind them, the trees were festooned with plebian onlookers, calling out the names of their favorites.

A herald dressed in a turquoise tabard strutted up to Jean-Michel from the stands, to ask his name and whom he wished to challenge.

Jean-Michel forced his parched mouth to speak. "Le Marichal."

The herald cocked his head. "Messire, he has retired from the field for the day."

Jean-Michel's stomach jumped. He stared ahead into the crowd, where every eye was fixed on him.

"Is there another?" the herald asked.

"Tell him Saint Germaine sent me," Jean-Michel insisted.

"Messire, I am sorry . . ."

"You will tell him." Jean-Michel surprised himself, with the hostility in his own voice.

"Custom permits him to refuse an unknown challenger."

"He knows Saint Germaine."

The herald returned to the stands. Pages ran at once to the tents of the *chevaliers*. When the people saw the runners strike the shield of the red gryphon, a great murmur arose.

Galbert Le Marichal punched his way through his tent flap and straightened to his full intimidating height. He was a broad, massive man, with a neck thicker than Jean-Michel's thigh. He had not yet removed all 125 pounds of his padded tilting armor. He glared at the upstart challenger with repugnance while tugging at his hauberk. His pitted face was squeezed like an angry fist.

Jean-Michel could feel his palms perspiring inside his gloves. Le Marichal might turn down a thirteenth bout to avoid bad luck. But on the other hand, since Jean-Michel was the thirteenth opponent, the bad luck could be his instead.

Signaling that he accepted the joust, Le Marichal plucked his shield from its post. The crowd cheered. Trumpeting heralds announced the two contestants. The betting began.

Jean-Michel steered his mare to the far end of the lists. Bobo held out to him his first lance, made of plain ashwood and tapered to a blunt, ball-shaped tip. Jean-Michel grasped its smooth handle in his glove, just below the cone-shaped rondel. He lifted the shaft and rested it on his right shoulder. He had tested this lance before, but now it seemed heavier and shorter than its actual eight English feet. Perhaps he should have affixed a pennant on the end to give it some lift in the wind.

Bobo assisted with the reins and shield, which Jean-Michel gripped in his left hand, and mimed some final instructions. *Stay low and forward in the saddle. Keep the shield up to your chin. Drop the point at the last possible moment. And, in the name of God, do not miss the target entirely or you will be forfeit.*

At the opposite end of the field, squires led Le Marichal's prancing war horse into position. The caparisoned beast wore a silver nose plate sporting a plum-colored plume at the forehead. Galbert, standing in the stirrups, wore a dark helmet etched in silver and fixed with upraised eagle's wings. The moveable visor, a recent innovation, was pushed upright, and Le Marichal's pitiless stare seemed to sear through Jean-Michel's shield. Galbert gripped his lance. It was as thick as an oak, tipped by an orb of iron, and ornamented with ladies' hair ribbons in place of a pennant.

Jean-Michel raised his shield to cover his light ring mail, which could easily puncture from a direct hit. He tilted his head to drop his helmet into place. It thumped painfully on his breastbone.

The gallery quieted. Commoners pressed against the fences. The squires nodded to the Marshal, indicating their men were ready.

The Marshal stood ceremoniously. He raised a white baton. "In the name of God and Saint Michael, do your battle!"

He waved the baton.

The horses sprang to life.

The crowd rose with a shout.

At the prick of Jean-Michel's spurs, Fidelity catapulted forward. The momentum pressed Jean-Michel back in the deep saddle. The wind whistled through the narrow slits of his helmet. The fence flashed past and the ground rushed up to meet him. The hooves thundered beneath him and he felt as if he were riding a storm. The earth quaked from Le Marichal's approach. Jean-Michel crouched. He lowered his chin to the top of his shuddering shield. The red gryphon swooped toward him. He dipped his lance point.

The crash deafened him. The scream of metal and splintering wood filled his helm. The ground fell from his sight and sunlight flooded his eyes. Fidelity fell back on her haunches, but she struggled up, her rider intact.

The spectators roared.

Each knight brandished a broken lance butt and a jagged mark on his shield. "Fairly broken!" the nobles cried. The villeins hooted.

Galbert jerked his stallion to a halt and veered about. He flipped up his visor to acknowledge the cheers and to gloat. But the golden mare cantered back to its station with its rider, and the bald-headed squire ran out holding a fresh lance. Galbert tossed his handle to the dust in disgust, dug in his spurs, and galloped to his end of the barrier.

Jean-Michel, shivering with elation, spun Fidelity to face Le Marichal once more. He pushed back his helm and wiped the sweat from his brow. The breeze cooled his face. His hand stung and his forearm felt as shattered as his lance. His shoulder flared in pain from the glancing shock he had absorbed, but he smiled nonetheless. He was probably Le Marichal's smallest target in a long while. That had given him another chance.

Making calming motions, Bobo passed the next lance up to Jean-Michel. He inspected the shield and knocked on the positions most likely to unseat Le Marichal. He held up two fingers. Two lances left. He made a spurring motion.

"Faster?" Jean-Michel asked.

Yes, Bobo nodded. He clapped his palms together and thrust one hand out like a javelin.

Jean-Michel guessed why. Because of his superior weight, Le Marichal could only be unhorsed by a perfect strike given with greater force.

Bobo patted Fidelity and scurried back behind the fence. Jean-Michel dropped his helmet over his face as the Marshal raised the baton again.

It swung down.

Fidelity bolted ahead, carving the air like an arrow. The cheering was drowned out by the rhythmic drumming of her hooves. She churned up sod as she flew down the track. Jean-Michel cleaved to her, her mighty muscles rippling under his knees, and her neck tendons as taut as bowstrings. He leaned into Fidelity's fluttering mane, a golden fire whipped by the wind. He swung up his shield. Took aim at the oncoming gryphon. Dipped the point. Braced.

Crash!

The shock lifted him from the saddle and threw him to the side. He clamped his feet onto Fidelity's hide but became snagged on the saddle straps. He hung there, the hammering of hooves close to his ear and the gravel crunching below his head.

The audience gasped. The equerries kicked open their gate to assist him, but Fidelity wheeled sharply in the direction of Jean-Michel's dangerous lean, re-seating him with a thud. Though dizzied by the rush of blood to his head, he held on.

The crowd's glee could not be contained. At the cheer Galbert spun about, flourishing his shattered hilt in victory. When Fidelity circled, Jean-Michel propped his helmet up on its leather lining. His spangled sight cleared and he saw his opponent's face harden. Le Marichal, gritting his pointed teeth, stabbed his splintered lance at the judges in an angry appeal.

The crowd joined the deliberation by cheering even more loudly. It did not take long. The judges, whispering among themselves for mere seconds, prompted the Marshal to raise the baton a third time.

While the guards used their pole axes to push the villeins away from the fences, Jean-Michel trotted Fidelity back to their post. The horse hesitated and tugged. She stamped and whinnied. Were the shrieking peasants scaring her? Jean-Michel bent down and patted her reassuringly. She felt sticky and sweaty. He raised his glove. It was stained crimson with blood.

It ran in glistening rivulets down her leg. A trail of rusty-brown hoofprints followed them from mid-field, where a bloodied piece of Galbert's splintered lance lay on the grass. Jean-Michel, suddenly sick with worry, urged Fidelity forward to meet Bobo. The mare limped and dipped her head in protest. The galleries, seeing the wound, murmured in unrest. Bobo hurried out to the track, grabbed the harness, made kissing sounds and led Fidelity to the end of the barrier. An assistant ran up, dragging a wooden bucket of water.

"How bad is it? Is anything broken?" Jean-Michel tried to dismount, but Bobo shooed him back. The groomsman worked a washcloth over the wound, searching. Fidelity shied, snorting. Bobo dabbed gently and shook his head.

She had taken a bad gash. It wasn't long, but it was deep. Bobo's compress could not staunch the blood, now pooling in the dirt.

"The bliaut," Jean-Michel said, unraveling the knot on his arm. "Tie it on as a bandage."

Bobo shook his head, his eyes darting, searching for something else.

"Do it quickly," Jean-Michel ordered, "before we are disqualified." He dropped the blouse to Bobo.

The valet kissed it, snapped it to full length, and twirled it into a long strip. Tenderly, he applied the folded wet cloth. Fidelity bucked. Bobo tried again, clicking his tongue as if explaining the procedure to the horse. He wrapped the bandage over the cloth once, then twice, his hands speedy and assured, quickly securing the bandage.

The equerry, gripping a new lance, stood ready. Bobo beckoned him to come, and raised one finger to Jean-Michel. *One try left.*

Jean-Michel, the last lance tucked firmly under his arm, pivoted toward Le Marichal. In spite of the distance, he could see the rage in the thief's riveted stare, the eyes black as coals, the fist as solid as a mace-head. Galbert spat in contempt and snapped down his visor.

Jean-Michel's bowels gnarled in fear. Le Marichal's lance was armed with a shining hooked coronal. The man intended this time not to aim for Jean-Michel's shield, but to try to rip him open. *He doesn't want to chance a draw*, Jean-Michel realized. He invoked Saint Denis, who empowered Purity, for protection, and he implored Saint Germaine, the hunter, for courage.

The Marshal stood and surveyed the arena. The squires nodded readiness. The white baton was lifted into the air like a torch prepared to set the field aflame.

It arched down.

The people rose up.

Jean-Michel spurred Fidelity to a charge. The pounding of the hooves matched the pulsing in his breast. Fidelity accelerated to a full, foaming gallop, as if trying to outdistance her pain. Jean-Michel's spine pressed back into the stiff saddle as her speed peaked. The barrier blurred. Through the whining slits of his helmet Jean-Michel saw Galbert's gleaming lance point flashing toward his heart like a comet. Briefly the lance point was the bear he had wounded in the chase.

Jean-Michel angled his shield. The vision of the bear faded, but not the feeling that he must protect Blanche.

In an instant he defied his training and raised his lance tip.

The collision bent the lance like a bow before it cracked in two. Galbert's coronal skidded off Jean-Michel's shield with a screech. Fidelity reared. Jean-Michel's helmet snapped from its laces and thumped on the grass. He was dazed but firmly seated. When Fidelity steadied and snorted out the dust, Jean-Michel looked across the field.

Le Marichal lay sprawled headlong in the dirt, his armor clattering, and his shield spinning away like a runaway cartwheel. His horse continued forward, leaping the fence and galloping through the shrieking spectators.

The galleries, wild with excitement, shouted their approval of Jean-Michel. Ladies threw garters and silk stockings to him; jongleurs began to sing impromptu songs about him; the rabble chanted his name.

He watched Galbert roll over. Had he gravely wounded him, like he had the bear?

Le Marichal's squires ran up to their master, with black-robed physicians close behind. Wielding pocket-sized scythes, they looked like grim reapers. Galbert, gagging, clutched his throat where the lance had struck him squarely. The squires unlaced his helmet from the dented neckpiece and pushed up his grimy visor. He coughed away a few teeth.

Now he tastes blood, Jean-Michel thought. *He wants it to be mine.*

Le Marichal said not a word when he surrendered the sword and reliquary to the stunted man with the shadowed jaw. Galbert burned into his memory every distasteful detail of this bold stranger's face which he had not noticed in the tavern: the slight build, the narrow nose, the quick eyes of a common kestrel. A darting bird had outmaneuvered the mighty gryphon. The diffused light inside the pavilion haloed the dark, disarrayed hair on Jean-Michel's reverently bowed head, and for a moment Galbert wondered if Saint Germaine really had sent him.

The formal exchange, supervised and recorded by the judges, surprised Le Marichal, not only because the victor, rather than the vanquished, was kneeling, but because the Angevin hardly demanded anything when he had a perfect right to strip Galbert of his expensive mail and more. Le Marichal felt oddly insulted for losing so little. Was he not worth more than this? Was it not enough to be humiliated in public, and now he must be disgraced in private as well?

He will wish he had asked for more, he swore, *for I will face him again.*

11

Eternity dwelt within it, but without, time had laid siege to the Abbey Saint Claude. A sequence of square battlements, scorched black by a long forgotten fire, surrounded it like a fortress. Rubble rolled out into the cemetery and mingled with rows of headstones. Moss-coated boulders that looked as if they were once flung, flaming with pitch, to batter down the walls, lay about. Smaller rocks the size of skulls lined the roadway to the monastery's entry.

A great tympanum crowned the double doorway. Two imposts and a central carved pillar divided the entrance and framed the two iron-rimmed oak doors. The sculpted stone depicted Christ's heavenly throne and four fantastic creatures at worship: an eagle with beak agape, a winged bull, a haloed lion, and a wide-eyed man who looked awed and apprehensive, much the way Jean-Michel felt.

He studied the granite visage of Jesus, the Judge of the Living and the Dead, the face stern and impassive. Majestic hair and beard flowed around the hard face and over the shoulders in symmetrical streams. The figure's crown was rich in gems and an intricately embroidered imperial cape fell in broad folds over the knees. The left hand hugged a sealed scroll and the right was uplifted in rebuke or admonition.

Jean-Michel saw in this Jesus the image of his father—distant, critical, judgmental, and never satisfied. The granite eyes glared at him, and he looked down to his feet, as he had done so often did in Philippe's fault-finding presence. Then he tugged at the ragged bellpull.

Two black-frocked Benedictines admitted him. They prayed aloud, "I was a stranger, and you took me in," then both gave him the kiss of peace. In their minds it was Christ they really received. The monks directed Bobo to the barns and led Jean-Michel across the courtyard toward the salutorium of the Guest Hall. A passing brother bowed and asked for Jean-Michel's blessing, then walked on, permitted to speak no more.

They passed the Aedificium, an octagonal building that from a distance seemed to be a tetragon, the perfect form to proclaim the steadfastness and inviolability of the City of God. Three rows of windows gave light to knowledge of the Triune Deity. Each corner included a heptagonal tower. The building was a sermon in architecture for each of these holy numbers communicated a spiritual lesson. Eight was the number of perfection; four was the number of the holy Gospels; three was the number of the earth's continents, each equal in size; and seven was the number of the spirits and gifts of the Holy Ghost.

"One night," Jean-Michel informed the hosteler.

"You are here for the fair, my son?"

"I was, but no longer," Jean-Michel said. "I have found what I was sent for—a holy relic."

The monk arched his brows as high as a cathedral's clerestory windows and his eyes brightened as when sunlight passes over a glass. "You have come to see Reverend Father Paulinus, then?"

Jean-Michel gave him a blank look.

"From Constantinople?" the monk prompted.

"I have come only for a place of safekeeping for myself and my relic, Father. If you please, may I see the sacristan?"

"You must see Father Paulinus right away," the monk said, clapping his roll book shut. "We might still catch him in the guest kitchen."

Reverend Father Justus Paulinus preferred the brick guest kitchen to the large wainscotted dining hall for three reasons. The food was better, the room was warmer, and it was always open.

He had traveled too much and eaten too many strange foods at irregular hours to ever be satisfied with the strictures of a refectory's rituals. Every night at the bell, the brothers salivated together. They washed their hands in dutiful turn, bowed to the high table in unison, and stood in stiff lines until the prior came to read Psalm fifty-one.

Every night.

Paulinus was more accustomed to dining among bluebells, cupping his hands into streams, and kneeling by campfires to hear the popping of wood and choirs of crickets. He felt closer to God on a ship's forecastle than in a cloister, although the galley fare at sea usually sickened him.

He cut the turnips floating in his soup into smaller pieces and wiped the knife on his bread. The soup needed more salt, but the kitcheners had left to welcome a late guest, and he did not know which cabinet to open. He shrugged. He had done without salt on mountain trails and ship-decks, even in deserts; he could wait a few minutes more. As Augustine once said, "Patience is the companion of wisdom," and patience was one of Paulinus' better virtues. It came from all the waiting a wandering scholar endured, with much of his life beyond his control.

This latest journey was a good example. He had spent two weeks on a Byzantine pier, waiting for a favorable wind. Then ten weeks at sea and two wrecks later, he had landed mercifully at Marseilles to begin his pilgrimage to Nola. He traveled partly on foot each day and partly on a lazy barge up the Rhone. Hardly anyone had believed he was headed north for Nola; most pilgrims traveled in the opposite direction. But he was patient with them, too.

And on the way, what painstaking perseverance he employed to catalog the relics of Constantinople residing at Cluny. It was an enviable collection. The Clunaic insistence on precision was maddening but admirable. The cowled bureaucrats there toiled endlessly to account for every holy prize in their far-flung jurisdiction. And as one fully acquainted with the treasures of Constantinople before it was plundered by the Latin invaders, Paulinus had provided information on authenticity that was almost as valuable as the relics themselves. There was always enough work to keep his feet moving and his belly satisfied.

Deo gratias, he said, thumping his barreled chest and belching.

The kitcheners were returning, chanting Psalm 104 to praise God for providing food for His creatures. Paulinus gave thanks as the new pilgrim guest arrived, for his safety and that no novice would be reading lessons on gluttony over his shoulder, as was the standard in the refectory.

The psalm ended and the abbot himself entered. Paulinus noticed Father Antoine's silver halo of hair and the porridge stains on his tunic. *The lodger will be glad for the kitchen fare*, thought Paulinus.

The men rinsed their hands in a basin by the door and shook them dry. Paulinus guessed the young visitor must be of some rank to merit the abbot's personal attention. Antoine was not in the habit of greeting latecomers, though he liked to socialize with pilgrims during daylight hours. The guest must be at least a knight and perhaps of good lineage, judging from the spurred boots and broad swordbelt next to his pilgrim scrip. But his eyes lacked the arrogance and wary suspicion so familiar in warriors. They seemed full of wonder, even at the sight of a common kitchen. The young man bowed shyly, like a novitiate meeting his confessor for the first time.

"Jean-Michel d'Anjou," Abbot Antoine announced and tapped his fingertips for food. The keepers of the kitchen ladled soup from the hearthkettle.

"God's peace to you, pilgrim," Paulinus said, liking the knight's humble manners.

"And to you, Father."

Antoine gestured for Jean-Michel to speak on. Something was on the knight's mind.

"Reverend Father tells me you are an expert on the relics of the Church," said Jean-Michel.

Paulinus smiled warmly. "Let us say I have seen as many bones of saints as a chef sees bones of fish and fowl."

The abbot prayed a psalm over his soup, then bid Brother Paulinus to continue. Such could not happen in the refectory, where silent monks scratched for salt and beckoned for bread.

Paulinus peeled a crust and said, "I, too, have been on pilgrimage, to visit the home of my namesake, Paulinus of Nola, the good friend of Saint Martin."

The knight looked up from his bowl, radiant. Paulinus marvelled at the change. *Could a few sips have refreshed him so quickly?*

"Then you must also know of Saint Germaine," Jean-Michel said.

"Of course," Paulinus replied. "The reluctant hunter. Saint Martin had to coax him to seek game, since he refused to harm the animals."

"And he perished in a forest fire?"

"Yes, while saving panicked creatures by showing them the way to safety across a stream. Why do you ask?"

"I have his remains," Jean-Michel said.

Curious Paulinus squinted. "Blessed Martin is at Tours, pilgrim."

Jean-Michel shook his head excitedly. He opened his leather scrip and, with trembling hands, lifted out a little case that looked like a woman's prayer box, only it was dirtier and dented in places. "The ashes of Saint Germaine," the knight announced solemnly. “May I put them in the sacristy for safekeeping tonight?”

The soup lost its taste for Paulinus. He put down his knife and stared at the box, then at the knight's beatific face. Should he tell the young man? Jean-Michel looked utterly sincere as he went on talking.

“It was stolen from me once, but I have recovered it by the grace of God. Now I must return it to my bishop so that the cathedral may be built.”

So it was not a private treasure. Paulinus might have let the matter go if it were, but now he could not. He pressed his fingertips together and looked gently into Jean-Michel's guileless gray eyes. “Do you know, pilgrim, that Saint Germaine is a dog?”

The turnips tumbled like stones in the pit of Jean-Michel's stomach, and he swallowed with difficulty. His high spirits wilted and his hands fell limply to the table. As dumb as his valet, he sat immobile.

“But Germaine still has a following,” Paulinus continued, trying to comfort him. “Hunters invoke him all the time.”

Jean-Michel wanted to close his ears the way he could close his eyes. His crushed heart felt as if it had taken a blow from Le Marichal's iron-capped lance.

“Brother Paulinus, are you sure?” the abbot asked.

“Quite sure, I must say,” Paulinus said, his weathered hands intertwined as if praying on Jean-Michel's behalf. “The stories of him are well-known in Nola.”

Jean-Michel wondered why the men did not burst into laughter and insults over his foolishness, like his brothers would, or rebuke him the way his father would. He tried to tighten his burning belly to close off the heat rising from there to his face. "There is no reason for me to stay and trouble you," he said, apologetic. He hoped to be excused before he felt any sicker.

"You do not trouble us, but honor us by your coming," the abbot said. "It is by the will of God that you have been sent at such a time as this. We invited Brother Paulinus here because of what he can do, and God has sent you here because of what you can do."

Paulinus' grizzled eyebrows curled like two fuzzy caterpillars caught by surprise. "So you suppose Saint Germaine has guided him as he did Saint Martin?" he asked Father Antoine.

"Who can tell?" the abbot said, shrugging. "But when we have a dispute with a sister abbey over duplicate relics, one of Christendom's most notable scholars is in our region to arbitrate." He nodded to Paulinus. "And when even a brother approved by Cluny speaks to our brothers to no avail because of the hardness of their hearts and vain avarice, one of Christ's soldiers arrives to enforce what is right." He nodded to Jean-Michel.

Jean-Michel looked at Paulinus and Antoine, seeking an explanation. The abbot coaxed Paulinus into speaking by waving his white hand.

Paulinus pouted and looked reluctant. "The Abbey of Saint Odom has claimed, as does this abbey, to possess the crown of King David. At the request of the abbots and under the authority of Cluny, I have examined each crown, with its records, and have decided that the good brothers of Saint Odom have a clever fake. Even the documentation is forged."

"And they will not admit this?" Jean-Michel asked, forgetting his own embarrassment.

"Their crown is plainly of a later date and make. It is Italian in design, not Hebrew or Philistine. The crown here at Saint Claude—what is left of it—is the true one."

"But," the abbot added, "they say it is a miracle common to relics to multiply themselves so as to bless many people. Our bishop agrees and refuses to intercede."

Jean-Michel glanced down at the dull box containing the ashes. "How can I do more than you, Fathers, or more than His Excellency, when I know nothing?"

"You know how to wield a sword, and you are sworn to defend the truth with it," said the abbot. "And it is the judgment of all concerned that the issue must be settled in a trial by combat."

Jean-Michel felt himself pale. A duel sanctioned by the brothers? Did they not uphold the truce of God, and frown on tourneys of all sorts?

"The chosen knights of each house will face each other on the morrow, in the melee of the fair," the abbot continued, sitting taller as if in a saddle. "And the side which possesses the true crown of King David will surely prevail, since David will fight for the side that is true, just as he fought Goliath." The abbot leaned toward Jean-Michel. "Will you join us?"

Paulinus appeared disturbed. By his pained look and constant shifting in his chair, he signaled that he did not like the idea of resolving a church matter on the field.

The abbot sensed that Jean-Michel was hesitant as well. "For your service to the truth and to Mother Church, a gift of gratitude to God on our part is appropriate. What would you say, then, if I released a relic of the Abbey Saint Claude to your cathedral?"

The kitcheners nearly dropped the kettle they were cleaning. Paulinus' eyes grew as big as onions. Jean-Michel judged that the scholar well knew the value of Antoine's treasures.

"Consider the stones from the road Jesu walked on the way to Golgotha," the abbot said reverently. "Imagine them as the steps to the altar in your cathedral."

Jean-Michel's hands, just a moment ago lifeless and drained of energy, trembled with hope. Relics of the Savior Himself, in Auxonne! Embedded in the floor, so the stones' blessedness would spread to every other stone in the structure! *The priests would walk where He walked . . .*

"Take your rest in your room," Abbot Antoine said. "And if you please, attend prayers at Compline with us tonight. Consider the will of God for you and for His cathedral." The lines of his face lengthened. "We need a righteous man on our side of the lists, Jean-Michel, to fight in the service of King David. The brothers of Saint Odom, God save them, have hired the service of a Goliath. Perhaps you have heard of him—Galbert Le Marichal."

The sword, like its knight, was honest and straight, double-edged with chivalry and justice. In battle it represented the cross, reminding the knight to use it to slay foes of the truth. The shield, like Charity, covered many sins. Placed between him and the enemy, it signified the knight's office, just as the knight stood between his prince and the people. The lance, which pierced the foe before he could come near, symbolized foresight—something Jean-Michel d'Anjou prayed for while a dozen war horses lined up along the outer lists.

He bore his lance, blessed by the brothers of Saint Claude, on the slope of his right shoulder while marching beside a score of fellow knights. In the arena, he brought the lance to a vertical position, resting its butt on the stirrup before the action began.

The galleries were full of gaiety as noisy pastry peddlers and bet brokers went about their business. Banners of each knight's noble house hung on poles on each side behind the stamping horses. Jean-Michel did not recognize many of them, but no matter. Except for the plumes on the helmets, no one could tell who fought for whom once the violent free-for-all began. Each knight, as formidable a fighter as ever shared the sins of humankind, was trained to fight alone. They did not maneuver in companies; they only massed and charged. They all disliked orders and distrusted strategy. Every man had his own honor to uphold, his own cause to affirm, his own lady to win, his own grudge to avenge—even if temporarily in the employ of an abbey. The trumpets blared, like Gabriel heralding Christ's return. Jean-Michel peered up at the clouds for a sign of the Savior's white courser and blazing face, but saw only the unblinking sun.

He dropped his helmet into place. It was hot and stuffy, and as sweat beaded on his lip he remembered how his face felt in the fire.

On the other side of the field, a shimmer of light passed along the front ranks of the opposing horsemen as their lances lowered in unison. Colorful pennants fluttering just below the metal heads would prevent the shafts from plunging too deeply into a man's body.

Jean-Michel checked his shield, aimed his lance, and tucked in his elbows. On either side he heard the swish of lances lowering and the snorting of impatient chargers. A breeze fluted in his eye slits, and he spied the flapping flag of the red gryphon directly across the arena.

Galbert had seen him, and he was laughing. Did not the Philistine also laugh at David? "You come to me with sword and javelin," Jean-Michel recited under his breath, "but I come to you in the name of the Lord of Hosts."

Paulinus processed into the church, chanting responses but hearing little of the Mass. Stepping across the floor stones in his worn sandals, he measured the line of monks ahead of him and imagined Jean-Michel was nosing his horse into line just about now. He looked down the deep nave, trying to picture what it would be like to look across the field. He felt his rosary swinging on his hemp belt and wondered what Jean-Michel felt with a real sword there. His was sharp and polished, not blunted for sport as was common in the melee—except for this one.

Forbidden by Benedict's rule to partake in violence, instead the monks would share in the mystery of Christ's broken body and spilt blood, on behalf of those whose blood would be shed and whose bodies would be broken on the field.

Paulinus grieved that the dispute had come to this. He had done all he could to resolve the rival abbots' impasse. Antoine took his position by the altar beside his concelebrants while Paulinus and the others filed into neat rows standing facing him. The abbot lifted his hands like a tourney Marshal: "The Lord be with you!"

"Do your battle!" the marshal yelled on the field.

Galbert Le Marichal let out a war whoop, jabbed his spurs, and propelled his charger forward. The ground beneath him shook with the pounding of many hooves. He chose a target from among the onrushing pack of bristling lances. The crowd roared when the first rank of gleaming points collided.

Clouds of dust and missiles of metal debris flew in all directions, obscuring the field. A score of drawn swords rang from their scabbards, and a percussion of steel on steel ensued. A discordant confusion reigned as halberds hacked wildly against hauberks, tri-bladed courseques, and against cuirasses.

Le Marichal, who had driven deeply into the opposing force, skewered a knight in the back. Once the man had crashed to the grass with the lance still quivering in him, Galbert saw it was not the Angevin. He cursed. He wanted it to be him. He reached down to his belt, groping for the spiked mace. In a whipping frenzy, swinging the bloodied iron ball overhead, he cleared a path through screaming horses and shouting riders.

The abbot swung the brass censer over the altar, back and forth, back and forth, filling the church with sweet-scented smoke and a haze of mystery.

Tension curled Paulinus' folded fingers. He tried to flex and relax them, pinching the fingertips the way the abbot did when he consecrated the pure Host.

The white disc of the sun, shining through a haze of churned-up dirt, had turned everything gray. The combatants all looked alike to Le Marichal. He scanned the tangle of men through his helmet holes but was unable to spot the Angevin's crest or horse. Frustrated, he smashed the head of a man on his left; then the one on his right. Riderless horses stampeded to one side, and through the clearing, Le Marichal centered the stout Angevin in his sights as a crossbowman would.

Shivers rippled up Paulinus' spine. A feeling crept over him like a spider crawling on his back, a feeling that warned him of a distant danger drawing near. He had felt the same tingle at sea before a squall. Paulinus swivelled in his seat, his teeth chattering, feeling the temperature plummet as though before a thunderstorm. A warning arose in his throat, but he could not shout it—not at the high point of Mass when the monks genuflected. The words, like trapped animals, raced to escape through his hands where they sweat out the palms, which pulled at unseen reins to turn around an imaginery horse. Paulinus clicked his heels, trying to spur away.

Le Marichal's snorting charger, its head low for the attack, bolted forward into the breach. The Angevin's shield had caught on a poleaxe and immobilized him. Galbert raised the chain mace and whirled it to a deadly speed. Suddenly a halberd's point hooked through his arm like a fishhook piercing a trout. With a back-breaking jar Galbert tumbled backward into the path of trampling hooves. The world went black.

"Father, he is awakening."

"Then stand clear, pilgrim, in case he is frightened."

Jean-Michel backed to the wall where Paulinus and the infirmarer conferred, as they watched Le Marichal stir from his stupor.

Galbert's huge head was wound in white gauze strips, stained by blood where hooves had pounded him. His cheeks were raw and bruised, his left eye swollen like a plum, his lips cracked and flaky. He convulsed with a cough, and then moaned in agony from the nasty tear in his arm and what was certain to be broken ribs. Paulinus and the infirmarer approached him with a pillow and a water skin as though stalking a wounded wild animal, even though Le Marichal's wrists were bound to the bed by strong leather thongs.

"Drink, my son," the infirmarer said. He put the spout to Galbert's rigid mouth as Paulinus slid the pillow in place.

Galbert's good eye squinted in pain, opened, and rolled around as if oiled, trying to get oriented. He jerked up, but the broken ribs ground into his gut and he fell back, gasping.

The infirmarer offered the water again. "It could be much worse," he said. "You might have been trampled to death. The others we treated have not fared so well as you."

Le Marichal took a few swallows before he turned away, his face contorted and his breathing sounding like a leaky bellows. He tugged at the leather thongs. He lifted his chin, a look of anxious anguish marring his face even further. But seeing no leeches, blood bowls, or evidence of missing parts, he settled back. He tried to speak. "Where . . . I . . ."

"You are in the Abbey Saint Claude," Paulinus said, bending over him, "which, by virtue of the true crown of King David, prevailed in the melee. The crown at Saint Odom is now believed by all to be false. It has been surrendered and destroyed."

They all understood the implications. The flow of pilgrims would no longer divert to Saint Odom. Saint Claude would regain the pilgrim traffic and tithing it had lost.

Galbert moaned, not from the news, but from his injuries. In an attempt to hug his ribs, he pulled at the straps and realized he was tied down. He growled and groaned again, this time not from pain but from the disgrace of having been vanquished and lived.

"We are sorry for this," the infirmarer said, "but you must understand our caution. We did not know how you would act when you finally awoke."

"How . . . long . . ." came the grimaced question.

"Two days. You took quite a kick in the head before Jean-Michel reached you and pulled you off the field."

"Jean . . . Michel?"

Jean-Michel genuflected by the bed, well out of Le Marichal's reach. "May God speed your healing and bring you to health to serve Him."

"Why . . . did . . . you . . ."

"Take more water and rest," the infirmarer said. "You will be with us for a few weeks."

Jean-Michel stood aside as the infirmarer adjusted the blankets. Paulinus clapped the young knight on the shoulder.

"God is most pleased," the scholar said. "As John Chrysostom says, 'Dost thou wish to receive mercy? Show mercy to thy neighbor.'" Jean-Michel rubbed the bruise on his forehead that had turned from purple to pickle-green. "And," Paulinus continued, "the abbot says he will make request for the relics he offered you."

"Make request? Of whom?" Jean-Michel asked. "Does not the abbot govern his own house?"

"A transfer of holy relics must be approved by the bishop and sent to His Holiness in Rome to consider."

"Rome?"

"There the papal committees concerned will examine the request and make a recommendation based on a thorough investigation . . ."

"His Holiness? Reverend Father, I do not understand," Jean-Michel protested.

Paulinus paused, his face rumpled like Le Marichal's covers. "Abbots and bishops are permitted to make gifts of relics entrusted to their care," he began tentatively. "But such gifting of the Church's treasure must be guided by strict rules of fairness so all of God's people will have access to them." The measured words came with effort, as if Paulinus were restrained like Le Marichal. His creased face suggested that he greatly disliked this awkward situation. "You could go and testify before the committees yourself by bringing the proper letters of introduction, which the abbot is prepared to write."

"Testify?" Jean-Michel said, still trying to absorb the impact of Paulinus' revelation. "In Rome?"

"Yes."

"How long would that take?"

"A year or two to get on each committee's agenda, provided they are not overworked. Another two years of document and affadavit research. Then hearings, reports, appeals . . ."

"All that?"

"After which, *if* the committees concur on a recommendation and *if* the Holy See decides to study the matter and issue a ruling, you *might* possibly acquire the necessary transfer. Unless the bishop changes his mind or His Holiness is called to glory and there is a conclave, in which case . . ."

Jean-Michel tottered to the nearest bed, his knees wobbly. "But the abbot said . . ." he attempted to speak, but his voice broke off.

"I am sorry, but it must be this way. It stops the bishops from going to war—usually."

Heavy with disappointment, Jean-Michel drooped his head. "And you knew this all along, Reverend Father?"

Paulinus held up his hands, claiming innocence. "I honestly did not, pilgrim. I thought that perhaps the abbot would be free to act alone in this case. But as you can see, I am not well acquainted with the ways of the West."

The infirmarer, wetting a washcloth in wine, overheard. "Mayhaps it is well for you, sire knight," he said. "A visit to Saints Vitus and Modestus in Rome brings pardon for a third of a man's sins. And at the shrine of Saint Veronica one may gain a nine-thousand-year indulgence."

But Jean-Michel did not wish to think of purgatory. The only fire in his mind was the one that fused the image of Saint Martin's sword on his sleeve and consecrated him to this mission. But to Rome? For such a long wait, for such an uncertain result? Even with the abbot's approval, would his bishop really authorize the transfer of the holy stones to another bishop's church? Not likely. Perhaps the abbot had known that all along. The fire moved to his belly and became a simmering resentment over having been used and misled.

The infirmarer dabbed at Le Marichal's raw face to clean it. Galbert bellowed. He kicked his legs once in protest, then stilled because the movement jolted his cracked ribs. Laboring for breath and wheezing, he called for Jean-Michel.

Jean-Michel went to his side, ever mindful of his distance and keeping a sword's length away.

"I know . . . where . . . there . . . are relics . . . for you."

Jean-Michel put up his hand to still the infirmarer's washcloth. "Why should I trust you?"

"You . . . saved me . . . so shall I . . . not save you?"

"It is God who saves."

Galbert squeezed his eye shut and a tear moistened his battered cheek. Whether it came from pain or repentance, Jean-Michel could not tell. It trickled down a shiny scar to his chipped ear. "Aigues-Mortes," he said dreamily. "In Aigues-Mortes . . . where the king . . . sailed to fight . . . the infidel . . . and I left . . . with him." His fingers clutched at the bedside as though clutching a rocking ship's rail. "Aigues-Mortes . . . where come riches . . . from the east . . . from Outremer." He opened his eye and fixed his gaze on the timber ceiling, envisioning the spoils of war carried by sea out of the Holy Land. "Silks . . . and spices . . . and relics."

Jean-Michel drew nearer. "But as you heard, the Holy Mother Church has her own way of alloting them."

"Not . . . there," Le Marichal said. "Traders of Genoa . . . and Venice . . . and Constan . . . Constantinople . . . sell them openly."

At the mention of his home city, Paulinus' wrinkly ears perked up. "Pilgrim," he said to Jean-Michel, "if you go, I will go with you. My work here is done, and I am ready to seek my passage home. Mayhaps you will have need of one who speaks an Eastern tongue, and—if I may say it—one who can tell a true treasure from a fraud."

Jean-Michel considered this offer. He could fulfill his obligation to Renard by moving on to the Mediterranean port of Aigues-Mortes. The Midi would not be a dutiful detour after all. And he could not be tricked again. *All things work together for good . . .*

"It is an easy journey by barge down the Rhone," Paulinus said helpfully. "We would arrive in just a few days."

Jean-Michel's strength drained from his legs, and the dread of a river trip made his knees watery.

"Go with God," Galbert said.

The blessing so surprised Jean-Michel that he thought it a sign of God's own leading. "So be it," he said, a spirit of thankfulness straightening him. "To Aigues-Mortes, the city of His Most Christian Majesty."

12

His Most Christian Majesty, Louis IX, King of the French, Heir of Charles Le Magne, Overseer of the Kingdom of Jerusalem, and grandson of King Philip Augustus who marched with Richard Coeur-de-Lion, smelled bad. His bodyguards stank of horse sweat and pork. His priests reeked of incense offered to the trinity. The foul odor of their corruption clung to the draperies like rotted garlic.

Nazim ad-Din felt polluted in their presence, and he resolved to wash himself twice before the *zuhr* prayers of midday. He ignored the stench as he had learned to disregard pain. He clutched more tightly the jeweled hilt of the ceremonial three-bladed knife. Each blade fitted into the handle of another. With a leap and a whip of his wrist, he could drive the topmost dagger deep into the king's heart.

But he had come today alongside the emir Husayn ibn Wafa' only to hurl a demand. If the king rejected the emir's proposals, Nazim was to present the knives as a sign of imminent death.

Sharaf, a year younger and still beardless, sat behind Nazim. He shuffled the stout roll of linen wound around his forearm. The young *fada'i* was to present this to the king as a winding-sheet for his majesty's burial if he refused to meet the requirements of their master, the Old Man of the Mountain.

The Old Man's emir sat cross-legged on a cushion in front of Nazim. His handsome robes flowed out from him on the tesselated tiles like shimmering waterfalls streaming into a golden pool. His turban, fringed by teardrops of lapis lazuli from Persia, sat on his head like a wasp's nest. Each jewel hung serenely while the emir fixed an uncompromising stare on the Frankish king as he occupied his canopied throne.

A circle of advisors cloaked in the blue of France and the black of the church gathered around King Louis. In the doorway stood Queen Margeurite, dressed in a long gown and a linen head wrap. She looked at the Arab envoys as if they were curiosities, exotic birds or odd fruits, from the *souk*, the open-air market. Nazim felt uneasy, not because of her stare, but because of her immodestly unveiled face. At least her attendants were properly covered by opaque veils and floor-length robes. By the fire in her eyes, he recognized Yolande among them. The sight of her put a glow in his belly, but for her safety he pretended not to notice her.

A mule-faced monk, ready to interpret, hovered beside the king. The king nodded to the emir. "Tell me," said Louis, "in the name of the One True God, why you have come?"

The king's voice was firm although the man himself was frail. Nazim's sensitive ear tuned to the sound of it. It was not the voice of a man dishonored in war that he had expected. Had not this king lost thousands of warriors in a humiliating rout in Egypt? Was he not sick from mourning for the masses of wounded and beheaded knights left behind in Mameluk hands? Wasn't that why he refused his royal robes, wore a penitential hairshirt, and had himself whipped daily by his priests? (How much Yolande had told him!) Didn't the foreign king realize that Allah, the most great, was bringing to ruin this arrogant quest to recapture Holy Jerusalem and would bring shame to Louis' revolting religion?

Nazim made a mental picture of the king's sallow, serene face, the straw-colored hair spilling down from the gem-studded crown, the cheeks hollowed by dysentery and defeat. The steady eyes, the color of the sea after a storm, looked peaceful. They were neither hardened nor naive, although the king's reputation as a negotiator was poor.

He had submitted too quickly, without haggling, to an outrageous ransom for himself and his captive army after the disaster at Mansoura. The astonished victors, in deference to his piety and the mercy of Allah, had lowered the figure from one million gold *bezants* to eight hundred thousand. Even more astonishing, the king had ordered his reluctant Templars to open their coffers and pay the ransom promptly. And they had.

So Nazim thought this was an opportune time to make the king pay for the neutrality of the Assassins.

The emir reached into his robes, and the king's guards stiffened, their swords at the ready. Husayn presented his letters to the monk. The cleric slit the seals and, bowing cautiously, confirmed the noble's credentials.

Not condescending to speak a coarse tongue such as French with its weak and whining tones, the emir spoke in the melodious cadence of the Qur'an. "My lord has sent me to ask you if you know him," Husayn said gravely.

"I do not know him for I have never seen him," the king answered through his translator. "But I often hear about him and his fortresses when I speak to the Master of the Temple and the Master of the Hospital, in whose lands his fortresses lie."

Nazim tensed. Mentioning the military Orders was a shrewd move on the king's part. Neither the Templars nor the Hospitalers had any fear of the Assassins, because they knew that if the Old Man of the Mountain had their masters killed, others just as capable would quickly replace them. The Old Man did not sacrifice his carefully trained killers on projects that would bring no public political advantage.

Husayn hardly blinked. "Since you have heard of my lord, I am greatly surprised that you have not assured yourself of his friendship with a generous gift, just as the Emperor of Germany, the King of Hungary, the Sultan of Cairo, and other rulers do every year. They know most certainly that they live only by my lord's permission, and they live only so long as my lord pleases."

Nazim wondered how this infidel king could refuse an offer to appease the Assassins? They had been the terror of Outremer since King Conrad of Jerusalem was knifed in broad daylight while escorting a young man he thought was a Muslim convert to his sickening religion. The *feda'i* had even taken Christian baptism to complete the ruse. "It is the Lord God who holds our lives in His hand, and Who numbers our days in His book," the king said resolutely.

Well-spoken, Nazim thought. *As the Prophet said, "No soul can die except by Allah's leave and at a term appointed."* But if the Franks truly believed it, they would not wear cowardly armor in battle to protect themselves from death.

The emir also acknowledged the pious reply with a courteous nod of his sharp goatee. But he did not back down. "If it does not suit you to do what I ask, then there is another way to secure my lord's continuing favor. Arrange for him to be released from paying tribute to the Hospital and the Temple. He will graciously consider your obligation to him fulfilled, and your life will be spared."

As tributes went in the balance of regional bribery, the Old Man's was a trifling token—twelve hundred *dinars* and one hundred *mudd* of wheat annually. Still, Nazim knew it was an annoying splinter in the Old Man's hand that he longed to strengthen against the Sultan of Damascus. If the tribute were dropped, the Old Man's prestige would rise in the Frankish dioceses of Tyre and Tortosa in the North and Damascus would be put at a disadvantage.

The king consulted the monk. "Such a request must be brought to the Masters themselves," he told the emir. I will consider it with them, and meet you again today at the tenth hour."

The emir's smile of agreement showed faintly, like a crescent moon on a cloudy night. He scissored upright as if levitated. Nazim and Sharaf followed him out, expressionless, holding high their symbols of death and defiance.

"If Allah is your helper," Nazim prayed from the Qur'an, "none can overcome you."

Allahu akbar!

After a pause, another *muezzin* somewhere in the direction of the Tower of Flies echoed the *adhan*, the call to prayer. *Allahu akbar!* "God is most great." Again and again, four times in all, the call wailed from the spired minarets of Acre just past midday. There was no mistaking this homage for pagan sun worship.

La ilaha illa Allah! "There is no god but Allah!" the creed thundered, and every cafe, alley, market, kitchen, well, stable, church, and brothel vibrated with the vehemence of the voices. The creed thundered again, and a light rain began to fall as a squall from the harbor dashed in and dissipated like a Bedouin raid. Lightning played on the horizon like bared swords.

"And Muhammed is the Messenger of God!" It sounded as if the *muezzin* were flinging defiance at the city's European rulers, who had to cease all actions while their Muslim merchants, servants, sailors, tailors, dray-drivers, dry grocers, cooks, and cafe workers rolled out their mats and prostrated themselves in a united witness, saying, "Come to prayer. Come to salvation. Come to security." *Allahu akbar*.

These were the first words Nazim had ever heard. His parents had recited the *adhan* in his right ear immediately after his birth.

"And I bear witness that Ali is the *wali Allah*." In keeping with the creed of the Shi'i sect, Nazim affirmed under his breath that Ali, Muhammed's son-in-law, husband of the blessed Fatima and murdered heir of the caliphate, was the Prophet's true successor and guardian of the True Religion of God. And the spilt blood of Ali's two sons, martyred by the Sunni, would never remain silent in the distant sands of Karbala. It happened over five hundred years ago, but the memory for all true believers was refreshed five times daily.

Stirred by the thought, Nazim laid his prayer rug facing the old battlefield in Mesopotamia instead of facing Abraham's altar in Mecca. The rug had worn spots where Nazim's knees touched, and where Nazim's teacher had knelt on it before him. He placed his prayer brick, a block of baked blood-red mud from the earth of Karbala's shrine, on the dirt floor. He stood silent a moment in meditation, exorcising worldly thoughts. Cool ablution water dripped from his hands and feet.

His mind cleared and Nazim fell rhythmically and easily into the exercise of the set prayers, the *Raka'at.* He touched his ears and announced his belief in the oneness of God, the *Takbir*, which joined all Muslims, even the errant Sunni. He clasped his hands over his navel, the left within the right, and declared, "There is none to be served beside Thee." He bowed, knelt, and touching his forehead to the hard brick at the right moments, recited the *Fatihah*, the opening *Surah* of the Glorious *Qur'an.*

Praise be to Allah, Lord of the Creation,
The compassionate, the merciful,
King of Judgment Day.
You alone we worship, and to You alone
we pray for help.
Guide us to the straight path,

the path of those whom You have favored,
Not of those who have incurred Your wrath,
Nor of those who have gone astray.

Seven perfect verses—three of God, three of man, and one to relate the two—it was a universal prayer for all people, who are fashioned from clots of blood at Allah's whim and whose blood is required at a time of Allah's choosing.

Nazim bowed again in satisfaction and submission, and then stood. He looked over his right shoulder, then his left, to acknowledge the angels who kept strict account of his good and bad deeds.

Sharaf stood behind him, following his lead. He smiled, the scar on his cheek deepening.

"Peace upon you," Nazim said by custom. He concentrated on the next sequence of prayers, the most important ones. Squatting in the *gada*, a reverential position, Nazim ad-Din quietly recited his list of hatreds.

It was a long list.

He began by cursing the Sunni, who altered the word of Allah. They had excised any mention of Ali and his spiritual successors, the Imams. What they did retain they read only on the surface, thus shielding their ease-loving minds from the word's deeper meanings. Though the Sunni claimed extra piety by saying the *Qur'an* was eternal, this was surely sacrilege, since Allah alone is eternal, "Who can have no equals or partners," as the *Qur'an* itself testified.

In fasting, the Sunni did not wait until the sun was fully down before gorging themselves.

In prayer, they touched their callousless foreheads to soft mats, not to the dust in true humility.

They gave alms to their corrupt leaders rather than to the poor.

Nazim was only too glad to have dispatched five Sunni officers to the Fire on the orders of his Master. He recited each of their names, bitter on his tongue, and felt his consecrated dagger vibrate from the screams of their well-deserved torment.

Yet, in solidarity with the Sunni, his brothers in the House of Islam, Nazim ad-Din abhorred the Franks.

Ignorant and unmannered invaders, the Franks showed no shame or modesty. The nobles permitted their wives to be tended in their baths by Muslim menservants. Men and unveiled women kissed in public as a greeting. They ate gross amounts of forbidden foods and drank copious amounts of wine. Did such things please their three gods—the Father, the Mother Mary, and the Son?

Nazim was nauseous at the mere thought of their perverted doctrine. Everywhere they had erected profane images—statues of saints they wooed and replicas of the wooden cross they worshiped. The hated sign ubiquitously declared their unbelief in the power of Allah, who would never permit his prophet Issa to die so shamefully! Did they not know that in justice Allah put the unrecognized Judas there in Issa's place? *Ignorant blasphemers*, he thought. As was revealed, "They did not kill him, nor did they crucify him, but they thought they did. Allah lifted him up to His presence; He is mighty and wise."

The house was cool, but Nazim ad-Din was perspiring as if sweating out a fever. He wanted to wash again. *Bismillah al-rahman, al-rahim*, he mouthed. In the name of God, the merciful, the compassionate, he would see the land purged of the Frankish filth. They would be driven into the Great Sea.

But did not the Franks have the same plans for Allah's true believers? Wasn't that why the French king was in Acre—to find a way to push the faithful into the desert, to destroy them, and then defile holy Jerusalem again? Yolande had overheard their devilish plans. The French king had already sent envoys to the East, intending to ally himself with the Golden Horde of the Great Khan and crush God's faithful between them.

The fire of anger in his belly crackled with a fear he would never reveal to Sharaf or the emir Husayn ibn Wafa'. Nazim had once faced the armies of the Khan.

He was five years old then. The raid on his village was a swift surprise. The scouts had reported Mongol marauders were days away, but at dawn, before the dung fires were lit, the Mongols attacked like demons. They put every man, maid, and mother to the sword, torched every hut and hovel, and carried off the goats and children, presumably to eat them. Or so Nazim thought. His father had warned that the warriors of Far Tartary did such things, and that when they ran out of food, they chose every tenth man from among themselves for meat.

But that night the Mongols were ambushed in turn by fearless clean-shaven men in white, screaming the prayers Nazim had only heard from the village *mullah*. The confused Mongols thought them to be *jinn* or angels, like Nazim did, until one of the men in white had cut his leather collar and carried him off to a castle higher than eagles fly.

There, he joined the household with other sons of peasants orphaned by earthquakes, disease, or Tartars. They learned Latin, Greek, Saracen, and the True Religion. If they were diligent and obedient, the Master of the Mountain would grant them the joy, the Garden of God, even before death. He remembered how it looked . . .

"Nazim."

It was not the voice of the Master or the doe-eyed girl in the Garden.

"Nazim." *As-salamu alaykum.* It was Sharaf, awakening him from his thoughts. "Nazim, peace upon you."

Wa alaykum as salam, Nazim responded. "And peace with you."

"It is time."

How could Sharaf tell? On this rare drizzly day, no point of sun crept across the mud wall.

"The *adhan* for the hour of *asr* has already sounded. Did you not hear it?"

So. He had spent all of midday in meditation. His stomach growled, but he would deny it a little longer. They had no time for the cafe, where they might take a bowl of mashed bean curd and camel's milk. By a different route and in different clothing than they wore when they came, they must meet the emir and take audience again with the king, who wished to join Nazim's father's and mother's murderers.

The meeting was brief, the tempers short.

On either side of the seated king stood the Master of the Hospital and the Master of the Temple, both grim and hostile, like great desert vultures. They folded back the wide wings of their cloaks, one all-black, one all-white, and waited to pounce.

The Dominican translator, standing between them, looked like a raven.

King Louis asked the emir to repeat the message he had delivered that morning.

Husayn ibn Wafa' scanned the throne room, unintimidated. "As you will. But only in the presence of all others who attended you this morning, that there may be witnesses to the full truth."

Renaud de Vichiers, the Templar, flared. "You dare to call us liars? We command you to repeat your message!" His hand went to his broadsword.

Nazim raised his knives.

The emir lifted his palm to calm him. "Since you command it," he said to Louis, "it will be as you wish. One command for another." He repeated his demand that the Old Man of the Mountain's tribute be rescinded.

The Masters, their proud faces pink with anger, gave instructions to the interpreter. They seemed to be confirming a pact made in private.

"In place of the tribute, there is one thing we ask," the monk said on their behalf. "You will come and hear the terms, alone, at the commandery of the Hospital tomorrow at dawn."

"After prayers," Husayn countered, "and accompanied by my witnesses."

The king approved. He looked overly pleased, and Nazim distrusted him. *Are they leading us into a trap? "The disbelievers schemed"*, he quoted to himself, *"and Allah schemed against them, and Allah is the best of schemers"*.

In the year of the Hijrah 550, or by the Frankish reckoning 1172, the Assassins sought an alliance with the Christian king of Jerusalem, Amalric. The Old Man of the Mountain of that day, alarmed by the rise of the great Sunni general, Saladin, promised an equally alarmed Amalric that with an alliance, his men would adopt Christianity. His only condition was that the Templar tribute imposed on Assassin territories be lifted. Amalric agreed, promising the Order of Poor Knights of the Temple that he would make up for their financial loss. Thus the alliance was agreed upon. But when the Assassin ambassadors returned to their mountain castle, Alamut—the Eagles' Nest—they were ambushed and slaughtered by a single Templar knight, the fanatical one-eyed Walter de Mesnil. The Master of the Order, Odo de Saint Amand, did not admit to ordering the killing, but he protected Walter in his commandery at Sidon. A furious Amalric demanded that Walter face trial for murder. The Templar Master refused to hand over Walter, declaring that the Order answered only to the Pope. Amalric, tired of the Order's arrogance and independence, marched to Sidon with an armed force. He burst into the Templar commandery and arrested Walter.

In response, the Templars held fast to their tribute, and the alliance between Amalric and the Assassins evaporated.

It might as well have been yesterday, Nazim ad-Din mused. *It is certainly happening today, only the names are different.*

The current Old Man was alarmed by the rise of the Sunni general, Baibars the Panther. It was Baibars who engineered King Louis' humiliating defeat in the flood waters of the Nile. It was Baibars who chased the Egyptian shiekh into that same river and chopped him to pieces while Louis watched in horror from his captured ship. It was Baibars who now commanded a vast white-skinned army of half-breed slaves, the Mamelukes, Sunnis all, who were pressing from Cairo in the South and the Caucasus ranges in the North. It was like the rise of Saladin all over again. Both men were Turks from the north, and not even true Arabs. They were uniting Arabs into a Sunni empire that might drive the hated Franks from Palestine, but it would also exterminate the Assassins, who were regarded by the Sunni as despicable heretics.

The situation began to clear like an oasis pool for Nazim ad-Din. The Old Man was seeking an alliance with Louis as a buffer against Baibars. In a land where alliances shifted as quickly as the desert dunes, the leader of the Assassins was about to do the unthinkable—wed himself to the infidels.

Nazim rolled up his prayer mat. A dull sickness gnawed in his abdomen, as if he had swallowed vinegar or eaten pork. He chastised himself for speculating upon the Old Man's political intentions, for his place was only to obey. If he did, the mission would be accomplished. The tribute of the Templars would be revoked, and the Old Man would consolidate his forward positions in Palestine, free to face the Mongol threat from the rear. How could he ever lower himself to join with the foul Franks? *It is foolish to think such a thing.*

Sharaf waited for him by the door. Together, they made their way through the labyrinthine alleys of Acre and paths as twisted and dirty and confusing as the politics of the Levant to the headquarters of the Hospitalers.

"Your lord, the Old Man of the Mountain, has acted rashly in daring to send such an insolent message to the king." The interpreter's words hung as coldly as the air in the vaulted stone chamber. The enraged Masters, dark and glowering, had shouted their message so that the echo of their voices still shook the pillared halls.

"It is only because our king received you with honorable intent that we do not drown you in the sewage of the bay," the interpreter finished.

Nazim awaited a signal from the emir to avenge these insults. In a wink, he could sever the Frank's offending windpipe and receive in return whatever blow that would transport him instantly to the Joy, to the lustrous fruits, and to the luscious maiden there who loved him.

Husayn ibn Wafa', unruffled, smiled disarmingly. "What then, is your decision on the removal of the tribute?" he asked.

"Impudent dog!" DeVichiers the Templar snarled, his rotted teeth bared. "Go back to your master at once! Within a fortnight, bring another message more pleasing to His Majesty, and bring jewels that may appease him and make him gracious toward you. If you do not, we will see to it that the Sultan of Damascus may have his way with you."

Nazim felt the sands shifting again. The only thing the Templars would lift would be restraint on the Syrians, permitting them to plunder at will the villages loyal to the Old Man. Even though King Louis favored Cairo because of the French prisoners still there, the Templars had a longstanding relationship with Damascus. They could easily secure a separate agreement.

No wonder they had requested a meeting away from the king's hearing.

The emir acknowledged the ultimatum with a deferential nod. He did not protest, or bargain, or threaten in turn—urges that thumped like drums in Nazim's taut chest. Husayn exited quietly, ignoring the smug scowls of the two warrior-monk Masters.

Beside Sharaf, Nazim reluctantly fell in behind the emir. They went out to the dusty street and into the *souk*, dividing, doubling back, then reuniting in a clay-walled cafe where the air was thick from the smoke of braised lamb, the haze of backroom *hashish*, and the clamor of Arabic conversation. The emir had changed clothes en route, exchanging his rich robes for homespun ones.

When the cups were served and the first bitter sips shared, Nazim spoke. "Which of them shall we slay first, my teacher?"

Husayn gave him a dark look. "Neither, for they have fallen into our hands."

"They deserve the Fire."

"In due time, by Allah's will," the emir said. "For now, they follow the Master's plan."

"But the tribute has not been removed. They are even demanding that we add to the payment."

"It is a small price to pay for a large prize. Did we not just pass through the *souk*, Nazim? Did you not hear the buyers make silly offers to lure sellers into a bargain?"

Sharaf slurped his drink, his eyes dull.

"I do not understand, my teacher," Nazim pressed.

"In asking to be unbound, we have bound them to us," the emir said. "In this way the king and the Orders of knights remain opposed to each other. So the Franks are divided and weak. They will ally with neither Cairo nor Damascus, but court them both, supposing themselves to be allied to us. So the Sunni will remain divided and weak. Our Master can now turn to the Tartars."

"To destroy them," Nazim said.

The emir frowned. "No. To ally with them."

Nazim's stomach filled with acid. "But the French king already seeks to ally with them," he warned. "He wishes to crush us in between."

Husayn laughed. "Do not be deluded like the Franks, Nazim. They place their hope in a vain superstition. They seek Prester John, the great Christian Khan of their silly legends. He does not exist."

"But the king sent monks . . ."

"If they return alive, they will report that there is no Christian Khan, and that the Tartars will bow to no foreign gods, since they expect all to bow to their gods."

"Why, then, should the Tartars ally with us?"

"Because they will fear us as all the others do."

Nazim put down his cup, lest it shake and spill. He steeled his face and summoned anger to fill his eyes, lest they betray his fear. He still heard the hellish whoops, still saw the fiery eyes, still smelled the sulfurous breath of the men begotten of devils in the flames of Tartarus itself from whence they took their name. Servants of Satan, inflicted upon the world as a warning of the Last Day, they would carry the damned off to the Pit of giant scorpions just as they had carried him off in the night so long ago.

What companionship had light with darkness? What demon deluded the Master of the Mountain into seeking an alliance with both the Franks and the Mongols?

He sealed his lips and shut the others out of his feelings. The Old Man had trained him well in disguises and deceptions. He had been chosen for this task because of his unquestioning obedience, but he was bound to obey the Highest Power.

"We return to Alamut," the emir confided, "to bring such gifts as the Franks require, and to receive our next instructions from the Master."

Nodding, Nazim knew where he would seek his next instruction. From Allah Himself, for no mortal could be trusted.

Within a fortnight, the envoys returned to Acre. They brought the Old Man's shirt to the king, and Husayn explained that as the shirt is closer to the body than any other garment, so the Old Man considered King Louis closer to him than any other leader. Husayn also offered the Old Man's ring, a gold band engraved with his Arabic name. By this ring he was united with the king as though wed.

Then Husayn clapped his hands, and to everyone's amazement, presented exquisite gifts to the espoused: an ivory elephant, an ebony giraffe, silver bowls full of crystal apples, table-sized gaming boards inlaid with costly woods, and finely carved chessmen. When Nazim and Sharaf opened the cases, little amber flowers tumbled to the tiles and a saffron scent perfumed the room.

A pleased King Louis sent the envoys back bearing a load of gems, scarlet cloth, golden goblets, and silver bridles. The mule-faced interpreter monk, Yves Le Breton, accompanied the party to their mountain stronghold to learn more of the king's new ally.

At first Nazim considered slitting the priest's throat and slicing out his translating tongue to send back to the king. Did not the slaying of the

Assassin ambassadors years ago annul the alliance then? Why not annul it now by killing the Frankish envoy? But without an order from the Master to do so, would he forfeit the Joy? If he acted on his own, would he be disobeying, and inherit the Pit?

The monk did not have the smell of prey, and Nazim's knife did not vibrate. He decided not to kill Le Breton.

Nervous under Nazim's scrutiny, he began to ask distracting questions about Nazim's doctrine. It was then that the revelation came.

"In your religion, what happens at death?" the monk asked.

"It is Allah's decision," Nazim said. "Some are given the Garden, where every drink is as the first drink of a man athirst in the desert, where every fruit is always as the first fruit of its season, where every embrace of a friend is as the first embrace after a long absence, and every kiss of the maidens is as the first kiss of a true love." He spoke wistfully, as if he had been there. For he had.

"What of others?"

"Others are given to the Fire, to be stung by scorpions and snakes, roasted and burned, then given back their forms to begin all over again. Such is the end for all unbelievers."

"Can one ever know which is his destiny?"

"None but Allah, Who is mighty and wise. He consigns some righteous to the Fire so that no one can trust in his own worth but in Allah's alone, and He spares some unrighteous for the Joy to show His mercy. He chose the soul of Abel, after he was murdered, to enter the body of Noah, and after Noah's death it passed to Abraham, and later it entered the body of Saint Peter, whom we both honor. Yet for all others, there is but one way to know their destiny."

"How?"

"If a man is killed while obeying his lord's command to kill an unbeliever, his soul is immediately given a more pleasing body in the Garden." Nazim grinned broadly. "So death is dear to us."

"By Saint Mary!" the monk exclaimed; Nazim winced at his impious oath. "Well did my king speak when he said that God alone prolongs or shortens our days, for to seek one's own death is a great sin."

To seek the Joy is a great quest, and to seek the death of unbelievers a great honor, Nazim thought. *And your king is the chief of unbelievers.*

As if conjured by Nazim's thoughts, a gust of desert wind from the east whipped at his face. It smelled like the hatch of hell had opened a crack and leaked its stench. At first Nazim thought it was only Le Breton, who smelled little better than the knights he served. But he was downwind. It might be the carcass of an unfortunate goat or pilgrim lost in these rugged hills, but the vultures were usually efficient. It could be the stink of the Mongols consorting with their rulers, the demons, just as they consulted with the Frankish filth. Yes, it was the breath of their laughter, plotting to drag the true believers into the door of doom. Nazim's tough skin pimpled to gooseflesh at the unthinkable.

There was only one way to prevent it.

A viper, coiled on the sun-bleached rocks, hissed in agreement.

The blade in his belt shuddered with expectation.

So be it. Even without the Old Man's order, he must kill King Louis.

Ins'Allah. It is the will of Allah. As the *Qur'an* says, "When He ordains a thing, shall it not come to pass? And where upon the earth is there a mortal who can oppose Him?"

13

Jean-Michel hung his head over the edge of the barge. His reflection was distorted by the gentle wash of the Rhone, but his misery was obvious. He had emptied his stomach many times upriver. Now he lay limply on the creaking plankwork like the sacks of apples headed south to Saint Gilles. Thankful that Paulinus was anchoring his ankles to the deck to prevent him retching himself overboard, Jean-Michel wondered how he had allowed himself to be persuaded to travel by water.

Paulinus tried to comfort the seasick knight by reminding him that good King Louis had made this same trip on pilgrimage to war. His sumpter beasts, supplies, and soldiers all had floated to the coast in a grand procession of flatboats. Jean-Michel imagined his father and brothers riding the boats and passing these same steep, scrub-covered hills. Limestone spurs protruded from the land like dead men's bones washed ashore after a storm. Clutches of poplars marched across green valleys. Sunny slopes of vineyards flanked by sentinel-like cypresses scented the air. His father and brothers would have smelled the aroma, too, and recalled their grapes in Anjou. He could almost hear the clinking of their armor while they joked about how Jean-Michel would be sick even on a lazy barge, and that he could never survive the sea passage to Egypt.

The clinking sound was really Bobo adjusting the bridles of the horses. Fitted with blinders, the beasts stood contentedly in narrow stalls.

Shamed by his inadequacy, Jean-Michel shaded his eyes too. "How much longer, Father?" he asked Paulinus.

Paulinus scanned the shore for a landmark. "An hour, pilgrim, and we shall be at Montverais."

The boatman, an olive-skinned Provencal who looked Moorish and sounded German, nodded in agreement. *Oc, einz heur.* "Yes, an hour," he said.

"May God make it pass quickly," Jean-Michel said.

"Come, sit up, and you'll feel better." The monk encouraged Jean-Michel with a smile and extended his hand to help. "Let the breeze blow on your face. Don't worry, I have a good hold on you. There, now lean against these sacks."

Paulinus uncorked a water flask and offered it to Jean-Michel. He sipped and then smiled sheepishly. "How can I be a good soldier for Christ, Father, if I can ride a fast horse but not a slow boat?"

"God our Father is not looking for good soldiers or sailors, but for good sons," Paulinus replied with a pat on Jean-Michel's shoulder. "Do you remember what John of Antioch said? 'God the

Son became a man in the flesh so that all men might become sons of God in the spirit.'"

"How can I be accepted as a good son?"

"One does not become accepted as a son by his own will. As Paul the apostle said, 'In Christ He chose us before the world was founded, and He destined us—such was His will and pleasure—to be accepted as His sons through Jesus Christ.'"

"How, then, may I please God as His son?"

"How did you please your earthly father?"

Jean-Michel turned away. "I have never pleased him."

Paulinus put away the water skin. "I see. And do you hope to please him through this quest?"

"He does not even know of it. He is in the Holy Land with my brothers. He left me behind."

Paulinus rumpled his brow, concerned. "Your heavenly Father knows of it. Do you not hope to please Him?"

"Only if I find a holy relic to rebuild His church."

"And if you do not?"

"I pray that will not be."

"'The Lord of heaven dwells not in temples made with hands, neither is He worshiped by men's handiworks, as though He needed anything,'" Paulinus quoted. "His desire is to dwell in our hearts. God wants you to find Him. Don't think that if you fail to find a relic your Heavenly Father will disown you."

"My earthly father did."

"Because you were the youngest?" Paulinus probed.

Jean-Michel's throat tightened in a noose of guilt. "Because I killed my mother."

"By accident?"

"By being born. She died in childbirth, and I never knew her. My father hates me for that."

The wrinkles at Paulinus' temples streaked his weathered face as if he, too, bore Jean-Michel's burden of grief. He looked away to where the river curved through an avenue of willows, their boughs dipped as though for a drink. Sweet summer jasmine, winking white from the hillsides like little angels, urged him to speak.

"Pilgrim, I have seen many people on the roads to the shrines, each with his own reason for going. Some take the staff and scrip to fulfill a vow or a penance. Some seek a healing. Some want to escape a debt. Some seek the truth, and some flee from it."

Jean-Michel looked quizzical.

"You do not merely seek a relic. Don't you truly, in your heart, seek to be accepted and forgiven?"

"Who doesn't seek God's forgiveness?" Jean-Michel said. "My bishop promised the remission of my sins when I return a relic."

"I meant your father's forgiveness."

"Why should he forgive, and why should I seek that?" Jean-Michel said defensively.

Paulinus sensed the knight's shields rising up. "Even if he does not forgive you, you must forgive him. If you cannot accept and forgive your earthly father, how can you be accepted and forgiven by your heavenly Father? Forgiving him will be far harder than finding a relic, pilgrim. But far more pleasing to God."

Jean-Michel knew it was true, and his fist curled as if to fight his own conflicted conscience.

Paulinus clapped him on the shoulder with a sign of reassurance and confidence that Jean-Michel had never known from his father. "Tell me, my son," the scholar said tenderly, "have you forgiven yourself?"

Jean-Michel looked as if he had just heard a blasphemy. "How can someone forgive himself?"

Paulinus shrugged. "Perhaps we can only stop blaming ourselves for what we were helpless to prevent. We all live with something we regret. All we get from looking over our shoulders at the past is a sore neck."

Renard lay on the apple sacks. He stretched and sat up with a start, as if ambushed. He blinked, trying to orient himself.

"We are nearly in the district of Montverais," Paulinus called helpfully.

"I know," Renard said. In this waking, unguarded moment, the troubadour's tone suggested to Paulinus that Renard also lived with something he regretted.

Renard's memories washed over him like the fragrance of the vineyards. Seeing the chalky bluffs, he remembered his escape along their narrow paths. He had traveled only by moonlight and had avoided the customary tavern stops for fear the Inquisition had alerted his jealous rivals that he, the once-wealthy Arnaud de Montverais, was a fugitive.

Had he really had a choice? Had he fled in cowardice or in prudence, hoping to one day clear his reputation and regain his properties?

He shrugged; the torture of his indecision and the agony of his compunction could not be worse than what the Chief Inquisitor, Pons Bernard, would have inflicted.

He heard that raspy voice again in his mind, as he had on so many nights when even the diversion of a woman could not help him to forget it:

"In the name of Jesus Christ, the righteous Judge, the Inquisitors of Heretical Depravity greet you. By summons delivered through your parish priest, Brother Raymond William, we enjoined you to gather here all those in the household and service of Arnaud de Montverais—men from age fourteen and women from age twelve."

"We are all here," Renard replied.

He winced now, recalling his impatient, angry interruption. It had set a bad tone for the hearing, and he had wondered since if he should have held his tongue.

Pons Bernard had knit his brow in response. "I did not invite you to speak, Messire de Montverais."

"I did not invite you into my manor," Renard had responded.

"Let the record show that Messire de Montverais, failing to answer the citation to appear voluntarily in the parish deaconry to answer for possible acts against the faith and to abjure heresy within the six-day period of indulgence, did formally object to a location of greater convenience to him and lesser expense to the commission of inquisitors."

The notary scratched in the record.

Pons Bernard steepled his fingers and waited for another incriminating reply. But Renard, restrained by the touch of his sister, kept his peace. What defense could he possibly present to the church's juggernaut of jurisprudence and power? A prince of Languedoc had little defense against land-hungry crusaders of the north ready to seize southern properties in the name of suppressing heresy.

What had he to do with heresy? He cared little for religion. He might be convicted of indifference, but not of collaboration with the Albigenses, Waldensians, and other sects allegedly "strangling the people's grain of faith with the weed of error", as the priests claimed. The friars had been sent to cull the tares with the hoe of preaching, and the princely, propertied troubadours were easily victimized. Many, it was true, exalted Lady Venus over Mother Mary. Convicted as heretics, their fields were legally forfeited to the church. The income financed "the greater harvest of souls," or so the friars claimed.

Renard recalled the interrogation, regurgitating it and chewing it again like a cow chews its cud. He wondered if there were anything he could have said, if there were anything he should *not* have said, to save his fief and, most of all, to save his sister.

Pons Bernard:	In the presence of these witnesses and God Who is Truth, you will answer this tribunal with the full and accurate truth. Have you seen any heretics or heard them preach?
Renard:	Who has accused us?
Pons:	A man's own conscience accuses him. Answer the question, if you please.
Renard:	My conscience is clear, yet I do confess contempt for those who are using you to confiscate my lands.
Pons:	If you will name your enemies, their hostility will be taken into

	account when the evidence is weighed.
Renard:	No doubt they are already listed in your register.
Pons:	Then you will confirm them?
Renard:	I will add no names to your lists.
Pons:	Do you wish to call a witness to list them for you?
Renard:	I will not.
Pons:	Let it be so noted. Have you given or arranged shelter, lodging, or comfort for heretics or their sympathizers?
Renard:	As good Christians, we give our help to all who are in need.
Pons:	Have you shared food and drink with heretics or their sympathizers or eaten bread blessed by them?
Renard:	Our stores are shared freely with all visitors.
Pons:	Have you held any deposit from them or acted as their financial agent or assistant?
Renard:	We do not charge our guests as the monasteries do.
Pons:	Have you received The Peace from them? Have you bowed your head or knee to them, or in any way received a blessing from them?
Renard:	If we impart a blessing to travelers and pilgrims, it is blessing enough for us.
Pons:	In welcoming visitors, did you at any time have reason to believe

they were, as commonly called, "good men," teaching a good faith?

Renard: I do not ask visitors for their religion just as I do not ask them for their money.

Pons: Have you heard them speak of the sacraments, of prayer, of the nature of Christ, of the origin of evil, or of the resurrection of the body?

Renard: I do not have a scribe at the dining table to record every conversation. I do not recall.

Pons: A faulty memory is no excuse. Brother Gregory, the dossier, if you please.

Renard knew someone had betrayed him. Perhaps it was a servant, fearing accusation or having been promised a reward. It might have been an envious neighbor, eager to gain from Renard's loss. Or it could have been a guest—he'd had many—who'd been offered clemency by the church. Renard remembered every word of the damaging testimony, but he could not discern who gave it. Of course, the Inquisitor who read it aloud was not obligated to reveal the source of the deposition.

I, the above named deponent, do plead forgiveness by the mercy of Christ and pledge to avoid and abjure all heresy and to support the True Church by exposing and opposing error.

To this end, I testify that, on or about the sixth day of March, there came to the manor in the night a wounded pilgrim, Yves by name. Thrown and tram-

pled by his horse, he arrived from a goodly distance on a broken leg, in a great deal of pain, drained of much blood, and in grave danger from the cold. Madame Rachelle de Montverais, sister of Messire Arnaud, received him into the guest house, where hot broth and bandages were brought.

This Yves drew close to death, despite the comforts offered by Madame Rachelle, and in the morning Madame asked the pilgrim if a priest should be summoned for unction. In the hearing of all attending him, including myself—God have mercy—this Yves declared that unction, like baptism, the Mass, and burial in consecrated ground, was a silly foible fostered by the clergy for their own profit. Prayer for the dead and the invoking of saints were likewise useless, he said. He further stated that the prayers of priests and people are equal to God, and that it is no better to pray in a church than in a guest house.

He did greatly improve with soup and the opportunity to preach. But he said he welcomed death, for he had received "The Peace," as he called it, so that his perfected soul would be a prisoner in the flesh only a little longer, passing from body to body, even to the bodies of animals.

Must I say more and defile my mouth with such blasphemies? For even as Madame tried to console him with the hope of the resurrection of the body, Yves replied that such a thing could never be, since this material world was formed by Lucifer, Prince of Darkness, and the body only serves the Evil One. For this reason, he said, Jesus Christ never took on human flesh and only appeared to be a man. Nor did Christ marry, as marriage only produces more bodies in this corrupt world, making marriage no better than prostitution.

Yves then failed quickly, for God's wrath was surely on him. Messire Arnaud sought in good will, for he is always kind, to cheer this strange guest with a song.

Renard remembered the injured stranger and how in a moment his silvered eyes could turn from peace to wildness. The tale of Renard the Fox seemed a way to calm his hysteria. Who can turn away a bleeding man at the door? Who would not seek to protect his household, even with a lute? In the hearing this had been his only defense.

Pons: Messire de Montverais, you have been heard by reliable witnesses to speak against the Holy Church.

Renard: I confess only to telling bad stories on a poorly tuned lute.

Pons: And reliable witnesses have seen you accept and adore a Cathar heretic.

Renard: I adore no man.

Pons: Nor God either. You have offered comfort and shelter to a heretic. And you have buried the selfsame heretic in your own family's plot.

Rachelle de Montverais: It was I who let him in.

Renard groaned aloud at the memory of his sister's damning words. When Paulinus and Jean-Michel looked up at him, he pretended to yawn and rolled over. He shut his eyes, but he could not shut out the echoing voices of his past.

Pons: Speak, woman, for it pleases God.

Rachelle: It pleases God to not turn away a bleeding man at the door. Is it better to heal on the Sabbath or to maim?

Pons:	I will ask the questions, Madame. Do you now wish to make a confession?
Rachelle:	I ask only that you be merciful as we were merciful to a stranger, as our Lord taught us.
Pons:	Is this what the stranger, the Good Man, taught you?
Rachelle:	It is what the Gospel teaches us.
Pons:	Let the record show that this woman attempted to instruct a priest. Her dossier, Brother Gregory, if you please. You are a widow, Madame?

The lawyer had done his research rigorously. Pons knew Rachelle was the widow of a physician known to have aided families persecuted by the heresy-hunters. Rachelle's husband had been killed in a city besieged by an army led by local bishops.

Guilty by association, was the verdict. The sentence still stung in Renard's ears.

Pons:	In the name of the Lord Jesus Christ, we, friars of the Order of Preachers, deputed as Inquisitors of Heretical Depravity in Montverais, through the public investigation which by apostolic authority we make of heretics and persons defamed, find that you, Rachelle de Montverais, espoused of the late Pierre of Toulouse and sister to Arnaud de Montverais, as you have confessed in legal proce-

> dures before us, have accepted heretics, adored them, harbored them, and offered them shelter and comfort. We direct you to do penance for these acts, by which you have shamefully offended God and His Church. You will betake yourself without delay and present yourself for holy orders in the Convent of Saint Mary Magdalene d'Aigues-Mortes. There you will make your permanent abode.

Rachelle was sentenced to a nunnery for former prostitutes. She might have been handed over to the secular arm to be burned, except that she had confessed. Did she do that to preserve herself? Renard thought it wasn't likely. She'd always been concerned for the needs of others, not her own. In a convent she would have plenty of opportunity to help those who needed help. The thought gave Renard little relief, for he had sought to preserve himself in a different way—a shameful way.

Declining to confess on the spot as she had, he was warned to reconsider the matter overnight and make his appearance for sentencing the following morning. Guards were posted outside his door, but he had slipped through the latrine hole in the wall and at great peril climbed down the stones on the outside. He whistled to Sylvester and was off into the night, hoping to reach his cousin Blanche. She was far away from the Inquisition's jurisdiction. He would hide with her until he was brave enough to return for his sister. All the way, he imagined the sentence of the tribunal once his escape was discovered.

> Having heard and carefully weighed the evidence for the crimes and defaults of Arnaud de Montverais, that he did knowingly harbor, defend, comfort, aid, favor, and bury a heretic, we relinquish him now, wherever he may have fled, to secular judgment, and by apostolic authority we not only condemn him as a heretic but also bind with the chain of excommunication, as receivers and defenders of heretics, all who henceforth knowingly hear, harbor, defend, shelter, comfort, aid, or favor him. All faithful Christians who love God and the truth are eligible for one hundred years' indulgence for information leading to the apprehension and arrest of Arnaud de Montverais, who is also known to some by the name *Renard.*

Renard surveyed the distant hills where he had once hunted. He could not tell the knight and the monk that they were passing through lands that once belonged to him. He could not warn them that if the authorities recognized and captured him, he could be burned, as the body of Yves had probably been exhumed and burned publicly in detestation. Why, if they knew the truth about him, this pious knight and priest might turn him in themselves. They would surely do it out of duty and to protect themselves, because, by being in his company, they were also in danger.

He wished them no harm. *Just a few leagues longer*, he thought. *Then we shall part, each follow-*

ing our separate quests. And God help us—if there is a God.

After passing Montverais, Renard remained quiet, introspective, almost contemplative. He shed his silks for plainer garb that was less conspicuous and more native to the region. Along the southern route to Saint Jacques de Compostelle and nearing the royal road to Aigues-Mortes, the singer thanked Jean-Michel for his protection and slipped away unceremoniously, begging his leave to visit a few local ladies. "No need to tell brother Paulinus," Renard confided. "Why risk offending the good father with such talk?"

For his part, Jean-Michel felt relieved to be rid of Renard. It would ill befit the dignity of a knight and a monk, two soldiers of Christ, to enter the royal city with a randy troubadour. Having Paulinus for a companion and guide down the Rhone, Jean-Michel considered Renard and his irksome horse to be only trouble in tow. Jean-Michel tried to forget how much he had to pay the boatman for the apples Sylvester had scavenged.

On the way to the Basilica of Aigues-Mortes, Jean-Michel sidestepped Paulinus' questions about Renard. He watched his feet to avoid both the monk's inquisitive eyes and the unpleasant surprises so common on the roads in French towns. Cramped houses with corbeled upper stories leaned over the narrow streets, where filthy waste vomited from windows collected. Horrid offal cast from kitchens and refuse from the tanneries splashed the unwary. The pigs roaming the alleys left their dung to drain in the channels running down the middle of the crowded streets.

Shopkeepers on Le Rue l'Epicurie leaned from their display counters to shout insults at their rivals' wares and assault customers with promises.

"Best prices today!"

"Don't listen to that thief!"

"He's worse than a Jew!"

"Watch out for the worms in his meat!"

Jean-Michel jostled among armed soldiers on horseback who fought with women for bargains. At the poulterers, geese tied to stalls honked and gabbled. Chickens and capons, their legs trussed, floundered on the ground next to the limp-eared hares resigned to their fate. The butcher's ax was busy today, so the paving stones at his stall were slick from blood and thick with flies.

Jean-Michel swatted away the insects while looking over the red-tiled roofs, keeping track of the basilica's spires. They jutted skyward like lances, a fitting feature for a military town. He brushed past a winking whore wearing a spicy smile and the distinctive armband of her trade. He ignored a man wearing an earring who was selling weighted dice. He avoided touching the dirty half-breed children with their dark hair and Saracen skins. But Paulinus patted their little heads and laughed with them while they circled a pile of cheap salt dried from the mosquito-ridden marshes that gave this port its prophetic name—Dead Waters.

Jean-Michel and Paulinus followed the grid pattern of the streets that had been planned meticulously by King Louis—Tanner Row, Glazier Lane, Parchment Place, Le Rue des Croisettes. They passed arched houses built from the brackish mud dredged from the clogged canals that led to the outer harbor. Among these forbidding flats, the only stone structures were the church, the palatium of King Louis, and the Tower of Constance, a perfectly round citadel as austere and uncompromising as the king. It dominated the lagoon-indented shore in the same way the king dominated his realm. It dwarfed the town's encircling rampart, a poorly-built wall made of wood hastily taken from the timberland of local heretics and put in place by conscripted carpenters. Located four miles inland, Aigues-Mortes was an undesirable launching point for an armada, since no big ships could ply its silted channels. Only vessels of shallow draught could approach the walls and ferry out to the unprotected bay, a place plagued by sandstorms, gnats, and uncertain winds. This all should have been warning enough for the ill-fated French expedition to Egypt, which had foundered in the reedy floodwaters of the Nile.

A warm gulf wind was blowing today, and a hint of fresh-cut lavender hung in the air. The smoke from burned stalks drifted through the hills of Provence into the plain of Camergue. Jean-Michel recalled the aroma of wild basil along the road from the Rhone, and the sound of walnut trees swelled with nuts clicking in the breeze like Spanish castinets. But here in the salt marshes, where nothing grew but reeds and mosquitoes, even the lavender was overcome by the stale brine of the sea.

At the church steps, the men passed a pair of washerwomen at the lavoir. The women rubbed and rinsed a paste of woodash on their linens and the vestments of the church's priests to bleach away impurities. Sheets and stoles hung out to dry on the scaffolding dangled like thieves on gallows. Beggars and hucksters crowded the double doors. Paulinus and Jean-Michel had to pass through their pressing offers just as one passes through the temptations of life to enter heaven.

"Goliath's tooth, messire."

"Peter's net."

"Half price today."

"Alms!"

"Just a penny."

"Pity the poor."

"Alms!"

Ignoring the tugs on his clothes, Jean-Michel followed close behind Paulinus, like a plowman behind an ox. Once inside, he brushed himself off. His sleeves were stiff from salt, as if the sins of those outside had become encrusted on them.

Galbert Le Marichal had been only partly right about the relics in Aigues-Mortes. Such treasures, purchased from Byzantine and Venetian merchants in the East, reached the royal town via Hospitaler galleys, under royal protection and registration. Each was accounted for and then stored in the basilica. Jean-Michel had at first despaired of obtaining one, but Paulinus had a plan.

The monk led the knight down the dim nave, a musty cavern of damp floors and bare walls. The plinths and pillars, like chapters in a book, told their stories along the way. A roaring lion, Christ the Judge, effaced his tracks with his tail, as during the incarnation God became man in secret in order to cheat the devil. Christ used His claws to take vengeance on a Jew, pictured as an ass. King Louis, acting in Christ's stead on this depiction, had banished all Jews from the city.

Paulinus stopped at the east chapel, where a line of lace-like windows depicted the life of the Virgin. "Wait here, pilgrim," he whispered. "Let me speak to the canon in private. In this hood and habit, I can get through more doors than you can."

"But my tunic bears the image of the Cross."

"And I will tell him. He will be impressed. But what will really impress him are my travel papers from Cluny." He winked. "And the authority they give me to declare that his relics are fake."

Paulinus crossed the choir under the skeptical stone eyes of apostles and prophets who were gathered like vassals around the Queen of Heaven. Pavilioned in splendor, she oversaw the nave like a great baroness at the head of her hall. The rose stone put a blush on her delicate cheeks. It was the same blush that had been on Blanche's cheeks at the banquet. The brocaded tent over her crowned head fluttered lightly like the taffeta gown had fluttered on Blanche when she walked. The Queen of Heaven wore Blanche's inviting smile while the winged archangels, Gabriel and Michael, offered her the twin scepters of temporal and spiritual power. Jean-Michel genuflected in fealty. Gratitude filled his soul. If only he might please the Holy Mother and return to Blanche with a relic, and hear her voice, and feel the touch of her freckled hand, and taste . . .

The scuff of sandals raised his head. At first he thought the Virgin had stamped her foot to rebuke him.

Paulinus approached with a heavy-footed prelate, a tall, hawkish man with an aquiline nose and a severe mouth. Jean-Michel stood to face him. His feelings of longing were replaced by rumbles of dread.

Paulinus looked chagrined as he used his most formal tone. "May I present His Grace, Canon of the Basilica, Reverend Father Pons Bernard."

14

"You seek a relic?" Pons Bernard rasped. Behind the canon, a pinch-lipped Paulinus signaled Jean-Michel with a solemn nod. Something was wrong.

"I do," the knight said, tentatively.

"I seek Renard," the saturnine canon said.

He sounded like Marcel the bailiff, hunting poachers, his voice like a file sharpening knives for skinning. "How do you know of him?" Jean-Michel said, chilled.

"Brother Paulinus tells me you have traveled in his company."

"We have."

"That you also have accepted his guidance and service."

"We have."

"And entered into financial agreements with him."

"We . . . that is . . . I have." Jean-Michel flexed his clammy hands. This was the unmistakable tone of an inquisitor. He looked to Paulinus for a clue as to what to do, but the jowls on the monk drooped defeatedly and his shoulders slumped.

"And what do you know of Renard?" Pons Bernard pressed.

"He is a jongleur, a clever fool who sings of love," Jean-Michel said.

"He is a lover of heretics," the canon entoned gravely. "As is his sister, here in the Convent of Saint Mary Magdalene."

Sister? Renard had never mentioned a sister, let alone a sister in the nunnery for prostitutes.

"He must be brought to sentencing," Pons Bernard continued. His fingers were locked together as if grasping prey. "The due process of law must be fulfilled." His hooded eyes examined Jean-Michel. "And those who have accompanied and abetted him must also be investigated thoroughly."

Jean-Michel's fingers trembled. His mouth went as dry as kindling fagots at the stake.

"Reverend Father," Paulinus said, "let us show good faith by assisting you in the inquiry. Let me take this young knight, a sworn soldier of the Church, to locate and detain this rascal who has so vilely deceived us, while you gather the proper papers and a party from the secular arm to arrest him."

Pons Bernard considered the plea, stroking his nose to a sharper point. "By your faith, then," he agreed, turning to the frightened knight. "You will no doubt find the fugitive at the convent. If you hold him there until I bring the bailiff and his men, it will incline me toward dismissing any motion for your own excommunication for consorting with a heretic."

"He is no heretic," Paulinus said, his cassock hiked up for speed. "This way, this way."

Jean-Michel and Bobo steered their mounts through the alley. "How can we know?" the knight asked, ducking the laundry lines. "Renard is a trickster, and he has never shown respect for God."

"I can tell a true relic from a false one, and a true heretic as well," the monk said puffing for breath. "I fear Renard's only error is to say that men and women may marry to fulfill their love, while the Church says they must marry to curtail their lust."

Hearing men's voices, "joy women" leaned from doorways to advertise their availability. Paulinus asked one for directions to the convent. The woman, a paunchy professional accustomed to having clerics for customers, pointed west without shame. She waved her Syrian silks at Jean-Michel, but feeling disgust and pity, he looked away and spurred Fidelity forward.

The convent stood serenely between two busy brothels, like a white-robed nun calming a quarrel between two peasant women. Above the high entry door, a statue of the Magdalene welcomed all penitents. Paulinus yanked the bell rope and, heaving like a bellows, leaned against the wall.

A sweet-faced sister opened the door's peek hole. "Grace and peace to you, brothers," she said.

"And to you," Paulinus replied, giving a sign of the Cross. "We come with an important message."

"I will take it to Mother," the nun said.

"It is for Renard the Fox."

The nun's face, framed in a white wimple and veil, went pink at the cheeks. "If you seek a tavern," she said testily, "there are many in the neighborhood. *Adieu.*"

"Tell him it is Paulinus and Jean-Michel who call," the monk said, too late. The little door clapped shut in his face. Paulinus rubbed his nose. "It is as James of Ephesus wrote: 'God guides us more by closed doors than open ones so that, in the knocking and waiting, we open the door of our hearts to God.'"

"Mayhaps Renard is not here," the knight said, relieved.

The latch squeaked and the oak door opened a crack. The nun peered out. "He speaks well of you, Jean-Michel," she said. "Come in."

They found him in the sick room covered with blood.

"None of it is my own," the jongleur assured them when he saw their startled faces. "Just cleaning up after a nasty delivery. It happens sometimes to the girls around here. This is the only place that will take them in and care for their little ones."

When Jean-Michel noticed the bloodied sheets, guilt gnawed at him. How had his own mother suffered in bringing his unworthy self into the world? "The girl," he said. "Did she live?"

"Yes, poor soul," Renard said. "She'll be back on the streets in no time if she doesn't become a nun. Come. To the *lavoir.*" He pulled off his stained smock and gave it to a nun, whispering an instruction.

In a tiled room with a large tub, Renard asked Paulinus to pour a pitcher of water over his outstretched arms. "I am not surprised to see you," Renard said. "It was only a matter of time before you learned the truth about me. I would be gone by now if the girl's labor had not taken so long. That towel, if you please." He dried his arms. "Have you come to arrest me? If so, I claim sanctuary."

"There is no sanctuary from the Inquisition," Paulinus said. "The canon of the basilica, Pons Bernard, is searching for you."

"He has more blood on his hands than I do," Renard said.

"He is on his way, and we are to detain you," Paulinus said, one ear cocked to the courtyard. The bell might ring frantically at any moment.

"It will be a while before he can find the bailiff and his men," Renard said, rubbing his fingers dry. "They are probably scattered in the neighborhood. No wonder he hoped you would hold me for a while." He took note of Jean-Michel's contorted face. "That is what you came to do, is it not? I suppose the canon promised to reward you with a relic."

"Not at all," Paulinus said. "We have come to warn you."

"Have you indeed?" Renard said. "And what is it that you gain in helping me? Surely I have no relic to give."

Jean-Michel remained silent, though his hand went to his queasy stomach.

"You must change quickly and be on your way," Paulinus urged. "We will stay and inform Pons Bernard that you are no longer here, and that we missed you."

"That you cannot do," Renard said. "Pons Bernard is a relentless man. He will wring the truth from you. No, you must come with me."

"Go with you?" Jean-Michel cried. "To where?"

"To Acre," Renard said. "There is a boat waiting for us in the bay."

"For us?" Paulinus asked.

"My sister and I," Renard said, as she entered the room. Renard took her hand and kissed it in greeting.

As with Renard, her chin dimpled when she smiled. Her Mediterranean skin looked as dark as olive wood against the pure white of her veil; she gave the visitors a cordial but cautious look. "Your friends?" she asked.

Renard introduced them to her, then held her hand while he told her the news.

"Thank you for helping my brother," she said, her doe-like eyes misting. "He speaks well of your faith and kindness."

"They will come with us, and we must go at once," Renard said, still holding her hand as if to lead her away.

"My place is here," she said. "How often must I tell you? It is the will of God for my life."

"It is the penance of Pons Bernard," Renard scowled. "You did not choose this."

"God has chosen this, Arnaud, and I must follow Him. How often must I tell you? All my life I have taken in the sick and the homeless, and there is no better place than this for such work."

"Follow me to Acre," Renard pleaded. "Rachelle, you will be safe there."

"I do not wish to be safe," she said. "I wish to be used by God. That is never safe."

It was an argument they had exchanged many times, thought Paulinus. He felt a shiver, but not from the water that spilled on his sleeve. It was the same icy tendril that touched his spine before a storm, or before a battle. He had felt it in the basilica, too, and dismissed it as being from the dampness. But it was not from wetness, either there or here. *Pons Bernard is coming,* he thought.

"Avram is waiting," Renard said to his sister.

"Tell Avram I am sorry," Rachelle said, her eyes brimming with tears. "Take your friends and go."

"I cannot leave you again in his hands."

"I am in God's hands."

Paulinus shuddered. His arm rippled with gooseflesh. "This b-boat," he chattered. "Where is it?"

"At anchor in the outer bay," Renard said, looking at him curiously. "It is a merchant ship belonging to an old family friend. He is removing Jews from the city, by order of the king, and he has reserved a place for us. He is in wait of the wind. Pons Bernard will not think of looking there. I have a flatboat at the pier now, to ferry us out. I think it can manage all our horses."

"There is a wind today," the monk said. "If we go, we must go now." His ears perked like those of a deer. "Come, pilgrim. To the stables. Let brother and sister have their farewell in peace."

Jean-Michel was shivering too, not from the strange foreboding that afflicted the monk, but from his terror of the sea. He stared at the sink as if looking upon his own grave. Paulinus tugged on his sleeve as though hauling up an anchor. "Pons Bernard has no power in Palestine," the monk said reassuringly. "No edict of his can stand there."

"How can we do this thing?" Jean-Michel protested. "We will be excommunicated for helping a heretic."

"They cannot do so without a hearing. Even if they did, I would absolve you." He grasped Jean-Michel by the shoulders. "And think of it, pilgrim. You can find your father."

The prospect struck Jean-Michel like a mace. Would he rather face the canon's wrath or his father's scorn? Aflood with conflicting thoughts, his head swam from indecision. He certainly did not wish to face the Great Sea. Before he knew it, Paulinus had led him through the cloisters to the alley side of the abbey, where Bobo presented them with their freshly-fed horses.

"Renard will be here in a moment," Paulinus told Bobo. Jean-Michel took Fidelity's reins. His knuckles were as hard as seashells and his face as white as the foam under a bowsprit. Like it or not, Renard was his passage to the Levant, where at last he could forgive his father, face to face. And where else in all the world but in the last stronghold of the crusaders in the Holy Land could he fulfill his vow to find a relic for the cathedral? Even now he could hear the bells of Auxonne rejoicing.

It was the front gate.

Paulinus peeked through the cloister pillars while Bobo and Jean-Michel waited at the alley gate. Indecision gripped him as the bailiff bullied the porter. If Renard were caught and they fled without him, surely they would be defenseless in an inquiry. Could they claim to have just arrived? Could they claim to have only apprehended his horse in the stable?

The gatekeeping nun was unable to forestall them any longer, and the bailiff's men burst through the door. With swords drawn, they clanked across the courtyard in their hastily-donned mail. They nearly knocked over a cowled priest who stopped to bless them. The priest shuffled quickly to the stable. *We are discovered,* Paulinus thought, gulping.

The priest slipped through the door and shook off his hood. "Turn left at the alley," Renard said. "My sister will get them off our scent."

At the hour of vespers, with an orange sun sitting like a bull's-eye on the west point of the compass, the freighter creaked out to sea. When the ship cleared the marshy basin and headed into the open Mediterranean, the rowers stowed their oars and stepped the double masts to unfurl the triangular sails. The canvas snapped and bellied full in the breeze. The ship lurched forward, and Jean-Michel's stomach lurched with it.

He clung to the open porthole of the cabin while his legs dangled under him. The sea churned below. Its salty tang could not disguise the odor from the livestock pens that supplied the galley with fowl, or the reek of onions swinging in the rafters, or the stink of bilge water in the ballast sand on the ship's bottom. Most nauseating of all was the thought that in the hold lay rows of refugee Jews. Who could tell what plagues they had brought aboard? What ills from the Almighty would befall their voyage in judgment for their rejection of His Son? Storms? Shipwreck? Saracen pirates? That scruffy captain Avram had given him the Evil Eye when he saw a Christian knight and a monk approach his ship on the barge instead of Renard's sister as pre-arranged. Remembering the merchant's impudent reluctance to receive them, Jean-Michel tried to pray away the curse. "Having them aboard will be like transporting swine," Avram had complained.

"You can use a ship's doctor, and the priest is handy with cures," Renard had argued.

"I have worked with the *bussola*, whose needle always points to the North Star," Paulinus said, "and I can read the periplus, if you have one. I have personally seen many of the landmarks and lighthouses shown on such a map, and I have some familiarity with coastal depths."

The captain was bewildered, not by the monk's nautical knowledge, but that he spoke it in passable Hebrew. "And I speak several languages," Paulinus concluded, "to greet other ships."

"We only need trade French," Avram harrumphed. "And what of this knight? What makes him so pale? I will take no sickness aboard. Look you, he shakes."

"My bodyguard," Renard said wryly. "A fine horseman."

"Of what use is that on the high seas?"

"He can handle an oar if he can handle a lance. Now, Avram, let us sail while the wind lasts." Renard's voice was as unsteady as his sea-legs. He looked toward the shore, remorse filling his eyes.

The captain's weather-beaten face softened. He studied the knight and the horses on the loading ramp with a shrug. "So be it, Master Arnaud, for your sake and for our long friendship. But I can tell he would prefer a Hospitaler's galley or even a garbage scow to me. Tell him it is better to go with Avram of Akko than with some crooked transporter who would change course and dispose of his pilgrim cargo in the slave markets of Tunis."

By his acid look, Jean-Michel suspected this captain was capable of plotting such vile treachery. *But what does it matter now,* he moaned to himself, the white whirlpools below spinning in his head. He had cast his lot; the loading gates were caulked shut. He could now only pray that sprites, dragons, and other dangers of the unpredictable sea might be stayed by God's hand, and that if he drowned en route Philippe would never learn of it, lest he suspect that the least of his sons had died of fright and not as a true man—in combat.

15

Nazim ad-Din sat cross-legged on the Bedouin cushion, his bare feet planted in the plush carpet. With the coolness of sundown, he no longer felt rivulets of sweat running from his light *quffayid* headdress to his neck. But the sandy-skinned man opposite him was perspiring like a goat in a kettle.

Nazim drew a curved blade from the sheath fixed to his jeweled belt, and stroked the ivory handle. "You can tell me what I want to know and die quickly," he said, his voice as sharp as his knife, "or you can remain silent and die slowly."

"By the beard of the Prophet, may he be blessed, only tell me what to do and I will obey," the man beseeched, bowing forward. Two thugs on either side of him thrust him back, one gripping him by the hair to expose his quivering throat. Nazim disliked using ruffians from the gambling den, but they were nameless and desperate and would do anything for a *dinar* or two. If he kept his face veiled, they would be no trouble to him later. "Are you ready to obey me as quickly as you obey your Frankish masters?"

"Faster, my lord." The prisoner was near to blubbering. He had just come from a hard day's work rebuilding the city's north wall intending to increase his meager pay by playing dice. A harmless diversion, that was all he had wanted. It would come at a very high price this night.

"I have been watching you," Nazim said, testing the knife-edge with his thumb. "You are a foreman on the wall."

"I take orders well, my lord," the man said with a nervous smile.

"You have orders to finish the repairs by a certain time. When, and why?"

The thugs pulled on the man's hair and his voice went up in pitch. "By the morning after the Christians' Sabbath, my lord," the man breathed. "For inspection by their king."

So it was true. Yolande had heard correctly. Nazim tried to control his excitement. "What time will the king arrive?"

"After worshiping his three gods, cursed be the thought."

"Has he come to your wall before?" Perhaps he might learn the route the king would take in order to plan his ambush.

"Never. He has been too busy with the walls of Caesarea and Saida. When he visits them, he goes with great ceremony, attended by many knights . . ."

"Enough," Nazim signaled. He had the information he needed. He reached into his robe. The man quaked. Nazim withdrew a shiny gold crescent. "How has Allah treated you in the games?"

"Allah deals with all men as He wills, and tonight He has willed that I lose."

It was a good answer. "Take this, and perhaps His favor will rest on you." He tossed the coin on the carpet. "Release him."

The henchmen unhanded the foreman. He picked up the coin, watching Nazim all the while. He stood shakily, and rubbed circulation back into his arms. "Thank you, my lord," he whispered. "A thousand blessings." He passed Nazim warily and was about to push through the beaded curtain when Nazim called to him.

"One more thing I have for you."

The man turned. Nazim's knife spun into his throat. The coin dropped and rolled. The man dropped to his knees and rolled on his back. Bubbling blood pooled in his open mouth. His startled eyes stared blankly at the ceiling.

Nazim retrieved the coin and the knife. He bent close to the drowning man. When the gurgling stopped, he searched in the empty eyes for a trace of the man's fate. He saw no tongues of flame, no stingers of scorpions, not the slightest glimmer of the Garden, where Nazim once felt the fountain's mist and the maidens' fans, the boys fed him fruits, and his beloved offered herself, as smooth as peach and as sweet as cantaloupe. Sometimes it seemed to be only a dream. But did that make it less real? He looked intently for its reflection in the dark liquid of the dead eyes.

Nothing.

No matter. He wiped the blade on the man's chest and replaced it in its sheath. He flipped the coin to the thugs and commanded the frightened men to remove the body. They wrapped it in the carpet and carried it out a back way.

Nazim squeezed the warm ivory knife handle. The Joy might be his again, and forever, if he could be martyred in his duty. He would send the knife singing into King Louis' throat just as he had sent it into the throat of this mercenary bricklayer. Let the bolts fly. Let the javelins come. In the presence of such an escorting procession of nobles and knights in all their pomp, what a passage it would be to Paradise.

Hired as a day laborer in the market, Nazim worked his way to the crew unloading broken bricks from the rampart into canvas slings. With all the last-minute details there was much confusion, and the loss of a foreman, found dead in a gambling den the night before, apparently over a lost bet, had complicated everything. Thus, Nazim could roam at will inconspicuously if he looked busy. This was easy with so many new laborers hauling mortar and stone on their backs down the sloping scaffolding, which needed to be clean for the king.

From the top of the north wall, between Saint Anthony's Gate and the square towers overlooking the Franciscan sector, Nazim could scout every approach. L'Avenue de Saforie slanted southwesterly from the sea, past the Templar stables and the quarter of the German Knights of Saint Lazarus. La Rue Montmussart intersected it at the Church of Saint Denis, surely a stop for the king to pay respects to the patron of France. It was a good spot to strike, especially if the alley between the basilica and the blockhouses remained clear. He could run up just as Louis dismounted. That would be a most vulnerable moment.

A reflection from the merciless sun blinded Nazim. A stale east wind, like a viper's breath, blew a flour-like dust in his face. He pulled on his hood and wished for a proper Bedouin *quffaya* to shield his eyes and shade his head. Squinting, he listened for the jingle of harnesses, the click of hooves, the bleat of French horns sounding like sheep caught under a fence. But he heard only the normal cacophony of the streets.

He gazed into a shimmering haze over the road to Safad. A company of Hospitaler Knights of Saint John of Jerusalem, cloaked in black, patrolled the perimeter. That was what had raised the dust. Nazim spat grit from his mouth. He hoped the foolish Franks would fry in their armor. He watched them enter Saint Anthony's Gate into the northern sector which they controlled, and where the citadel of the king presided over the town.

Sure-footed as a mountain lion, Nazim jumped up from the catwalk to the wall's brink. He felt no fear of falling. He faced the sun and the sandy flats. He remembered when he had stood at the edge of the precipice to Paradise itself.

While the dignitaries from Damascus had sipped their snow-cooled juices under silk canopies pitched far below the castle heights, the young *feda'is* had lined up at the rim of the parapet. The stones on the wide, gravelly top had cut Nazim's calloused feet. He had recited the Surahs more fervently. A bracing mountain breeze carried his prayers into the blue sky. He considered the young devotees in front of him, in similar attitudes of prayer for what seemed hours.

Finally, from the central pavilion, a mirror flashed. The first *feda'i* leaped boldly, screaming Allah's name.

The line of men shuffled forward. The mirror sparkled again, and the next man dived into eternity crying, *Allahu akbar!* The splintering of bones on rock, like the snap of dry kindling, ended his triumphal cry.

A third flash. A third martyr.

Nazim stepped forward. The young *feda'i* in front of him took his position on the wall. His martyr's robe shimmered white, aflutter like a proud banner. The boy swayed, dizzied by the height, his balance dulled by the hashish which Nazim alone had refused. The boy clenched and unclenched his fists. His breath quickened. Nazim drew in a patient draught of air and exhaled words of the *Qu'ran* to encourage him. They waited.

The mirror blazed like a star. The boy thrust his hands sunward. *Allahu akbar!* he whooped, launching himself into the air.

Nazim moved resolutely into his place and curled his bleeding toes over the chalky edge. He slid forward on the loosened dirt, uncomfortably close to falling. He dared not plummet by accident and be humiliated in the sight of God and his Master, the Old Man. He pressed down his heels to balance himself. Pain shot up his legs. He stiffened them. *Wait for the signal. Then obey. The Joy is given to the obedient.* He did not look down to the serrated slope below, but stared straight ahead to the hills mantled in spring green. Already the Garden's date palms, lemon trees, and ribbon streams of milk and honey shimmered in his sight like a distant oasis. *I come, my beloved,* he called in his mind, *into the Eternal Light.*

But the light never flashed. The Old Man's guards appeared and pulled him safely away. The visitors, deeply impressed that the Old Man could ask his followers to kill or be killed without fear or hesitation, conceded to his political demands. But Nazim did not feel relief or pride. He felt disappointment. To be so close to The Glory only to be denied. At the time he had nursed an agonizing doubt about the purpose of Allah's mercy. But now, on the north wall of Acre, he knew he had been spared for this moment.

A noisy procession of horsemen tramped into view from the direction of Saint Catherine's Church. It was a Hospitaler escort, in full battle array. Among their streamers and pennants flew the blue and gold *fleur-de-lis*, the emblem of the French royal house.

The king was coming.

"You! Get down from there!"

A Frankish overseer on a wooden platform pointed at Nazim with a chisel. He called again in choppy Arabic, beckoning him down.

Nazim noticed the other workers being herded into the grassy area between the double walls. It would be a temporary prison for security reasons, until the king's inspection was finished. There was no way to reach the target from there. He needed to be at close range, in the crowd.

He descended, shrugging all the while, pretending not to understand the Frenchman's scolding. The frustrated mason gestured to the row of men being prodded at lance-point into the stone pen. He wanted Nazim to be in that group. He indicated a ladder and poked Nazim with the chisel, forcing him down. He climbed down after Nazim, watchful and distrusting. The man seemed wary and on the lookout for help. Nazim saw soldiers arrive in greater numbers, taking up positions to clear the street of merchants, sailors, pilgrims, beggars, and prostitutes, all crowding for a look, hoping for a souvenir or a sale. The overseer took too great an interest in the soldiers.

Nazim landed, cat-footed, on the first platform. A huge crane, all beams, pulleys, and ropes, was operated from here by a wide winch. Like a monstrous catapult, it held a huge canvas sling filled with bricks. Surely the entourage would pass by here to review this impressive machine.

Two infantrymen took up posts below the platform. The overseer called to them.

The bray of camels distracted them. Halfway up the filthy street, a loose camel wandered into the king's line, causing no small commotion. Horses reared, soldiers blasphemed, vendors shouted, camels kicked, women screamed.

The soldiers turned away to look.

The overseer lifted his chin to see.

Nazim swung his knife in a swift arc, slicing the mason's windpipe. He caught the slumping body and wrestled it into a pile of brick bags. While everyone watched the panicked camels, Nazim covered the corpse, using his spattered robe. The blood had not stained through to his tunic of martyr's white. Sand and wood soaked up a crimson stream, though some trickled through the planks to the soldiers' feet. Laughing at the stray camel, they took no notice of the gruesome dripping. They chuckled, their hands on their sword hilts.

Nazim cursed. He could not climb down past them to blend into the crowd, nor could he kill both of them without drawing attention. He would have to stay on the platform. They were not liable to climb the scaffolding. But if the king stopped at Saint Denis for a dedication ceremony, they might look around and discover him.

He squatted behind a beam. If Louis passed by, the platform might provide a fine vantage point for hurling his knife. He calculated the distance. A goodly way to a mounted horseman, but he had struck birds in flight. He felt his knife handle, tracing the abstract engraving on it with his thumb. It was warm, having tasted Frankish blood.

The procession moved on, orderly once more. Would they stop at the church? Nazim watched the pennants bobbing. No, they marched past the doors, and no patriarch appeared. Nazim's heart thudded against his ribs. He sat on his haunches like a lion, his muscles coiled for a pounce. His acute ear was atuned to every footfall of his unsuspecting prey. He saw no gleaming golden crown, but the figure in blue, mounted on the white stallion, flanked by knights of the Temple and the Hospital, was obviously the king. In the haze and dust, Nazim could not make out his face. But he recalled Louis at court and knew he would recognize him at closer quarters. He kept his keen eye on the blue banner that preceded the king. When it reached the crane, he would make his move.

The banner bounced toward him. The jangle of mail and squeak of leather filled his ears. His thighs began to burn and his arms felt aflame. The flag fluttered into full view before him, the gold irises sharp and the stitching distinct.

Nazim shifted to the balls of his feet.

Now! *Allahu akbar.*

Nazim sprang. He whipped back his arm. He fixed on the white stallion and its rider.

A dark bearded man in a mail hood stared back at him.

He was not Louis.

Nazim's eyes darted from horse to horse in vain. A Templar shouted. Swords rang out. A javelin whistled past his ear and thunked into the crane.

Nazim kicked out the linchpin from the crane's windlass. The hand cranks, geared to the drum, spun madly. The sling of stones dropped like an anchor, the ropes screeching through the pulleys. The bricks crashed into the platform and ripped it from its mooring in the wall. The entire scaffolding collapsed into the street in a choking cloud of mortar dust and bits of bricks.

Nazim was already on top of the wall and running hard. He ignored the frightful noise of horses' screams, men's cries, the clatter of broken wood. Knowing that no javelin could reach him, he did not look back. Since the knights despised bows, he had no fear of arrows. By the time any foot soldier could crank a crossbow in the confusion, he would be gone.

Arab workers in the pen below shouted and pointed to him. Guards from the next watchtower rushed out to the wall. Nazim leaped onto a roof and skidded down the clay tiles. They broke up like old pots and gashed his legs. Nazim gnashed his teeth in pain and frustration. He tumbled and crawled to the edge of the house. It joined a flat-roofed terrace with stairs going down two stories to the street. He jumped down to it and rolled, his cut legs throbbing. He dragged himself to the stairs and stumbled down. Some Arab men who were lounging at the bottom, alerted by the breaking tiles, looked up at him. Nazim shoved them aside and raced down the crowded street. It reeked of manure and swill. He slipped in something spongey. His head hammered and his leg felt swollen and heavy, like a brine barrel.

The guards, fat from Acre's luxuries, tried the same leap to the tiled roof. Two made it, but slid over the loose tiles and plunged into the street. Two more followed, dropping their spears and landing squarely on the pitch and gravel beneath the tiles. The sunsoftened pitch stuck to their boots. They scrambled across the ceramic tiles in pursuit.

Nazim weaved through the crowd, keeping his face down to conceal it. He glanced behind him anxiously. He slammed into a woman and upset her head basket of melons. He went into a spin. The knife was knocked loose from his hand. He growled and searched for it on his knees among the horse dung and sandaled feet now clearing away from him. The guards, spotting him, waved their swords. Shoppers scattered like roaches. The guards had a clear view of him now.

Nazim grabbed his knife. He slid on a melon rind. From one knee, he steadied and threw the weapon.

The blade whined through the air into a guard's knee. The Frank crumpled, yowling. His companion tripped over him and sprawled in the sewage. Nazim thought to retrieve his knife, but the guards were getting up.

The cobblestones shook with iron hoofbeats. His leg protesting, Nazim dragged himself up, punched aside onlookers, zig-zagged through narrow alleys piled with rubbish and dropped exhausted behind a hayrick. He heard horsemen thunder past the alley. Dogs were chasing them and snarling. When the barking and the pounding receded and the buzz of commerce resumed, Nazim leaned into the hay and examined his leg.

It looked as if a wild animal had clawed him. The parallel lacerations, not deep but stinging, were clotting already and turning an ugly black. Flies began to swarm. He drug himself up and limped away. His martyr's white was soiled, like his honor. He rubbed the bloodstains on his robe into the dirt to disguise them, and then made his way into the faceless masses of the Muslim sector. It was best to remain anonymous there until sundown when he might meander back to the city proper. He resisted the urge to return to the wall and survey the damage. Knowing that news traveled in Acre's streets like a desert wind, he would wait.

He wished to cleanse, cool, and conceal himself in a mosque. But most prayer houses had been converted in part to churches, and he refused to share space with befouling images. As much as he needed to wash his wounds, he would not stain his soul to do it.

He found asylum in a Turkish bathhouse, which swirled with rumors of many men, some of them prominent, killed at the wall. Most of the gossipers had heard it was an accident involving a hoisting crane. How strange was the will of Allah. Some said the king was dead; others argued that Louis was not even there. Nazim remembered the dark man on the king's horse who bore the king's standard. Had they discovered Yolande was his informant? Did they make her tell them that she gave notice of the inspection to him? Some bathers were speculating that it was a foiled assassination attempt. Nazim kept his distance and kept his peace.

At the call of the midday *muezzin*, Nazim joined the ranks of the prayerful in the street. Kneeling on his tunic, he bowed on the slimy stones. He was ashamed and angry. He had stood at the edge of the wall again, but had failed to enter paradise. No, it was worse. He hadn't merely failed; he had run away like a frightened hare. Would Allah grant another opportunity to a coward who had blackened his face with shame?

Prostrating himself, he bloodied his forehead in repentance and self-rebuke, and the men around him quietly admired the young man's tearful piety.

16

The Holy Land glowed. Necklaced by golden beaches, crowned by verdant hills, and perfumed with blossoms, she was adorned like a bride awaiting the advent of her King—in Jean-Michel's imagination.

But Acre was a cheap harlot, dressed in dirty brown and reclining on a divan of dull yellow dunes.

Jean-Michel held his nose as the professional rowers maneuvered the ship around a lighthouse and into the busy harbor. Like in a hideous soup, chunks of garbage and offal bobbed in the brackish waters, shiny from grease and stinking of dead fish. Squadrons of noisy gulls fought over the floating trash.

"Just like the Genoese, the Pisans, and the Venetians in the city," Paulinus said, gesturing toward the gulls. "All quarrelsome rivals, brawling in the streets for the most profits. Even the knights fight each other. No wonder the Saracens could take the city at will."

"But the king is here," Jean-Michel said, searching the spire-studded skyline for the castle. "Why doesn't he stop it?"

"Conrad of Jerusalem is not really a king, but just a boy who lives in Sicily. The real rulers here are the merchants, the military orders, the papal legate, and the various patriarchs and princes whose lands have fallen to the Saracens. As James, Bishop of Vitry, has said, 'Acre is a monster of many heads, each one biting the others.'"

Avram barked orders to the oarsmen to direct them through the clutter of vessels into the small inner harbor reserved for native citizens. The experienced captain knew how to clear the huge submerged chain that could close the basin to traffic. Once they slicked past the Tower of Flies, Paulinus said, "Soon we will be on land. Your legs will be unsteady at first. Don't worry if you feel the ground under you swaying. It's perfectly normal after a few weeks at sea."

But Jean-Michel was not thinking of his bowed legs or the pitch of the deck. He was fighting a nauseous dread of his father's reprimand. He glanced toward the hold. What would Philippe say if he knew his son had taken passage from a Jew?

Paulinus noted his anxiety. "Ah, yes, your horse. Come then. We must prepare to debark. We will go straightaway through the customs house and seek lodging with Hughes. Do not worry about that. He will not refuse his wife's cousin or the son of one of his nobles."

At the docks, flotillas of lighters unloaded merchandise from the larger galleys anchored in the outer bay. The Italians unloaded goods, bound for their own warehouses in their own fortified, self-governing communes, at their own quays. Avram's pier teemed with ragged men, their faces like well-tanned leather. They jostled each other at the gangplank, waving their arms and calling out in a cacophony of languages.

"Carry your bags, messire! *Mein herr*!"

"Porters! Wagons!"

"Take you to the inn! Which quarter?"

"Stables for horses!"

"Guides who speak French! Provencal! Farsi!"

"Beautiful women! Good prices!"

"Camels!"

Acre, a penal colony, crawled with felons aiming to swindle gullible pilgrims. Bobo beat them all away from the horses, his fiery face communicating more than the forceful command he could not utter. Paulinus and Jean-Michel hired three of the least dangerous-looking porters. Renard, having said his farewells to Avram, joined them and waved away the other job seekers, who left shaking their fists and muttering insults.

"May you choke on pig meat!"

"May a thousand fleas find refuge in your armpits!"

"May scorpions make nests in your boots!"

The party entered the customs house, a colonnaded yard spacious enough for winding caravans. In the Chain Court, named for the barrier across the harbor's inner basin, the noise of travelers and the smell of livestock overwhelmed Jean-Michel. Without the cooling breeze of the sea, the heat was oppressive; he dragged himself to the first station.

Seated on carpets, the clerks inspected baggage and levied duties. All Christian, all fluent in Arabic, the men clicked beads on abacuses and dipped their heron quills in ebony inkstands to register imports. Ivory and silks. Aloe, camphor, ammoniac, tumeric, and other medicines. Ginger, pepper, nutmeg, cloves, and cardamon were used for currency when the exchange of coinage could not be calculated on the scales. Everything was entered in the ledgers in strange wormy letters. Polite and thorough, the clerks searched all luggage—especially of those who were not merchants—checking for smugglers. The efficient agent who cleared Paulinus said he knew of Hughes.

"Who does not know of Hughes of Ptolemais?" the clerk said in hushed tones. "It is a wonder that you did not land at one of his piers like most pilgrims do, and pay the storage and transfer fees required to move your goods here."

It was Hughes duVal, to be sure. In Acre he was engaged in a far more profitable venture than raiding villein villages could ever be. The agent whispered discrete directions to Hughes' residence in the Venetian sector at the foot of Mount Joy.

Paulinus dismissed the porters and instructed workers to load the horses. He watched them to be sure they did not walk off with more than their pay. For an exorbitant price, the travelers refilled their canteens at a cistern. Jean-Michel poured the fresh water down his throat and neck. After the filmy green water on the ship, it tasted like new wine.

The city smelled fouler than the harbor. The vaulted streets stank of stale urine and swill. Rats skittered in the broad daylight, and mangy dogs roamed everywhere. Vendors sitting on their rugs lined the alleys, shouting out their bargains—wrinkled oranges, pastries in cloying syrup, clumps of figs, pilgrim palms. Beggars displayed their infirmities to their best advantage and clawed at passersby, begging for handouts. Scruffy, irascible camels, the oddest and orneriest creatures Jean-Michel had ever seen, shuffled through the rubbish and shouldered the newcomers against the walls. Herders bleated curses and whipped the miserable animals into line. People of every color loitered in the doorways, arches, and corners, shouting at the tops of their lungs at each other. Some talked of trade, some argued politics, and some were threatening fisticuffs.

"Just like in Constantinople," Paulinus called above the din. "A few people of every tribe and tongue. Look, pilgrim—there is a black man, an Ethiop, likely descended from the treasurer that Saint Philip converted. There is a Greek woman. Do you see the ringlets in her hair? The man beside her is probably a Persian. Acre is full of odd couples. But you will never see a Jew and an Arab together. The women who walk about in tents are Muslim, but not all veiled women are Muslim. Many are Christians who cover their faces to protect their delicate skin from the sun. But these," Paulinus indicated the women they were passing, "are probably wives to that man in the white turban. And did you just hear those men talking? They are Maronites and Jacobites, arguing about whether Christ is of *one* substance with the Father or of *like* substance as the Father."

Jean-Michel could not tell the difference in theologies any more than he could distinguish Armenians from Syrians. In the babel of languages he did not hear the war horses cantering carelessly through the crowd. Bobo pulled him aside just as the riders, with a chink of mail and creak of leather, hustled by, without warning or apology. The blood-red crosses on their dove-white surcoats identified them as Knights of the Temple. The lead rider cleared a path with bursts of Arabic curses. Jean-Michel marvelled at his knowledge of the infidel speech. *How demeaning*, he thought, *to have to speak like a man swallowing his own tongue.*

The irritating sound rang in his ears. He began to feel vulnerable, sensing that he was a member of the minority among the crowd's exotic complexions.

A piercing wail cleaved the air like a call to attack. Jean-Michel braced himself. Dozens of dark men suddenly dropped their business, kicked open little mats, and lined up in snaking rows, their faces, then their backends, uplifted in prayer. The torrent of words, a continuous, deafening roar, rushed through the streets like water in an aqueduct. The few Europeans stood like Jean-Michel on the banks of this awesome river of devotion, listening to it pass. In time the mats were rolled up. The men became vertical again and business resumed. Across the alley, two squat men wrapped in tawny skins watched Jean-Michel through almond eyes. They had not bowed to the call of the *muezzin*, either.

"Mongols," Paulinus explained.

Could it be? The demon-begotten bogeymen Jean-Michel had been taught to fear in childhood? The mongols tore at some *shish-kabob* purchased from a street grill.

"Probably one of their own companions," Renard said, "sold to the vendor in return for a small portion."

This grisly thought made Jean-Michel's stomach gnaw with a renewed fear, that within moments he would be knocking unannounced and unexpected at Hughes' door.

The Hill of Montjoie rose to his left. A Genoese possession except for its highest spur, it was occupied by the ancient monastery of Saint Sabas. The other obvious landmark was the open Venetian market, decorated gaily with shade-producing canopies for an autumn harvest festival. Pools and baths abounded. Since Muslims had a religious duty to wash four times a day, a practice advisable in such a hot country, the pools were fed by conduits of running water. The square was paved with mosaics of colored stones. Jean-Michel checked the surrounding houses for Hughes' residence. The stately homes showed signs of mercantile prosperity. Glass windows glinted from frames of imported wood. Gardens and citrus trees decorated the terraced roofs.

"There, as the clerk said." Paulinus strode toward a house with a pink marble portico.

A dignified Arab with a pointed beard and dressed in a flowing garment answered his knock.

"Peace upon you, and welcome," the man said in refined French, guessing their language.

"And peace upon this house," Paulinus replied.

"May Allah grant you strength."

"God's strength is ours, as is His blessing, which we give to you."

"This unworthy servant wishes it may multiply to your account and be added to my Master's kindness."

How long will this flattery go on? Jean-Michel wondered. When would Paulinus get around to asking this infidel of Hughes' whereabouts? After more bowing, Paulinus gave their names and made his request.

"My master, the Sheikh Hughes, is occupied with market business for the day," the servant said. "But he will surely welcome you graciously to his humble feast tonight with his other guests." He leaned out to count their horses and snapped his fingers. A line of young Saracens filed behind him. "These obedient servants are at your bidding and will afford you and your animals every convenience. I will be your personal servant. My poor name is Ahmed; may you not speak it with much loathing."

Renard readily agreed to Ahmed's suggestion of a rosewater bath and an oil massage before dining. Jean-Michel declined such unhealthy indignities, not wishing to be kneaded by hands that lifted in prayer to a false god. And he did not dare meet his father smelling like an effeminate Saracen prince. Philippe might even object to the Muslim-like beard that had grown on Jean-Michel's face. However, since it made him resemble a Templar, the association might do him some good. His brothers had always admired the Templars. Perhaps they would admire him, too. Or would they simply laugh at him for trying to impersonate a warrior monk?

He caught himself twisting his beard and wandering in thought. He returned to prayer. He faced Jerusalem and tried to feel the warmth of its radiance on his cheeks. But he felt only the coolness of the descending desert evening.

"I thought it would feel different to pray here," he confessed to Paulinus. "I find it is harder."

"Perhaps that is because you are thinking more of your father on earth than your Father in heaven."

"We do not even know if my father lives in these quarters. Will my heart be hard and my prayers cold until I see him?"

"No. Only until you forgive him." Paulinus rose from his knees. "And if he does not accept your forgiveness, then as Miletus the Anchorite says, 'True forgiveness is the fragrance the violet sheds on the heel that has crushed it.'"

Renard appeared at the door behind Ahmed. The jongleur's skin glowed pink like that of a newborn piglet. "They scoured and rubbed until the soot crawled out of my pores like thin gray eels," Renard reported with great satisfaction. "A pity you did not try it."

Jean-Michel turned his nose away at the odor of musk, and wondered why, if the Arabs were so fastidious about personal cleanliness, they lived in such a fetid city.

On the way to the banquet hall, Paulinus cautioned Jean-Michel in a low voice. "There will be common bowls," he said. "Use only the thumb and first two fingers of your right hand to serve yourself and to eat. The left hand is nasty. It is reserved by the Arabs for cleaning yourself. Chew slowly. Avoid looking into the eyes of other diners. It is insulting to them and makes them lose their appetite . . ."

Jean-Michel nodded but paid scant attention to this advice on Arab etiquette. Why should he act like a Saracen in a French baron's hall? In a moment he would be face to face with his father's *suzerain*, and possibly Philippe himself, who would never approve of such behavior. Crossing the courtyard gardens, walking through the scent of lemon trees, Jean-Michel prepared himself mentally, as he would before a joust. He steeled his nerve. He set his jaw and narrowed his eyes like eye openings in a helmet. He braced his heart for the blow he would take from his father, who would undoubtedly censure him for making such a foolhardy journey with such unmanly companions as a priest and a harper.

He rinsed his hands in the fountain, shook them dry, and crossed himself as he entered the dining hall. His feet padded on the tesselated floor, on which each tile, freshly oiled and feeling more like carpet than rock, abutted neatly against its neighbor. His sight adjusted to the lambent glow from the silver candlesticks. The flickering tapers animated the enameled miniatures of Persia and tapestries of Byzantium on the walls. Such luxuries even His Most Christian Majesty would not think of having for himself; such riches were only sung about in poems such as the *Pilgrimage of Charles Le Magne*, which still seemed to echo Hughes' drafty hall in France.

"So it *is* you," a voice bellowed like a bull's snort. Hughes was enthroned on floorcushions placed around a gold-threaded linen cloth. Clad in a cascading burnoose and corded headdress, he presided over a spread of platters like a caliph. His braided beard, dyed with henna, had the hue of a Judean sunset. Around him sat three nut-colored men wearing silks and looking like the Magi themselves.

"Sit you down, let me look at you," the squint-eyed Hughes beckoned with a bone. "By my beard, you do look like your father. Come now, refresh yourself." Hughes invited him to sit. Swaying his sausage-fingered hand, he pointed out the food. "Lamb and honeyed lentils here. Roast camel calf there, stuffed with goose, stuffed with raisins and pistachio. Better than the venison in France, you'll see, and of course, there is no pork to be had at all in the East because of our friends, the Arabs." Hughes crafty eyes noted Jean-Michel's hesitation. "Do not look so suspicious, Jean-Michel. You are like all newcomers to Outremer. You must learn that there are good Arabs and bad. The bad ones, such as the Mameluks, are engaged in a *jihad*, a holy war, to exterminate the Christians. The good ones, such as these," he said, gesturing to his guests, "profit too much from the feuding to take sides."

He introduced his business associates, their names sounding to Jean-Michel as if Hughes had food caught in his throat. The baron speared a hunk of meat on a curved Saracen knife and, in the Arab manner, shoveled lentils onto his plate with his right hand. "And who are these companions of yours?" he asked.

Jean-Michel found his voice and squeezed it up like water through a dry well. "Messire Hughes," he croaked, "this is Father Paulinus, a guide and interpreter from Constantinople. And Renard, a singer of songs and cousin to your wife, the Lady Blanche." When he said her name, he felt his face warming. Perhaps it was only the hanging oil lamps. He seated himself with the others.

"Ah, yes, Blanche," Hughes said, spitting out a date pit. "Do I take it that a cousin of my wife and a monk trained in audits have come under your escort to bring me the accounts of my fiefs?"

"No, messire," Jean-Michel said.

Hughes raised an eyebrow. "But of course," he said, apologetic. "You came to see your father. But I cannot help you." He paused.

"Philippe is dead."

Over a confection of sweetened pomegranate pulp, Hughes described the accident at the North Wall that had crushed Philippe d'Anjou. Jean-Michel listened but seemed unable to fully comprehend the details. He obviously had no appetite for food.

Why has he come here? Hughes wondered. His stomach had soured, and he knew it was not the spices. He belched, and out of courtesy, his Arab guests followed suit.

With a bitter taste in his mouth, Hughes explained the king was due to review the repairs, just as he had inspected the other Frankish fortifications. A rumor had persisted that he would be retiring from Acre within the year, and that he wished to leave the city secure. Hughes himself had negotiated with the Genoese and the Hospitalers to provide ships for the royal departure. The Italians are stubborn and expensive, he explained. They are worse than Byzantines. He had yet to get the price down to the king's liking and still make a good profit.

And who is this nosy friar from Constantinople? Hughes wondered. *An investigator for DeBeauvais? Did they catch Gascon and not tell me?*

"The king never quite overcame the dysentery that plagued him in Egypt," Hughes continued. "His Majesty took ill—again—and appointed others to visit the walls in his stead. He chose Philippe because he had stayed in Outremer this whole time at the king's side, instead of not running back to France, like most of the nobles had been and even the king's own brothers, Alphonse and Charles."

Hughes studied Renard with distaste. *Did Blanche send her cousin to spy on me and see if I am ever going back to France?*

"The reason Philippe stayed so long," Hughes went on, "was not because of loyalty to the crown, as the king supposed. *Mais non.* Philippe kept trying to get his sons to return to Anjou with him and take up their proper duties in the estates, but they have found life in the East to their liking. The king learned of Philippe's disappointment and asked him to carry his banner before he departed; he knows it can be hard with sons—a son was born to him during the war in Egypt, you know. And when Philippe passed the site, somehow the scaffolding collapsed, and . . ."

He paused. "Some say it was a spoiled attempt on the king's life, perhaps even by the *Mulahidet*, the misguided ones."

The Arab merchants gasped and muttered among themselves.

"Who are these misguided ones?" Paulinus asked.

Hughes calmed his Arab guests in stuttering Farsi, then turned to the monk. "You may have heard them called Assassins, or *hashishiyim*; they kill for the Old Man of the Mountain. Which mountain? No one is sure. He has always been called by that name, as his successors will be. The Muslims consider the Assassins to be loathsome heretics, greatly to be feared. When the Old Man commands a follower to kill, the follower obeys. If the killer fails and is killed, another comes, then another, until the deed is done. They have no fear of death; they even desire it."

"How can this be?" Paulinus asked.

Hughes leaned toward one of the merchants. The Arab tapped his lips on a napkin and spoke excitedly in rough trade French. Whether from nervousness or eagerness, it was hard to tell.

"To understand these things," the merchant began, "O men of the book, you must know of the greatest of books, the Glorious *Qur'an.* The Prophet, blessing and peace upon his name, promises to every man of faith that if he is just and devout, then once in his life he may enjoy the Night of the Garden, a night of miracles, in which he will receive a foretaste of Paradise." The merchant's eyes gleamed as if in a dream. "It is a night filled with every delight—the best foods and the most beautiful women."

Hughes grinned lasciviously. "That is a heaven I can believe in."

"O, believe this, *effendi:* The Old Man can give this Night of the Garden to whom he wills. In secret, he gives a most faithful young follower a powerful opiate in a drink, and he swoons. Later he awakens in the most blissful garden at the Old Man's castle. There, comely and compliant ladies serve him fruits and forbidden wines. When he falls into a swoon again from pleasure, he is carried off to his former room and life, and promised that if he is killed in obedience to his master, the garden he has known in his dream will be his forever. Thus the followers kill without question and with great zeal."

"Misguided, indeed," Paulinus said.

"I recall a story," Renard said, "that two of these assassins slipped into France years ago to kill King Louis when he was yet a boy."

"That is only a rumor," Hughes said, "but this is the truth: while king in Acre, Louis has made a pact of peace with the current Old Man, the Shiekh al-Jubal. So it is not likely that one of the sheikh's martyrs made an attempt at the wall on the king's life at the direction of the shiekh."

Attention turned to Jean-Michel, who was sitting in grave silence. He drew a short breath. "I want the body."

Hughes leaned back on his cushions. "You would have to get the permission of your brothers and then claim it from the king himself," he said.

"Then you will arrange it?" Jean-Michel asked.

Hughes shifted in discomfort. The pulp dessert turned pasty in his mouth. "It could take weeks, even months, to be granted an audience with His Majesty. Would it not be a greater honor for your father to be buried in the Holy Land?"

"My father wished to return to France, and he will have his wish," Jean-Michel said resolutely. "If you have indeed been in charge of His Majesty's ships, then he will see you."

Hughes considered his merchant guests, who were studying him intently. He was too close to a profitable deal with them to risk earning their disfavor. Refusing a son's request to honor his father would seriously diminish his standing with the merchants.

Hughes spread his arms in feigned magnanimity. "So be it," he said. "I will bring you to the royal court."

17

With the king weakened, Yolande guided the knight into the best position for attack. Not even the queen, standing nearby grasping her hunting horn, could prevent the inevitable. Yolande withdrew her hand from the chess piece and smiled with satisfaction. "The king is in jeopardy," she answered.

"Don't say that," Queen Marguerite replied, studying the array of whalebone warriors. "Not while he is away in Saida, and subject to ambush by Saracens." She checked her speech and blushed a little, accenting the rose cosmetic Yolande had applied to her pale cheeks. Marguerite meant to cast no aspersion on Yolande's mixed parentage; she had merely forgotten for a moment that her chief perfumer and advisor on Eastern matters might be considered part Saracen.

Yolande pretended not to notice. "If you move the warder two spaces to the right, you will protect your king," she said. She noticed that her hand was nearer the color of the inlaid acacia wood of the board than the ivory of the chessmen.

The French ladies-in-waiting cupped their creamy hands and whispered to one another. Yolande wanted to believe they envied her skill and were commenting on the cleverness of her move. But she knew they were criticizing her. She was a *poulain*, a blend of two cultures, and she knew there was nothing she could do to win the acceptance of the milky maidens. They would not invite her into their elite circle.

"My dear, is there anything you don't know?" Marguerite asked. "You play chess. You hunt gazelle, read the sky, and mix lotions for our faces that dry so quickly in this awful heat."

Yolande bowed demurely. She knew these snowy-skinned intruders did not belong in the land of her birth. She also knew logarithms that went far beyond Frankish finger-counting, philosophers whose names these women could not even hope to pronounce, and poetry that made their singers sound like braying donkeys. "I cannot embroider as you do," she said. "In sewing gold and silver thread, you set an example for all women with the needle as the king sets with his sword."

The queen brightened, but without the acquired refinement of replying with a similar compliment she was silent. It was a custom of the East that escaped the crude women of the Continent. "Ah, my dear, if only the king would allow me to wear such finery," Marguerite said. "He expects us to disregard all worldly vanities, and has taken to his pilgrim robe again, forsaking his furs and scarlets. So then, must I." She fingered her bangles and neck chains, made of precious metals worked into a delicate lace.

Yolande moved the knight into a deliberately dangerous position, near the queen's bishop. "It is only because he is fighting his fever again that the priests have made him take the sackcloth. He will get better, and then you may wear the silks again."

"That may never be," Margeurite said. "I fear his is a sickness even your herbs cannot cure. He has a sickness of heart over all the nobles still held captive for ransom in Cairo." Absently, Marguerite touched her queen. Yolande pointed to the vulnerable knight. Marguerite made the move and captured the knight, but distracted by concern for her tormented husband, she looked downcast.

Yolande regretted choosing a game that reminded Marguerite of the French debacle in the Egyptian delta. A round of tables might have been a better amusement, although the rectitudinous king disapproved of dice. She had seen him break a backgammon board over his knee, then kick away his brothers' bets like an angry Christ among the moneychangers. He lectured them on the sin of gambling, but Louis was the biggest gambler of all. He had recklessly gambled human lives on a grand scale and lost because of his ignorance of Eastern ways and Eastern lands. It was the same with all the stupid Franks.

"Be of good cheer," Yolande said. "The Seneschal de Champagne will persuade Our Lady of Tortosa to work a miracle for the prisoners."

Recalling the special mission of the king's good friend, Marguerite smiled with hope. Mary had worked a miracle for Louis before at Tortosa, where several of her relics were enshrined. It happened that when a demon-possessed man had beseeched the Holy Mother there for deliverance, the fiend inside him had cried out, "Thou prayest in vain, swine! Our Lady is not here! She is afar in Egypt, to help the King of France and the Christians, who this very day will land and fight on foot against the horsemen of the heathens." The declaration was written down and the date attested to by the papal legate himself. Sure enough, it was the very day Louis landed at Damietta and routed its Muslim defenders.

What message will come from Tortosa this time? Yolande wondered. The *seneschal*, just back from his pilgrimage there, promised to deliver one today.

From her expectant look, Marguerite was having the same thought. She stood up. "Let us make ready for our guests," she said. "Isabel, my mirror. Anne-Marie, my cap and robe. Yolande, my colors, if you please."

The maidens busied themselves in meeting the queen's requests. Yolande, testing the camel-hair brushes with her umber thumb, fetched the cosmetics case and palette. Louis disliked his queen in a painted face. He called it a prideful distortion of God's image. But when he was away, the young queen found pleasure in eyeliners, lip balms, perfumes, and rouges.

Yolande stirred an aromatic rose powder and delicately stroked it onto Marguerite's cheeks. When the queen lifted the looking glass and angled, Yolande saw her own reflection. Her cinammon skin and onyx hair contrasted with the queen's lightly freckled fairness. Yolande firmed her subtle mouth. Was she not proud to be the daughter of a baron of Edessa and a Syrian princess? Did she not personify the ideal of East and West, of Latin and Levant?

The French women admired her artistry, but at a distance. They waited for her to move away before affixing the queen's fluted cap and fastening her collar with a brooch of Damascene silver. Her back turned, Yolande put away her paints. She was shunned again. Her *Saracen* knuckle wiped away a tear and her *infidel* fist nearly snapped a brush in two. She thought how easily she, a half-breed, could crystallize the arsenic in the hair dye for other purposes. Her tutor, an Arab physician, had shown her that, too.

"Visitor in the antechamber, Ma Dame," a servant announced.

Yolande subdued her resentment the way Nazim curbed his passion for her—a tense spring of nerve and muscle under control like a flare-hooded cobra hypnotizing his prey.

Marguerite tugged her muslin veil straight. "Admit him," she ordered.

A knight entered. He bore a package wrapped in white linen. Standing at attention, he said: "A gift, from my Lord Jean de Joinville, purchased in Tortosa."

When the queen saw it, she knelt in reverence.

The knight knelt also, presenting the gift. "Rise up, my good knight, it is not seemly for you to kneel when you are the bearer of relics," Marguerite said.

"Ma Dame," the knight replied, "these are not relics, but pieces of camlet cloth."

The queen and her ladies began to laugh. "Tell your lord Jean that I wish him the worst of luck," Marguerite said in jest, "because he has made me kneel before his camlet." Giggling, she rose from her genuflection, and motioned for the maidens to unwrap the cloth. There were four pieces in different colors.

"Tell me, sire knight," Marguerite said while admiring the purple, "did your lord receive anything else from the altar of Our Lady?"

"One hundred pieces of camlet like these," the man said, "by order of His Majesty, to give to the Franciscans when he returns to France."

Marguerite stopped feeling the cloth. This was not the divine message she had expected. It was better. "Then Louis is making firm his plans to return at last. We shall not be much longer overseas in this dismal Acre."

"It is what my Lord Jean also believes, to his great relief," the knight said. "I heard him say it to the prince of Tripoli when we returned through his city and took meat with him. The Prince gave us small relics as tokens of farewell from the Holy Land."

"The *seneschal* never wanted to come east," Marguerite said, thinking aloud.

Nor did Marguerite, Yolande thought silently. In France, the pious king in a delirious fever had vowed to take the Cross if he recovered. When he did, no reasonable argument by his friends or pleading by his wife could deter him from his obsession to liberate the Holy Land and recapture the greatest relic of all—Jerusalem. What else could be expected of a king who had emptied his vast treasury to buy the Crown of Thorns and house this simple plait of rushes in its own cathedral of glass in Paris?

During Yolande's musing, the knight left and Marguerite returned to the chess board in high spirits. "Come and finish the game, Yolande," she invited. "Is my king still in jeopardy?"

Yolande curled her lips into a smile. "No, Ma Dame," she said, anticipating Nazim's joy when hearing that Louis might soon be leaving Outremer, and picturing his bronze arms accepting her in a grateful embrace.

The meeting with the king was delayed, not by Hughes' reluctance, but by news of the Queen Mother's death. Louis returned from Saida prostrate with grief. He spoke to no one for days.

His mother had ruled as regent until he assumed the throne at the proper age. Then she ruled again in his absence. She disapproved of his crusade, but could not publicly oppose it. A popular legend held that the last and greatest successor to Clovis and Charles Le Magne would unite the Romans and the Greeks, convert the Jews, and lay down his sceptre on the Mount of Olives as a sign of surrender of the earthly kingdom to the rule of the returning Christ. Everyone believed her saintly son, Louis, would fulfill the legend.

Nevertheless, she had appealed to him twice by letter to come home. Once she wanted him to resist the saber-rattling of England's King Henry. Another time she felt she needed him to suppress a "crusade" of shepherds gone awry and rampaging under an ambitious Hungarian madman. But Louis had stayed in Acre. He was convinced of his duty to fortify the remains of the kingdom of Jerusalem and to regain its lost capital, where the Holy Sepulchre lay.

So Louis did not hasten to his mother's funeral. There were other burials to be conducted. The heads of the crusaders killed at La Forbie, which had become trophies on the walls of Cairo, were taken down, put in boxes, and shipped to Acre for Christian interment. Louis dug the graves with his own hands and refused to hold his nose against the smell.

At the same time, Louis arranged for many fine services in his mother's memory, at which various patriarchs concelebrated. He addressed letters to all the churches in France, asking them to pray for her soul. Gradually, at the urging of his wife, he resumed his schedule of appointments.

"No doubt Marguerite is glad her mother-in-law is gone," Hughes told Jean-Michel while the men traversed the tangled streets on their way to the castle. The baron loosened his white-fur-lined cloak, which proclaimed his rank but made his corpulent body sweat all the more. "The Queen Mother hated Marguerite for taking her son away. She kept the two of them apart day and night, if she could work it out. Here in Acre, they could meet as they wished. But in France they could only see each other at the manor of Pontoise. Their bedrooms had a secret staircase between them. Whenever the Queen Mother approached, a lookout rapped in code on the door. Then one or the other could quickly escape and be found alone. Everyone in France knew about this ruse except the Queen Mother." He guffawed, but being out of breath, fell into a fit of coughing.

Hughes was wheezing by the time they reached the forecourt of the castle, a fortress as somber as its chief occupant. Paulinus noted the knights of various orders lounging about, some throwing dice, others quarreling, still others obviously drunk even though it was still early in the day. None seemed eager or alert enough to engage in a sortie against the Saracens. The drowsy knights at the main door eyed the priest and knight with indifference, but frowned at the sight of a jongleur, for Louis forbade pagan poetry in his hall. When Hughes announced his appointment with the king, the guards said nothing, but jerked their hairy chins to indicate that the men should enter.

Inside, Hughes explained his business to one squire and servant after another, until finally a nervous friar with fidgety hands ushered the group into a vaulted room hung with battle flags and the oriflamme banner of Saint Denis. Beneath this flame-shaped pennant, the king administered justice from a plain wooden chair raised on a dais.

Louis of Poissy was a slight man with stooped shoulders, burdened by the cares of all Christendom. His gaunt face, fully whiskered, emanated a gentle grace. He wore no crown over his fair bobbed hair. Dressed in the undyed wool habit of a pilgrim, he looked more like a monk than a monarch.

A barefoot supplicant clad in penitential white and on his knees before the king, offered his sword to the king and held out his wrist so that his hand could be cut off.

Louis raised the sword and swung it around. Then he returned the weapon hilt first, forgiving the knight. "How can I not forgive you in this small matter, since Christ my King has forgiven me all my debt?" Louis said.

Most onlookers whispered in admiration, though a few stone-faced soldiers bit their lips. The bushy-bearded Templars, accustomed to harshness, shook their heads and tucked their thumbs into their broad sword belts, as if to prevent themselves from carrying out the sentence. The Knights of the Teutonic Order grinned happily and chattered in German. One of their own had been exonerated. Perhaps the king recognized the order's right to issue its own indulgences, or had taken into account the knight's severe self-flagellation, evidenced by the crisscrossing stains on his tunic.

Jean-Michel scanned the crowd to find his brothers, but he did not spot them. In turning, he noticed a peculiar smell, like rancid meat. He wondered if infectious lepers milled about, seeking to have the king invite them to his dinner table, as he was reputed to do.

The friar saw Jean-Michel sniffing. "I am most sorry," the jittery man said. "His Majesty earlier received an embassy of the Tartars, whose stench even the mint in the floor rushes cannot hide."

"That explains it," Paulinus said. "We marveled to see Mongols in the city."

"His Majesty hoped to enlist their alliance against our common enemy, Islam," the friar said from behind his gnarly knuckles. "And he wished to give them preachers to convert them to the Holy Faith. But today they asked only for tribute to be sent annually to their khan, who has no interest in foreign religions. Another disaster."

Jean-Michel wondered if this friar of the Order of Preachers was not more relieved than disappointed, since he no longer faced the prospect of being sent to Far Tartary. But Louis' dream of recruiting the Tartar's fearsome hordes had clearly evaporated. "Then we have come on a bad day," said the knight.

"Take heart," the friar said. "Since so many knights have left Acre in disillusion and disgust, the king will rejoice to see a French knight arriving. Ah, come this way. He is ready to see you."

Jean-Michel marched to the dais, his stomach somersaulting and his head spinning from self-consciousness. Paulinus granted a blessing, Renard gave a courtly bow, and Jean-Michel dropped to one knee. Hughes introduced them.

"Rise up, sire knight," Louis said, "for today we are not king and vassal, but two sons who have lost their parents."

"Majesty, I mourn with all of France for the loss of the Queen Mother."

The king smiled acceptingly. "It is well for us that we always have the Mother of God to watch over us. I have asked Her to look with favor upon both my mother and your father, because they labored to teach their sons how to honor Her and love Our Savior." Louis acknowledged Jean-Michel's companions but seemed to look past them. "Philippe had two other sons, did he not?"

"Yes, Majesty. I thought to meet them here."

"We are here." Two men emerged from the cluster of armoured knights. Behind the stiff whiskers, Jean-Michel recognized Guillaume and Roger. Both had aged a great deal. Their faces were battle-worn and browned by the sun and their skeptical eyes looked as hard as polished stones.

Roger spoke first. "You came by sea? A wonder you survived."

"You were told to stay home." Guillaume said, sounding like Philippe and using the same derogatory squint. "Why have you come here?"

Jean-Michel, hurt that they would not accept him as a brother even in grief, replied evenly, "I came to honor our father's wish to return to his own land."

"Is this your request also?" the king asked Guillaume.

The elder brother glowered, angry and vengeful. "It is true that our father asked us to return with him to our fields in Anjou. And you may take him there if it pleases you, Jean-Michel. As for us, we will remain, and avenge his death tenfold among the infidels who caused it."

"Our request is that you send us to Ramleh, Majesty," Roger said, his fists clenched tightly. "We are not afraid to punish the Saracens encamped there, and remind them that the men of Acre are not weak-stomached."

Jean-Michel felt like he'd been jabbed in the belly. "Still, you do not object to returning the body?" he asked.

"We do not," Guillaume gruffed. "We object to cowardice."

"Then let it be," Louis said. "The Lord says, 'vengeance is Mine,' but even David the King says, 'Let me smite them that hate Thee.' I will enjoin the Marshal of the Hospital to provide you with passage to his garrison at Ramleh."

Concerning the other request, Louis consulted an elderly cleric wearing a red skullcap and samite cope. As the king listened, he stroked his beard, an Arab sign of solemnity. Then he issued his judgment. "Since the legate does not object, I will instruct the canon of Saint Denis to transfer the remains to you. And when you have a Mass chanted for Philippe in your home cathedral, remember my mother."

"I would gladly fulfill your request, gracious Majesty. But I cannot. The cathedral of Notre

Dame d'Auxonne was destroyed by fire, and all its relics with it. I have come overseas to find a relic so that we may consecrate a new church."

Hughes gasped in astonishment, his fat eyes bulging.

The king looked upon Jean-Michel with esteem and empathy. He addressed the assembled clerics and nobles. "Here is a knight worthy of his vows and spurs, who seeks nothing for himself but all for the Holy Church. As Lot could not find ten righteous men in Sodom, which is but three leagues to the east of here, how rare it is to find a righteous man in this city, where a stone thrown in any direction is sure to strike a brothel."

Roger and Guillaume laughed, but stopped themselves when they saw the king's stern expression. He had not meant what he said as a joke.

Louis' silent rebuke gave way to wonder, for the mention of relics had stirred his imagination and zeal. "The Feast of the Annunciation is nigh," he said. "Should I not pray for my mother's soul in the very place where Our Lady learned she was to be the Mother of God? And what would be more honoring to Her than to find a relic there in Nazareth to restore Her church in Auxonne?"

A Templar, the skin of his face seamed with scars and as tough as saddle leather, stepped forward. "It is not prudent for His Majesty to venture outside the city walls at this time."

"Does the Master of the Temple fear danger?" the king asked.

The armored knight scowled as if stung. The warrior monks boasted of their reputation as ruthless men who feared nothing. "As guardians of the pilgrim routes, we are concerned only for your safety . . ."

"What better time than this, while we have a treaty with Damascus?" Louis answered. "The sultan promised safe conduct to Jerusalem itself, if I wish to see it, but I have resolved not to look upon the Holy City until I take it for Christendom. Even Richard Coeur-de-Lion put his tunic over his eyes when he was within sight of Mount Zion, and cried to Our Savior, 'I pray Thee to suffer me not to see the Holy City since I cannot deliver it from the hand of Thine enemies.' O Jerusalem, Jerusalem."

The king's eyes glazed over, as if beholding a heavenly vision. The room hushed awkwardly while the priests closed rank around the throne, mumbling *Ave's.* Minutes passed before Louis's azure eyes cleared, the way fog lifts from the sea. He spoke as if nothing had happened. "And the Old Man of the Mountain is appeased for now. Thus may we proceed to the holy places without looking under every rock for one of his foul Assassins."

Nazim's slap knocked Yolande against the wall.

"You lied to me!" he snarled. "I am shamed because of you!"

He raised his hand again and Yolande flinched, her eye puffy and tear-filled. "I tell you all that I hear . . ."

"You tell me nothing!"

The next blow split her lip, and Yolande tasted her own blood. She slid down into a crouch. "I heard too late that the king took ill," she sobbed. "I could not warn you . . ."

Nazim dragged her up by the shoulder and pressed his iron face against hers. "Perhaps you warned the king that I was waiting for him at the wall."

"Never, my lion." She lifted a trembling finger to stroke his rough cheek. He swatted her hand away and released her. She slumped, wounded to think he now distrusted her. How could he believe she would ever betray him and lose his love? "I . . . I am sorry . . . ."

"There is no forgiveness for liars," Nazim said, pacing like a caged predator.

"I told you the truth as I knew it, and I tell you the truth now. The king is leaving Acre."

Nazim froze, the way great cats do at the scent of a gazelle. He was listening, giving her another chance.

Yolande wiped her mouth and summoned her dignity. "The son of one of the barons you slew has come from France. He has persuaded the king to leave Acre with him for a pilgrimage of prayer in the Church of the Annunciation in Nazareth."

"When will this be?"

"At the new moon, on the Feast of the Angel's Visit to Mary. The king will hold vigil in the grotto chapel for two days. He will be alone."

Nazim spun, his eyes blazing with disbelief. Yolande shut her eyes and tensed, ready to take another blow, but it did not come.

"Two days?" Nazim said, incredulous.

"Yes, my lion." When she opened her eyes, she saw Nazim's face soften. His burning fury had been transformed into radiance.

"Alone?"

"Yes. Fasting and in a hair shirt, to pray for his mother. His physicians are begging him not to go, but he is adamant." Yolande could see Nazim's nimble mind at work, considering possibilities.

She stood up straighter. She was winning him back, and she felt needed again. "Of course, the king will travel in a company of men at arms, knights of the Temple, attendants, and the newcomer."

"Tell me of him."

She knew little, but spoke with confidence. "He is a knight of some standing, since he can influence the king to leave the city when all his advisors oppose it. He journeys with his own scribe and poet. He is a trader in relics." A growl of disapproval rumbled in Nazim's throat. Yolande switched the subject.

"This knight appeared in court with Hughes of Ptolemais, who is charged with the task of preparing the king's passage back to France. It may well be that the king wishes to see the holy sites before he leaves Acre for good."

"It may be," Nazim said, pondering.

"He is sorely disappointed that the Great Khan refuses to ally with him." Yolande described the failed Mongol mission, hesitating when she saw the hatred flashing in Nazim's eyes. "Without gaining the help of the Mongols, Louis is without hope."

"He still must be punished for the attempt."

Nazim padded to Yolande and brushed back the tousled strands of hair from her face. Yolande submitted to his touch and to the delicious thrill of his claw-like fingers combing her sable mane, his exquisite power infusing her quivering limbs. His thumb circled her ear and found the pulse in her neck. She felt it throb from desire. Her breathing matched its rhythm. She knew he enjoyed her unveiled beauty and savored her forbidden body. Her yearnings had not been numbed by the childhood circumcision that mutilated Muslim women to diminish their responses and ensure their chastity. She alone could please him in a way that matched his energy and ferocity.

But Nazim stepped back, his eyes closed in meditation. Yolande realized he would have taken her, except that he exalted her womanhood. With a restraint more muscular than his passions he was pledging himself to remain pure until he fulfilled his vow.

Enraptured, Yolande listened to him pray the Surah used before battle:

> Had Allah willed, He could Himself have punished the unbelievers.
> But He has ordained it thus that He might test you.
> For those who are slain in the cause of Allah,
> He will not allow their works to perish.
> He will admit them to the Garden He has made known to them.

18

"A safe-conduct is no guarantee against bandits, horse thieves, or treachery," the Templars said.

The travelers dressed in full armor.

Over his usual breeches and tunic, Jean-Michel strapped on a padded vest made of thick folds of linen stuffed with cotton wadding soaked in vinegar. "That will take any Saracen arrow," Hughes assured him. Over the vest went his flexible mail hauberk. Then he tied on borrowed *cuisses*, quilted leggings, and attached iron shoes with long tongues to protect his shins. Over all of it he pulled his crested surcoat. "Take this gauze for your helmet," Hughes advised. "Wrap it around in a turban, like this. You will be surprised how hot steel can get in the sun."

King Louis, in a plain pilgrim habit and cotton sun veil, processed to the Church of Saint Denis for commissioning prayers. The knights dismounted and stacked their iron-studded shields by the entrance before making their way to the dark chapels, where they knelt and received a blessing. The priests intoned a psalm in Greek and Latin:

> Happy the men whose refuge is in Thee,
> Whose hearts are set on the pilgrim ways.
> As they pass through the thirsty valley
> They find water from a spring,
> And the Lord provides even men who lose their way
> With pools to quench their thirst.

After crossing themselves, the knights returned to their horses. They assisted Queen Marguerite and her attendants into their saddles.

Louis, on foot, led them into the wilderness.

Nazareth lay a mere sixteen English miles south of Acre. It was accessible only by a single trail through a swamp fed by the *wadis*. These natural runoff riverbeds, dry for most of the year, bloated and overflowed in the late rainy season. Once again, as in Egypt, Louis had called for a pilgrimage during the flood period.

An experienced Templar took command in the swamps. The thin file of pilgrims threaded its way through the marshes with the knights leading their horses on a narrow but solid footpath. Their advance frightened swifts from their nests. Long-plumed egrets and regal herons waded among the tulips, lupine, wild orchid, and priest-in-the-pulpit—a slender olive-green plant whose leaves looked like the Sacred Heart of Jesus and whose striped canopies hooded what looked like a little gray monk.

Paulinus noticed Jean-Michel wilting in the midday heat. He was dragging his feet and barely keeping ahead of Fidelity. His helmet was pushed back on his sweat-soaked hair. His pallid face glistened from the humidity. His arms swayed limply by his sides, and he panted—no, he was praying in short breaths:

> My guilt has overwhelmed me,
> like a burden too heavy to bear,
> I am bowed down and brought very low,
> all day long I go about mourning.
> My heart pounds, my strength fails me;
> even the light has gone from my eyes.

Paulinus recognized the psalm and dropped back to speak to him. "Why is your face cast down?" he quoted. "If you do what is right, will you not be accepted?"

"Father, I have not done what is right, and would make confession now except that the whole line would have to stop for me."

"There is no hurry, my son. I hear from the front that we will camp in Sepphoris, on the other side of these waters. I can hear your confession then, if you wish."

"I only pray that I can reach it."

"If the heat troubles you, didn't you face hotter in the cathedral?"

A wan smile crossed Jean-Michel's parched lips.

"And if it is the waters, you faced deeper on the Great Sea, didn't you?"

"'I am troubled by my sin,'" Jean-Michel recited from the psalm. "It is a mire, like this swamp."

"Don't mistake grief for sin, my son. If you feel anger or failure or guilt because of losing your father before speaking to him, that is not sin at work. It is sorrow. As the Shepherd of Hermas says, 'Grief wears out the Holy Spirit.' If it be of any consolation, it is the same with the king."

"Grieving for his mother?"

"Yes, and for Mother Church. Today I heard him lament: 'If I alone could bear the reproach and adversity of my acts and my sins did not redound upon the universal church, I could endure with equanimity. But woe is me; for by me is all Christendom confused.' It is as Gregory of Alexandria wrote: 'A knight bears his own wounds, but a king bears the wounds of all the knights whom he leads. Thus are the wounds of Christ's soldiers borne by Christ their King, and He alone can bear them away.'"

Though pale and enervated, the knight appeared encouraged. His steps quickened.

"Sing a new psalm, my son," Paulinus said. "'Extol Him who rides over the desert plains, be joyful and exult in Him, Father of the fatherless.'"

Jean-Michel continued reciting, but from his earlier choice:

> Those who seek my life set their traps,
> all day long they plot deception.
> I wait for you, O Lord;
> You will answer, O Lord my God.

At the rear of the train, jouncing on a stout horse, Hughes of Ptolemais searched in vain for snakes. The wet weather had driven them all to higher ground. He could find no adders to slip into Jean-Michel's boots overnight. Hughes mulled over another way to ensure the young knight's failure.

The splashing of storks awakened them early.

Jean-Michel watched the huge birds lope along the grasses, leap into invisible columns of rising air, and rise in broad spirals to the high currents for their migration to Germany and France. With their pink bills thrust forward, their ruddy legs trailing aft, and their white wings outspread, they looked like flying crosses. Louis remarked that they were an omen of a safe and speedy return to Europe. But Renard predicted that many would end up on the dining tables of nobles who preceded them in flight from Palestine.

On firm ground at the far end of the swamps, they marched through countryside rich with green olive groves shimmering in the sunlight. Seeing sparrows flit through the branches, Jean-Michel recalled Jesus' words: "Are not sparrows two a penny? Yet without your Father's leave not one of them can fall to the ground. Are you not more valuable than they?"

Three great mountains ruled the landscape like three great kings. Majestic Mount Hermon, wearing a white crown, presided in the east near domelike Tabor, the Mount of the Transfiguration. From its stately cone long ago, Deborah had directed her general, Barak, to lure the Canaanites into those now-familiar marshes in order to neutralize their chariots. To the west Mount Carmel oversaw the plains of Esdraelon. Jean-Michel thought the clouds above its gentle peak could be the lingering smoke of Elijah's burning altar.

They stopped in Cana for water and worship. They recalled the miracle of the wedding wine and pledged themselves to obey Mary's injunction to do "whatever my Son tells you." Descending the Tiberias Road, they paused at Mary's Well, Nazareth's only natural source of water. The

Greek Orthodox revered the site as the authentic place of the annunciation.

In a proper royal welcome, red poppies carpeted the way through the graceful Galilean hills. Purple thistle and yellow daisy blinked their pollen eyes at the men, and the pilgrims remembered Jesus' words, "and even Solomon in all his splendor was not attired like one of these." Riding the crest of a path between two knolls, the men suddenly beheld the town of Nazareth at their feet. White buildings reflected the sunlight with a blinding intensity that drew the king to his knees in praise. His men left their saddles in genuflection.

"*Nazareth* means 'flower-bearing shoot,'" Paulinus said, shading his eyes. "As Joses the Sainaite wrote, 'It is the stalk on which blossomed, like Aaron's rod, the finest Flower of earth.'"

Sharing the soul-stirring view, two vultures, their huge wings fanned out to cool themselves, rested like angels of death in the nearby cashew trees.

Nazim studied the scorpion.

It had found its way to the surface of the soil because of the rains. Usually nocturnal and preferring tight, hidden places, the creature tucked itself beneath a loose, flat stone near the foot of Nazim's bedroll. It held its powerful forelegs in vigilance, the pincers open and ready. Curled over its crusty back, the five segments of its tail tapered to a pointed, venomed stinger. On the ventral side of the abdomen, comb-like pectens, able to detect the slightest ground vibrations, brushed the dirt. It waited, immobile, patient for prey to come to its lair. If another scorpion came instead, it would fight to the death, the victor devouring the victim.

And thus would Nazim lie in wait for the king.

A quiet town on Friday and Sunday, the Muslim and Christian sabbaths, Nazareth became a frenzy of activity on Saturday.

Arab peasants flocked to market with sheep and produce. Donkeys and dromedaries ferried in barley and oats from surrounding farms. Damson plums, apricots, and late melons sold well in the boisterous *souk*, because of the influx of feast-day pilgrims and now the presence of King Louis.

Nazim scouted the Franciscan compound where the king had taken up residence. At the north end of the walled garden stood the Church of Saint Joseph, a squat Romanesque shrine built over the cave traditionally identified as Joseph's carpenter shop. Linked to it by a colonnaded cloister, the spacious monastery housed dormitories, stables, and hostelry for distinguished visitors. At the southern extremity rose the fortress-like Basilica of the Annunciation. From its square belfry clanged the regular call to hours, which tonight would be Nazim's signal and Louis' death knell.

Nazim knew from Yolande's crude map that the church measured thirty English yards from north to south, and eighty from east to west. It was divided into a nave and two aisles that terminated in apses. There were no ambulatories or radiating chapels, and no transept or choir to speak of. It was a simple rectangular stone vault, heavy and earthquake-resistant. It was a giant mausoleum.

Though her geometry was good, Yolande's information was poor, and the basilica sketch looked as though it had been drawn hastily in fear of discovery. All she had noted about the Sacred Grotto was that it lay in an adjoining courtyard in a garden of cypress and citrus trees. The Franks had not built over this holy place, fearing the weight of a building might crush the network of caverns below. A simple man-made tunnel joined the lower grotto to the crypt beneath the main altar in the basilica. After taking communion there at midnight Matins, the king would descend the double stairway flanking the altar and walk alone through the tunnel to begin his solitary vigil in the Grotto of the Virgin.

A scorpion could not have chosen a better place for a trap.

Bishop DeBeauvais swung his crosier as if it were Moses' rod striking the Nile. "These are the words of the Lord of Hosts: Consider your way of life and build a house acceptable to me!"

"Mayhaps we can use the knight's burnt tunic for a relic," Anseau the canon said, spraying sand from a bucket as though he were sowing seeds.

"You have sown much and reaped little!" DeBeauvais scolded from the pulpit.

"So long as the accounts are in order," Hughes said, sitting atop a pile of rice and lentils, "that is all that matters—not relics and their miracles."

"The money was a miracle," Blanche said. "But it will be a greater miracle if Jean-Michel returns alive."

"Then you *do* love him!" Hughes shouted, mashing the rice with his fist. "He'll hang for this!"

"He will hang, or burn, anyway." Pons Bernard emerged from the sacristy, carrying a blazing torch. "He consorts with heretics."

"I am not a heretic," Renard said, tuning his lute in the nave. "I am a tenor." His music spilled out the pregnant-bellied lute and puddled blood-red on the floor. "And you, messire, are a murderer," he added as he showed Jean-Michel his mother's grave, marked by a stone from the ruined cathedral.

Philippe kicked in the transept doors and burst into the choir. "See what you've done? Can't you do anything right?"

"If you do what is right, will you not be accepted?" Paulinus asked, trimming the sails on the church's mainmast. The church tilted like a ship in the wind.

"Do whatever you like," Guillaume said. A helmet covered his face, but the voice was clearly his. "We're going to Ramleh. We want revenge, and kingdoms of our own."

"I want you, but I am afraid of Hughes," Blanche whispered in Jean-Michel's ear. She handed him her blouse, woven with her own golden hair.

"If you do what is right . . ." Paulinus began.

"Show the Saracens that there are a few men left in Acre who are not weak-stomached," Roger laughed, a sword in his hand.

". . . will you not be accepted?" Paulinus continued.

"You'll never be a real knight!" Philippe shouted. "Who the devil do you think you are fooling?"

"To the devil with you!" Jean-Michel shouted back.

"If you do what is right, will you not be accepted? Not be accepted? Not be accepted? Not accepted?"

"Father!" Jean-Michel cried, bolting upright in bed and sweat pouring down his face. "Father! *Father!*"

"I am here, my son."

Paulinus pressed his palm to Jean-Michel's forehead. "You are feverish."

Jean-Michel's teeth chattered. His arms felt as if the fever had burned off his muscles and only dangling bones remained. His tongue, dry and cracked like old leather, scraped the roof of his mouth.

"It is warm in here, but not that warm," Paulinus said quietly. "You need water, some fresh air, and a cool place to rest."

The bell for Matins rang to begin the Feast of the Annunciation. The few men curled in the straw nearby stretched, brushed their clothes, and shuffled out for the midnight service. Jean-Michel pushed up to his elbows, but Paulinus restrained him. "You are in no condition to attend Mass with us just now," the monk said firmly. "And fasting did not help you when you were so fatigued. It has made you weaker. I will help you to the grotto. The dampness may reduce your fever."

"My sword . . ."

"Leave it. You cannot fight a fever with it."

The robes itched and restricted his range of movement, but Nazim ad-Din did not mind. Once the bell for Matins had atolled, he pulled on the priestly cowl and slid his curved dagger into his belt. The knife, suddenly heavy, seemed to shudder, as if it were self-conscious and aware of what it would do.

From the courtyard garden, Jean-Michel and Paulinus heard the solemn procession tramping over the basilica's stone threshold. It was worn smooth from centuries of pilgrims treading there. Knights and squires, cloaked in frankincense, trailed the long parade, while every monk, friar minor, priest, and prelate on hand, led by the Legate of the Holy See, Odo of Tusculum, chanted the *Ave*.

"With God's grace, the Legate will finish his sermon by sunrise," Paulinus said, half joking. "But I hope to return here sooner to check on you. You must be gone by communion—before the king goes down to the grotto for his retreat." He pushed aside an iron gate. "I feel the cold already. The stairs are steep and wet. Let me help you down."

"I will be fine," Jean-Michel said, then stumbled on the first step.

Gripping Paulinus' elbow, Jean-Michel reached the foot of the staircase carved in the rock. The vestibule, vaulted by a low stone roof, contained two altars, one dedicated to Saint Anne and Saint Joachim and another consecrated to the archangel Gabriel. By the glimmer of the votive candles, Jean-Michel could see enough to avoid bumping his head against the hanging brass lamps and iron chandeliers. His heart thumping and hands trembling, he mustered enough strength and nerve to cross a pointed arcade resting on two twisted columns of marble. Then two steps down and he stood in breathless awe on the site of the greatest miracle and mystery of his faith, where the work of Redemption had begun through the Incarnation of the Son of God.

The singing, distant and surreal, seemed timed to the dripping of water from the rock-hewn walls. Small pools glittered like crystal mirrors at the base of the grotto's red granite columns and white marble altar. Jean-Michel read its engraved message in the light of the suspended lamps:

VERBUM CARO HIC FACTUM EST

"Here the Word was made flesh."

He thought he heard the rocks repeating the angel's holy pronouncement: "Hail, Mary, full of grace, the Lord is with Thee; blessed art Thou among women."

She alone, the new Eve and mother of mankind, eternal woman made beatific and celestial beyond Helen or Guinevere or Iseult, exalted above angels, yet possessing complete and benign understanding of the human heart, would accept him.

Nazim strode into the compound with the dignified gait of a cleric who knew where he was going. Mentally he rehearsed his Latin and Greek, mimicking the pilgrim accents he'd overheard in the market. He was prepared to say, "Peace be with you, my brother." "I have lost my way." "Can you direct me to the hostel?" But there was no one to question him; even the porters were attending the king's splendid service. Likewise the knights and squires, from duty and devotion, had packed the nave—leaving the stables unguarded.

Bobo shifted dreamily in the hayloft. The incense made his nose twitch. Why the knights compelled their groomsmen to accompany them to Matins escaped him. Would there not be a Mass celebrated in the morning for all? The midnight service was to initiate the king's private hair-shirted retreat. What if one of the horses took ill this sultry night? Did the knights expect him to look after them all?

A short whinney and stamp came from below. *Sylvester, hungry again.* Bobo knew that neigh. *Five more hours, you glutton,* he said in his mind.

At the squeak of an opening stall, Bobo blinked his eyes open. In the dark, without even a candle to use because of the hay, Bobo strained to see in the shadows. A hooded figure was leading Sylvester out of his stall toward the garden terrace. It could not be Renard, not in that robe. Was it a priest? Of course not.

Mon Dieu! Bedouin horse thieves. Aware that every knight and his squire was in the church, leaving their fine chargers alone and unprotected, thieves have chosen to strike.

But why take only one horse? Are there more thieves outside? Get help and ask questions later. Renard would not be in the church. Bobo scrambled to his feet. Barefooted he slid down the loft ladder and peered through the doors. Seeing only Sylvester and the thief silhouetted at the basilica's courtyard entry, he raced the other way into the hostel.

"My horse? Sick? No? Stolen! By who? A priest? Someone who *looks* like a priest?"

Renard, fully dressed, dragged himself up, cheap wine sloshing in his head. "Where are they?"

Bobo pointed down emphatically. He circled his arms and made trees with his fingers. *The garden courtyard.* Oh how he wished he could speak.

"The grotto?"

Yes, yes! Bobo nodded.

"They've come to steal relics as well as horses, then," Renard said. "But not on my horse, they won't."

He reached beneath his saddle blanket and yanked out the bronze hunting blade.

From behind a cypress, Nazim watched a monk cross from the grotto gate to the basilica door. He supposed the cleric had lit the candles below for Louis, and was surprised that the monk did not post himself as a sentry on the stairway. The whole courtyard would be sealed after the service. Still, he might reach the horse in time to escape, and they would not discover the royal body for two days unless they smelled it.

Silent as a scorpion, Nazim crept to the craggy rock entry of the grotto.

Jean-Michel felt baptized all over again; the water from the damp ceiling spotted his face like the Virgin Mother's teardrops. Surely she empathized with the full dimension of his father's tragedy—how he had lost his wife, alienated his youngest son, and lost his elder sons to greed and ambition. All he had worked for and fought for would now be forfeited to others eager to gain from his misfortune.

Finally, Jean-Michel forgave. Once he had forgiven, he no longer saw his father as a devil but as a desperate man holding on to what little he had left in this transient world. Jean-Michel's own tears wet the mosaic tiles and mingled with the Holy Mother's. He murmured the words of her Magnificat: "His mercy extends to those who fear Him, from generation to generation."

Someone was praying in the grotto.

Nazim drew his knife.

The king was not due to come until after the communion. Had the plan changed? Or had two monks lighted the candles and only one departed?

The praying figure knelt in a puddle, weeping and shivering with cold. It did not matter who it was. If it was the king, he must be taken. If it was a monk, he must be removed.

Nazim crouched in the archway. He raised the blade. It glinted in the candlelight.

"Jean-Michel!"

Startled, Jean-Michel swivelled about. Bobo stood in the vestibule. His hand was clapped over his mouth and his eyes were large with surprise. Renard leaped down the steps beside him, a sword in his hand.

A hooded man, poised in the archway with a knife frozen in the air, cursed in Arabic. Indecisive for a second, he started toward Jean-Michel.

Renard flung the bronze sword to Jean-Michel. It landed, ringing, on top of the altar and spun to a stop.

Jean-Michel seized it and parried the first blow from the dark stranger. The intruder struck again, and again, his crescent knife screeching as it scraped on the cross-shaped sword. Jean-Michel dodged and landed against the Column of the Angel. The stranger paused, casting a furious glance at Renard and Bobo, as if calculating how to dispose of them.

Jean-Michel struggled up, his thoughts racing. *Bobo shouted. His voice is restored.* He tightened his grip on the sword and glanced at it. Sudden recognition flooded through him. It was the miraculous sword—the sword of St. Martin!

Its strength surging through his arm, Jean-Michel lunged. The stranger slashed, and the blades sang. Jean-Michel forced the stranger up the steps with a flurry of blows, hardly noticing Bobo and Renard scurrying further up the stairs out of harm's way. The man's hood shook off, and beneath it his savage face contorted in rage and contempt. Jean-Michel rammed an iron chandelier into his head, and the man howled. His knife clattered to the tiles. He rushed Jean-Michel, knocking aside the sword. He clutched the knight's beard in his claws and they crashed to the floor together. Jean-Michel heard the sword tumble away. He snatched for it but the strength emptied from his arm as the attacker shoved his face underwater in the drainage gully at the base of the wall.

Jean-Michel panicked. He kicked spasmodically and screamed. The water swamped his submerged mouth. The hand clutching his head shook, releasing the pressure; Jean-Michel twisted his head for a single desperate breath. The powerful hand plunged him down again, then slid to his neck. The man was stretching for his knife. Jean-Michel jerked and bucked, splashing frantically and refusing to faint and drown. The hand jarred free. Jean-Michel heaved up, gasping and coughing up water. He whipped the hair from his eyes.

The killer, armed with the glittering knife, towered above him.

They both heard footfalls. The killer pivoted to face the stairway. He growled and hurled the blade. It whistled into a knight descending the steps. The warrior's sword rattled down to the vestibule, and the lax body thumped after it.

The killer whirled, looking for the sword to finish off Jean-Michel. But its point was at his belly.

Jean-Michel drove it in.

The brass lamps burst into stars, their brilliance burning away the last illusions of the present world. The scent of cypress enveloped Nazim, and the standing water on the tile against his face was transformed into a stream of effervescent wine. The angel voices were dim and the call of his beloved faint in his time of transport, but he embraced their welcoming words.

Ah! Thou soul at peace!
Return unto thy Lord, content in His good pleasure!
Enter thou among my bondmen!
Enter thou My Garden!

19

Blanche looked as if she were dressed for a festival. From beneath her saffron-colored veil, held in place by a golden circlet, two great braids of hair weighted with an extra intertwining of gold thread, fell over her breast. An elegant long-sleeved bliaut of green silk tapered to a train of elaborate flouncing. Her mantle, dyed a royal purple, glittered with good-luck stones: agates for happiness and health and sardonyx for the safe return of a loved one.

Jean-Michel nearly broke his dignified stride when he saw her. He steadied his nerve and pressed the velvet-draped ivory box to his surcoat. In a moment he would present the miraculous sword, now cushioned in his flame-branded tunic, to the baroness and the bishop.

His Excellency DeBeauvais, having been summoned for the occasion, stood beside Blanche. He was as straight and stately as a cathedral belfry. Amazement and skepticism alternated on his face.

Nervously he tapped his pointed vermilion shoes. Next to him Anseau, the sacristan, glowed with expectation. He might have rushed forward to embrace Jean-Michel save for the decorum of the meeting.

Jean-Michel and Bobo passed the courtiers and stewards of the castle who'd been assembled to witness the ceremony. Marcel the bailiff and Gascon the falconer eyed Jean-Michel like vultures hoping for a meal.

Jean-Michel wished for Paulinus' comforting presence to bolster his confidence. But drawing upon the blessed virtue of the relic and the royal authority of the documents Bobo carried, Jean-Michel kept his bearing and did not stumble as he feared he would when he knelt in fealty at Blanche's satin-slippered feet. He gently drew back the reliquary's slipcover and lifted the engraved cover.

DeBeauvais gasped. "It *is* the sword of the holy Saint Martin." He signed the cross, and everyone in the chamber blessed themselves.

Blanche's admiring smile seemed brighter than the galaxies of candles that lit the room. But the stamping of boots behind Jean-Michel dispelled the radiance of her welcome.

Like twin pillars of the prisoner stocks, Marcel and Gascon stood side by side behind Jean-Michel and Bobo, blocking all retreat.

"In the name of Hughes, Master of DuVal, I declare these rogues under arrest," Marcel said.

The blush of Blanche's excitement deepened to an angry red. "How dare you bring a charge so dishonoring to one who returns the holy relic. Stand aside and repent of your jealousy."

"Well it is that the holy relic is returned to its rightful place," Marcel said. "And we are satisfied that it is genuine, given that His Excellency knew it upon sight. Yet what is not genuine is this man's intent in presenting it. Why must we believe, as is the common word of this court, that an angel of the blessed Martin himself transported the sword to the Holy Land just so that this man, out of all men in the world, would find it? This scoundrel seeks to play upon our piety and earnest wishes for his own profit by returning the sword, which he himself stole."

A murmur rumbled through the audience.

Jean-Michel froze in his genuflection, unable to move.

Blanche's face paled.

The bishop's face went as hard as cut cathedral stone. "What proof, bailiff?" he challenged.

"You must forgive my forwardness, Your Excellency and Your Grace, at so happy an occasion. Yet it would be to all our grief if we consented too easily to this rascal's fraud and sin. For who else had the opportunity to remove the relic except a trusted guard of the cathedral grounds? Who else had the motive to dare such a desperate and despicable act except a disinherited son who longs for glory and proof of his manhood?"

"Still no proof," the bishop said, "without a witness."

"Were it not for the wit and quick eye of Gascon, your trustworthy servant, we should not have known of this evil scheme," Marcel continued. "For he sent us wisely in pursuit, and we learned that this thief had in turn been robbed of the precious sword in a tavern where he was celebrating his roguery."

Such effrontery was almost unbearable, but Jean-Michel resisted the screaming urge to spring up with Purity drawn to maintain his honor. He locked his knees. Paulinus had warned him to expect this. He was ready.

"What say you, sire knight?" Blanche asked. Her voice pleaded, urging a defense.

Jean-Michel stood to face his accusers. His heart hammered in his chest and his bowed legs felt wobbly. His only weapon now was his voice. "As God is my witness I did not take the blessed sword, nor did I lose one save for my own, which I regained rightfully in tournament. The sword brought to you this day I received from the blessed Martin himself, in battle against the enemies of our faith and our king. And I call upon both Saint Martin and His Most Christian Majesty himself to witness."

A rush of whispers swirled in the vaulted chamber.

"How can you say such things?" the bishop objected. "Do you mock us? I would have him seized," he added, facing Blanche.

She turned to Jean-Michel. Her jeweled eyes sparkled with trust and hope. "Let him speak," she said.

"I bear the testimony of the king in a message sealed by his ring. I beg Your Excellency to read it for our hearing."

Bobo withdrew a rolled parchment from his jacket. He passed it to Jean-Michel, who presented it to DeBeauvais.

The bishop received it with a trembling hand. He inspected the lead seal of Louis IX. Nodding approval, he broke it. Anseau stepped in front of him to hold the document steady and flat. Tracing the words with his finger, DeBeauvais read aloud:

> Louis of Poissy, a sinner, to all who hear, greetings. Praise be to God, the Lord of Hosts of armies, and to His soldiers the saints, who fight for us when we are weak. For blessed Martin, bishop and general of Tours, did battle against the infidel when he, by miracle of transport, supplied this Jean-Michel d'Anjou with his own sword to defeat the Saracens who schemed against the royal person. This timely miracle of grace is confirmed by Odo deRouen, Legate of the Holy See. And the blessing is all the more affirmed as a miracle worthy of praise in how it reveals the sin of some and restores salvation to others. For Hughes duVal, wounded gravely unto death in the selfsame battle, and convinced of the sword's virtue and also of the certainty of perdition awaiting those who depart this brief pilgrimage of life with sin unremitted, did confess to one Paulinus of Constantinople to a conspiracy to destroy by fire the Cathedral of Auxonne, by the hand of one Gascon, for whose soul he pleads mercy.

The bishop looked up from his reading, aghast. Gascon whitened. He grasped for his sword. Marcel, his mustache flapping like a live animal, seized Gascon's wrist and wrenched it up to his shoulder blade. Screeching, Gascon fell to his knees. He thrashed about like a snared eagle.

"Take him away at once!" Blanche commanded.

The assembly made way as Marcel barked orders for his deputies to assist in hustling Gascon out the door. The falconer's protests, sounding like the cries of a sparrow in the clutch of a hawk, faded behind the oak doors.

Thunderstuck, the audience turned back to the bishop. "There is more, your grace," he told Blanche.

Much more, Jean-Michel thought. But it was not in the letter. Hughes did not die in "battle," but had followed Jean-Michel to the grotto in secret, intending to murder him and foil his mission. Hughes stumbled into the assassin, instead. It was of but small comfort to Jean-Michel to have overheard Hughes confess his mortal sins in his last breath to Paulinus. "Mayhaps," the bishop suggested, "because of the news of your husband's loss and your present sorrow, the reading should continue another time."

Blanche stood taller, as though a yoke had been removed from her. "Read on," she commanded.

DeBeauvais found his place.

> Whereas Hughes departs to the company of the saints without heir, his properties in Acre are decreed forfeit to his nearest male relation by marriage, one Renard.
>
> And whereas Sire Philippe d'Anjou is martyred in loyal service to his Lord and his king, and his elder sons decline their inheritance in favor of adventure among the Saracens, we decree this Jean-Michel d'Anjou fully vested in his father's properties and free of the mortgage to the

> diocese in exchange for the sword of Saint Martin.

Jean-Michel watched for the bishop's consent to this arrangement. The room hummed with anticipation.

"Let it be so done as His Majesty and our Lord please." DeBeauvais held up a hand to calm the chattering crowd. Everyone knew that the cathedral could now be rebuilt, and that Gascon would likely be hanged from its scaffolding.

"There is one more line in the letter," the bishop announced:

> Let us, with gladsome hearts, give thanks to God for the restoration of holy Martin's sword to its rightful home, for by its virtue it hath both restored justice and restored speech to the mute, that God may be praised by all.

DeBeauvais looked up, his eyes round as Norsemen's shields.

"It is true!" Bobo cried. "And by your leave, I seek orders in the abbey that I may forever tell of God's goodness to me and my liege, Jean-Michel d'Anjou!"

It was too much for a few ladies-in-waiting, who fainted. Men dropped to their knees, sobbing *aves*. Anseau blinked incredulously, breathless at the miracle before his eyes.

"One matter remains," Jean-Michel said. He gulped, his mouth suddenly as dry as Syrian sand. He prayed he would not forget the words Renard had rehearsed with him weeks before. He knelt again, facing Blanche. He extended his right hand, the palm upturned in beseeching.

"Gracious lady," he began, "the more the desire in which I languish grows because love is denied to me, the more my heart swells to praise your worth. Full joy cannot come to me, beloved, if that worth is denied to you. I hold your noble worth so dear that my deepest yearning is to preserve it. Thus do I give myself to you who are without equal in virtue and worth, and I would prefer to die in sorrow than to receive happiness from you that might damage your noble worth. So I beg you, beloved, spare me not if I dishonor you in the least. But if my joy in seeing you might overflow somehow into your own heart to displace your present grief, then I shall be honored if the privilege is granted to me to call you my lady."

He bowed his head. He shut his eyes. Faith failed him and he did not dare to believe she would reply. *She cannot, she will not, she–*

He glanced up through brimming tears as Blanche reached out and clasped his hand in hers.

THE END

About the Author

John J. Desjarlais is an award-winning audio-visual producer, scriptwriter and author. He holds a bachelor's degree in Communication Arts from the University of Wisconsin and masters degrees in Intructional Media from Columbia University and Writing from Illinois State University. His writings include a mystery, *Bleeder*, and *The Throne of Tara*, a book nominated for the *Christianity Today* Readers Choice Award. His essays and stories have appeared in magazines such as *Student Leadership Journal*, *U Magazine*, *The Critic*, *The Upper Room*, *The Karitos Review* and *The Rockford Review*. A former producer with Wisconsin Public Radio, he teaches journalism and English at Kishwaukee College in northern Illinois. A member of Mystery Writers of America, he is listed in *Who's Who in Entertainment* and *Who's Who Among America's Teachers*. Readers may contact him at www.johndesjarlais.com

www.ingramcontent.com/pod-product-compliance
Ingram Content Group UK Ltd.
Pitfield, Milton Keynes, MK11 3LW, UK
UKHW020806120325
456141UK00004B/261